Sarah Blue
The Fang Arrangement
I0698848

Copyright

Spotify Playlist

Vampire - Olivia Rodrigo
Anti-Hero - Taylor Swift
She's so High - Tan Bachman
That Don't Impress Me Much - Shania Twain
The Only Exception - Paramore
Never Be Like You - Flume, Kai
Bullet With Butterfly Wings - The Smashing Pumpkins
Lightening Crashes - Live
MakeDamnSure - Taking Back Sunday
Just My Type - The Vamps
Fade Into You - Mazzy Star
There She Goes - The La's
Creep - Carolesdaughter
Heartless - The Weeknd
Down Bad - Taylor Swift
Fuck the Pain Away - Peaches

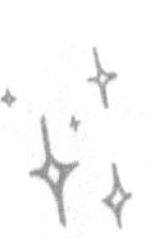

Foreword

Welcome back to the Celestial Witches Universe. This is book two, however it can be read as a stand-alone.

This book features a vampire and the witch he is obsessed with. If you are squeamish about blood, this book may not be for you. For a list of content guidelines for this book you can view all content warnings at authorsarahblue.com

To anyone who thinks their pussy power is strong enough to bring a morally gray, old asf vampire to their knees.

Chapter 1

8 Years Ago

I wasn't the smartest witch in my coven, or the most gifted, but I was, however, the most curious.

But as I stand beneath the bright, glowing red neon light, I wonder if this peculiar interest of mine might just be my demise.

My coven wasn't receptive to my incongruous thoughts, so I learned to keep them to myself. I hid folklore books under my bed as a teen, hoping my mother and grandmother would never find them. If they did, I would've had to face the High Priestess for questioning anything outside of coven life. In fact, if the High Priestess knew what I was up to, she'd probably threaten to burn me at the stake or do something even more drastic to teach me a lesson.

Witches are supposed to be happy with the platonic relationships within our coven, not intermingle with other supernaturals, we merely tolerate ordinary unmagical beings. If we want to bear a child, we make use of a human man, but nothing beyond procreation.

I hate it.

As much as I love being a witch, I want more.

I want someone who is only mine.

While my fellow witches, the women I walk through this life with, love me wholly, I yearn for a romantic attachment. My best friends, Violet and Iris, would follow me to the end of the world, but I'm not sure if they would follow me *here*.

A vampire bar is the last place a witch should be, especially one from the Celestial Coven. This isn't a place I should be looking for a romantic connection, far from it, yet here I am, standing in line to enter. I drove three parishes over just to come to this particular bar, mostly so no one in my coven would find out about my little foray into the dark. I don't know how to explain why this particular type of darkness calls to me.

Curiosity may just kill the witch, but at least it will be one hell of a story.

Heels click behind me, and I turn. A tall, raven-haired woman who doesn't look a day over twenty looks me up and down. She's wearing a sleek, sophisticated black dress. Meanwhile, I'm wearing the strawberry peasant dress that pushes up my over abundant chest that Violet bought me for my birthday.

Her smile is wicked, just a hint of fang pressing against her full bottom lip as she tilts her head at me.

"Come, you'll be my plus one," she says, not even waiting for an answer as she grabs my wrist, her perfectly manicured red nails slightly digging into my skin.

I should decide right then and there that I'm in danger, that this isn't where I should be. Yet, the idea of uncertainty, of doing something I shouldn't, thrills me even more.

She tugs me in front of the bouncer. "She's with me," she says easily.

"ID," the man says. He's huge, his muscles fighting against his black shirt as I pull my ID out of my purse and hand it to him. He shakes his head and hands it back as the strange woman pulls me through the doors.

"Um. Hi? I'm Ember. What's your name?" I ask her. She laughs too.

Yup. It's official. Stupidest fucking witch of a generation. These vampires are going to drain me of every drop, and I'm the dumb bitch who willingly served myself up as a feast.

"Samantha, and I'm taking you to meet my dad."

I blink, trying to both capture her words and all the surrounding chaos of the bar.

A game of pool is happening on the left of me so fast it takes me a moment to realize that vampires are actually playing the game. There's no way to ignore the blood bags hanging behind the bar top being poured into martini glasses for well-dressed vampires to drink. I swallow thickly, whispering an incantation for safety under my breath.

Humans are here too, most of them in a daze, but I can't quite put my finger on it. They all look happy, but like they aren't completely coherent with their glazed stares.

"Your dad?" I ask, wondering just exactly who her father is and why we need to be introduced.

She snorts. "Well, my father, in the sense that he made me what I am. Though, he really fucking hates when I call him that, so obviously, I do it as often as I can."

She continues dragging me through the bar; I get a few interested glances my way, but no one touches me or the woman ushering me to my very likely death. We reach a dark corridor and she drops my wrist.

"You know, maybe this was a mistake, I should probably—"

Before I can finish my exit strategy, she flings the door open. Multiple men in suits turn to look at her so unearthly fast I think

I imagine it. At least I know one thing from all the fairytales I've read is true. Vampires are indeed faster than a blink of an eye. I wonder what else is true and what's fiction when it comes to the most infamous supernatural beings in the world.

The man behind the desk is the first to speak. "Samantha, darling, what did I tell you about knocking?" he says, a smile on his face, but there's clear irritation there.

He's ridiculously handsome, and not someone you would ever consider being someone's father. He has shiny, medium brownish-blonde hair, cheekbones that could cut glass, and blue eyes that almost look ethereal. His gaze turns to me, his smile more predatory now as he uses his fang to grip the end of his black leather glove and free his hands, steepling them on his desk.

It's more attractive than it should be, and I try to calm my breathing. Can these vampires hear my heart beating like a hummingbird's wings?

"You're dismissed," the man says to the other vampires. He's clearly higher up in the food chain, which has a mixture of fear and wonder flicking through me. Samantha pulls me to the side and all the men are gone before I can even gather my thoughts. "What have you brought me?" he asks.

Hopefully not your next victim, I think to myself.

I swallow thickly, my hand trembles as I debate pulling out my wand. At the very least, I could call for help. I'm not great with teleporting magic, but I think if I really needed to, I could use it. Fuck, I should have taken Violet more seriously about learning the skill.

"A witch," Samantha says, ushering me to the chair on the opposite of this man's desk.

The man rubs the bridge of his nose with his now bare fingers and nods.

"Leave us," he says to his…daughter?

"You need—"

The man stands up so fast it barely registers as he grabs Samantha's arm and drags her out of the office.

"Go home. I'll send Betty to follow," he says. Who the hell is Betty? And why would a vampire need an escort?

Samantha rolls her eyes, crossing her arms over her chest. Okay, so maybe they are father and daughter in some strange way. He doesn't look much older than her; he was probably turned in his mid-twenties, but who knows how long he's been roaming the earth.

I should be pissing my pants right about now, sitting in front of a who knows how old of a vampire. Yet, I feel a keen sense of adventure and, well, I'm quite nosey.

Before I even get a moment to glance around his office, the door is shut, and he's taking the seat next to me, instead of in his high back chair on the other side of his desk.

My breath hitches as I take him in. Now that I think about it, every vampire I saw in the bar on my way in was effortlessly gorgeous. But he takes the cake. His beauty is timeless and classic, like a European prince, back when they used to be hot. Though his sinister smirk tells me he's far from refined royalty.

He tilts his head at me, analyzing me, while I sit here stupefied and wondering why I couldn't curb this interest in vampires in another way. Why did I need to come here to see what they were all about, let alone by myself? No one in my coven knows my whereabouts.

"Tell me, are you suicidal or stupid, witch?"

Valid question.

My mouth parts in shock, and he stares at my lips for a long moment. He leans forward, his cold fingertips gently gripping my chin to face him. His skin is cool, but not unpleasant. I wonder if he could effortlessly crush my jaw if he wanted to.

"What? Did you come here for a drop of vampire blood? Or something even more nefarious? It makes sense they would send you," he says, glancing down at my cleavage that is sitting high in the pink frilly dress. "Tell me, does your cunt of a High Priestess want a war with me too? Cause I can tell you right now, we're nothing like those wolves. Oz would destroy your coven in a night."

He comes even closer, still holding my jaw as my heart races in my chest. "I could kill you right now, so easily. I'd take my time too, devouring every drop of your magical blood. Then I'd go to each and every home of your coven and do the same thing."

His hand slides from my chin to my neck, his thumb on my pulse point. Fear lacing through my veins, along with something else I've never truly experienced. I can't pinpoint the emotion as I blink, staring into his aqua eyes.

"It's weak of Aster to send a messenger in such a pretty, tempting package," he says, drawing his thumb up and down my beating pulse point. His chest doesn't move, he doesn't breathe, and is eerily still as he stares at me.

I lick my lips and finally find my words.

"No one in my coven knows I'm here."

He pulls back, smiling with bright white fangs.

"Then what's stopping me from locking you in my basement for eternity as my pretty, little magical blood bag?"

This is embarrassing. Not only am I probably going to die, but how do I convince him I came to the bar for a one-night stand or something more? Not to start a supernatural war between vampires and witches?

His hand is back on my chin again, this time it's rougher as he forces me to stare into his gaze. They dilate quickly, the pupils nearly trembling as he speaks.

"Why are you here?" His tone is pure magic, commanding my obedience, and I find myself wanting to comply.

"I wanted to have a night of fun." The words slip out of my mouth involuntarily. "It's my twenty-first birthday."

His brows pinch and his head tilts to the side curiously as he stares at me.

"Does Aster Delvaux have any intentions for conflict with the vampires?"

"Not that I know of," I reply. Again, it slips out of me unconsciously.

"What's your name?"

"Ember…Ember Hallow."

He releases my chin and adjusts his suit jacket before sitting back down and looking me over once more. He seems to relax, no longer viewing me as a threat, but I can't read his face.

The reality hits me. He just compelled me to tell him all of those things. How didn't I know vampires were capable of something like that?

"It wasn't wise coming here, Ember Hallow."

"No?" I ask, trying to figure out how I'm going to get myself out of this mess.

I make a quick little vow that if I survive this, I'll stop being such a reckless, foolish witch.

He smiles before standing. It seems like vampires don't do well with sitting still. He heads to the wheeled bar at the corner of his office.

"What would you like?"

I scrunch my nose, looking at all the hard liquor.

"Silly of me, of course, you would drink something far more

delicate. I myself have a bit of a sweet tooth," he says and I swallow thickly as he comes back to his chair. "Let me have a taste and I'll let you go."

"Sorry. What?" I say without even thinking.

The vampire grins, grabbing my wrist, holding a thimble with a sharp prick on the end.

"Just a finger…just a taste…and then I'll let you go. You have my word."

"Why would I trust a vampire?"

"Ah, so you do have some fire in you. But you're still the pretty little idiot who walked in my bar. If you'd like to walk out of here completely unscathed, I'll be needing a taste of your blood."

Okay, Ember, what would Iris do?

"Magically bind our promise," I say, and he tilts his head as I take out my wand, flipping my hand so we're holding each other's wrists as I point the tip toward our skin.

I could easily start a fire, use the distraction to run away and attempt to teleport out of here. But the brain rotted part of me wants to see what happens.

"Vow to not harm me. For a taste of my blood, you are granting me protection," I say, keeping it extremely vague. "Vow that you will *never* harm me."

His lip twitches as his hold on my wrist tightens, and he pulls me closer. He smells rich, like aged whiskey and warm vanilla.

"I vow it."

My magic zips through us and he inhales deeply. He brings the thimble to my pointer finger, making a painless cut. A bead of red blood pools to the surface as he brings my finger to his lips, sucking the tip.

His eyes are closed as he does so, his body going soft, before he stills completely. He doesn't let my finger go, as he opens his eyes and stares at me. It shouldn't be so erotic, the feel of this stranger sucking on my finger or noticing how affected he is. But yet, it's single-handedly the hottest experience I've had in my life.

His demeanor changes completely after he's tasted my blood. I expect him to give me my hand back, but instead he tugs me closer to his face, his pretty eyes staring into mine.

"What are you doing?" I say quickly, actual fear hitting me now.

"What needs to be done."

I try to pull away, but he doesn't let me, not as my heart races or as I hold my wand against his chest.

His eyes lock with mine, doing the same thing they did before, and I can't help but to be captivated by his words.

"You will forget tonight. You'll forget me. But you won't forget your desire for vampires, what my blood felt like. No one can give you what I give you, Ember Hallow. When the time is right, I'll come to collect what is mine. You will not put yourself in danger and you will not come here again. Till we meet again, sunshine." His soft words rattle my brain as everything goes black.

Chapter 2

Present Day

I charm the box of all the herbs and flowers to be lighter as I ride my bike downtown to Goddess Apothecary. I'm regretting riding my bike as sweat trickles on my neck, spring is an illusion in Louisiana.

The major plus side is I can park my bike right in front of the shop and not have to deal with parking. My finger tingles as I do and I shake out my hand, every now and then I get this phantom feeling in my pointer finger. I glance around the lot, thinking I see something in the distance, but when I look back there's nothing there.

I shake my head at myself, this happens way too often. Maybe my grandmother is right, I have an overactive of an imagination, always seeing things that aren't there.

The feeling of being watched leaves me as I head down Main Street. My best friend Violet's husband, Silas, who happens to be the Alpha of the Moon Walker Pack, basically owns the town now. He's made major improvements, but all good things take time. Just like our relationship with the wolf shifters. Even though our coven is no longer a cult run by a psychopathic witch with outdated views, there's still a long way to go with our relations with other supernatural beings.

The bell chimes over the door as Iris yells out, "Just a minute!"

I place the box on the counter and look around.

Iris built this shop from the ground up. Her mother and grandmother weren't highly skilled potion makers, her grandmother was a seer, and her mom, well we don't talk about her much. My smart and too-wise-for-her-years friend is impressive and talented. Then there's Violet, who's the future High Priestess of the coven, she picked up magic like it was nothing, and is the most talented healer we've had in generations.

Comparison is a slow killer, and I try to not let it bother me, I really do. It's not that I feel jealousy toward my friends' gifts, I just feel like out of the three of us I have less to show for myself.

Sure, my herbs and flowers are important to the coven, but I'm replaceable. I'm a completely average witch, and it's been a tougher pill to swallow as of late. Maybe it's because of the huge shift in our coven, and watching Violet bridge the gap between the witches and the shifters. There's this deep down yearning in my gut for adventure and figuring out where I fit in the grand scheme of things. Not that I've shared what I'm feeling with anyone else.

I'm always happy when I'm around anyone in my coven, always ready to crack a joke or lighten the mood. Suppressing feelings is way easier than saying them out loud. Even if that means I'm like a slow cooking potion in a cauldron, simmering until my emotions boil over the smallest thing.

I take a look at all the beauty products on the shelves and sigh, guilt churning in my stomach for all my negative thinking.

"Hey Ember, thanks for bringing these all down," Iris says as she opens the box and starts taking everything out on the counter, organizing different plants and flowers based on what she'll need them for.

Iris is beautiful with her skin glowing as it normally does, but her amber eyes look haunted, like she hasn't been sleeping.

"Just because you live above the shop doesn't mean you have to work all the time. You're getting enough sleep?" I ask her.

She waves me off, as she usually does. It seems like I'm not the only witch bottling my feelings up around here. "I'm fine, just been working on some potions that require more around the clock care."

She's lying, and I don't know why, but I won't push her.

Iris, Violet, and I may be sisters in our own right, but we're all the same with having our secrets. I mean, hell, Violet was married to our enemy and didn't tell us until she had to. Her marrying Silas and uniting the wolves and witches is one of the best things to happen to the coven.

Whatever Iris is hiding, she'll tell me when she's ready.

"Alright, are we going to test this new hair potion out or what?" Iris asks, changing the direction of the conversation.

"Let's do it," I say, sitting in the worn, brown chair in the corner.

The chime dings with someone's arrival, and I smile, realizing it's Violet.

"Oh perfect, let's see if this is strong enough on the white pieces of your hair too," Iris says excitedly as she swirls the pink bottle.

"You know it won't work. How many potions have you tried now?" Violet says, but still sits down, knowing that Iris has to test the theory.

"I think about fifty. Can't hurt," Iris says, putting it on my hair first, running her fingers through my long wavy strands. "Let it sit for twenty minutes," she tells me before taking a test piece of Violet's hair and placing the potion on.

A timer goes off in the distance and Iris curses.

"Twenty minutes. I'll be right back!"

Violet and I give each other a look, one that clearly shows that we're both worried about our friend.

Violet clears her throat, neither of us verbally addressing what's going on with Iris. "So…A few new shifters joined the Walker Pack."

"Oh?" I say, trying to spur some excitement, placing my fist on my chin and resting on the arm of the chair.

I've wanted a boyfriend for a long time now, even more so that Violet has paved the way by getting married, changing the rules about relationships within our coven.

Yet, every guy I try to make it work with is lackluster. There's always a missing spark, and I don't know what it is.

None of them compare to what I fantasize about, how could they? Every now and then I drink a little too much and let what those fantasies are slip out, but only ever to Iris and Violet. They always laugh it off, thinking I'm joking or talking a big game. Which is fine, because what I dream about will never become a reality. Even if the coven has become more accepting, there's no way they would approve of the type of man I've been craving.

He doesn't have a face, not in my dreams, but the things he does to me, no human man or wolf shifter could compare. My visions of him feel so real, that sometimes I think I get reality and fantasy confused.

"What's his name?"

"Bobby," she says with a smile as I grimace. "Okay, maybe you can give him a different nickname? He's really nice, cute too. He was a nomad and has no issues with witches. I was thinking maybe we could set something up?”

I smile at Violet. “How tall is he?”

“Six foot five,” she says with a smirk.

“Alright, I’m in. He’s cute?”

“Yes, and very nice, too. I’ll give him your number.”

I nod at her with a smile, grateful that she wants to set me up with someone. Maybe he could replace this mystery man of my dreams.

I can’t even lie to myself convincingly.

“How are things at home?” I ask her, not wanting to get her too excited about this guy, if I wind up not liking him, it’s no one’s fault but my own.

“Good, really good. I’m happy, Ember. I want you and Iris to be happy too,” she says softly.

I grab her hand and squeeze. “I’m happy, I promise.”

She gives me a weak smile as Iris walks back into the room. Starting with Violet, she casts a quick spell, drying the potion on her hair.

“Well, damn. It didn’t work,” she complains and Violet shrugs her shoulders. “Let’s take a look at you,” she says, casting the same spell, and as soon as she does, they both gasp.

“Oh, Hecate, is it that bad?”

“No, Ember, it looks stunning,” Iris says, handing me a mirror. What used to be a mix of red and strawberry blonde locks is now nearly completely pink.

My mouth parts as I look at myself.

Somehow this feels like an omen for more change to come.

“I love it, Iris, thank you.”

She lets out a relieved breath. “Phew. Good. Well, I have to get back to some potions. I’ll see you two at the ritual later this week?”

It feels like she's kicking us out, but we both agree as we leave the shop.

"I'll make sure Bobby gets your number. The hair really does suit you, Em," Violet says, her light blue eyes shining with happiness as she gives me a hug before going the opposite direction.

I ride my bike home wondering what is wrong with me, why I feel so off-kilter. As I open the gate to the front yard, a small voice whispers my name and I crouch down onto the garden grass. Multiple garden fairies flutter in my direction.

"Miss Ember, the bat is back. It's in the shutters," Tabitha says. I hold out my hand and she stands on my palm.

She is the biggest busybody out of all the garden fairies that live in my garden. I give them somewhere safe to live and they help me take care of the vast property.

"The bat isn't bothering anyone. It just needs a safe place to stay," I tell her.

The bat has come and gone throughout the years, taking shelter in different places in my cottage. The shutters are their favorites.

"What if it eats one of us!" Domingo shouts and some other fairies nod in agreement.

I try not to smile too hard as I stare down at the small little garden fairy that's dressed in Barbie clothes they modified for their wispy, membranous wings.

"If the bat causes any issues, I'll handle it, but for now consider it another creature seeking refuge in the gardens."

Domingo and Tabitha both glare at me, which has no heat, considering how small they are. I'm not even sure they could wrap their arms around my wrist.

"Do you want to wake up one morning to us all slaughtered?" Tabitha complains and I sigh.

"No, Tabitha. I'll ward the garden to ensure that our little bat friend can't eat anyone," I say, compromising.

She has her arms crossed over her chest. She's wearing a formal gown and her long, blonde hair is plated with small flower petals woven in.

"Fine, we accept," she says, irritated, before fluttering away.

I stand out of the dirt, dusting off my jeans and head over to the main cottage.

"The fairies are out for blood. Watch your back," I whisper to the bat, before entering my home.

It's no surprise that Gus, my raccoon familiar, is eating peanuts while he watches *Pocahontas* on the TV.

"Gus, how many have you had?" I ask, looking at the container.

He makes a huffing noise, grabbing the bag with his tiny raccoon hands.

"Mind your own business. You need to get out of the house more," he says to me telepathically, and my mouth drops.

As my familiar, he communicates only to me through magic and I speak out loud to him. Every witch has one, and they come in a variety of animals and personalities.

"Excuse me, where is this attitude coming from?"

He grumbles, crunching on more peanuts. *"The fairies need to learn to shut the fuck up. They're hindering my daytime sleep."*

If there is one thing to know about Gus, it's that he loves cursing, eating, and animated movies.

"I'll talk with the fairies," I say, feeling exhausted from the day.

I plop down on the couch next to Gus, sending him in the air a little, and he side-eyes me.

"I'm not wrong. You do need to get out more."

"Violet is setting me up on a date with a wolf shifter," I tell him

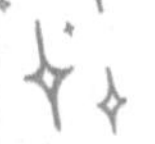

proudly.

The racoon snickers at me.

"What?" I say, exacerbated.

"*I wonder what will be wrong with him. Will he chew too loud? Will he be too tall or too short? Will he be too masculine or not masculine enough? Oh, I bet he won't be as big of a freak—*"

I grab his little nose gently.

"That's enough."

I let go of his nose, and he climbs his hefty self into my arms, using his hand to pat my arm.

"*I'm not complaining. I love being the man of the house.*"

I scratch his chin and ignore his words as my phone chimes with a message.

> **Unknown:** Hi this is Bobby. Violet said you might be interested in getting dinner tonight. How does Howl at the Moon sound?

Gus laughs in my arms. I ignore him, add Bobby's number to my phone, and type up my reply.

> **Me:** I'd love to. Is 7:30 good?

> **Bobby:** Looking forward to it.

"*Poor bastard doesn't stand a chance,*" Gus says, petting my arm, and I wonder if he's right, and what's so wrong with me that I can't let anyone in?

Howl at the Moon is not my ideal location for a date, not even in the slightest. It's somewhere I go all the time, nothing about it is special or screams romance. It's a wolf dive bar/restaurant that is conveniently downtown.

But I'm keeping an open mind.

Even if he isn't a vampire…I swallow that thought down, like I do every time it rattles in my mind. I need to get a grip.

I might over exaggerate when it comes to my encounters with men. I'm sure most of the coven assumes I'm promiscuous with the way I talk and joke about sex, but the fact is I've only had sex once and that was a one-night stand with a kind human boy when I was nineteen. Then of course there are my endless fantasies about being with a faceless vampire.

Maybe I should seek therapy, or maybe I just need to try harder with men who still have a pulse.

It's just every time I do, this instinctual thought rips me back and pure disgust fills me. The fantasies I have aren't filled with human men, or semi-appropriate supernatural men. What I want is a desired taste that I'm too self-conscious to bring up to most. Only Iris and Violet have heard me bring up vampires before, and only because I trust them with my life.

Even if the rules of the coven have changed. Vampires are still secretive and dangerous, and they should absolutely not be considered for my dating pool. It's a fantasy that needs to stay just that—a fantasy that gets locked away.

Damn, I need this date to go well.

A bat flies over the entrance of the building and it feels like a bad omen as a tall man in jeans and a plaid shirt approaches me. He's handsome enough, dirty blonde hair, and brown eyes. There are no tingles anywhere, but I plaster a smile on my face and shake his hand.

"I'm glad you could meet me tonight," he says, no southern twang in his voice at all.

"Of course, Violet had nothing but nice things to say," I lie. All she told me was his height and that he seemed kind enough.

"Shall we?" he says, holding out an arm as we walk through the busy restaurant.

We sit at the table and order our drinks as the small talk starts. He's friendly, and handsome, and yet, I feel nothing.

I don't feel attraction, butterflies, anything. I never do.

"So, Violet tells me you have a penchant for earth magic. What does that mean?" he asks.

I give him a smile, he's a good date, asking me questions and not making it all about himself like I am internally. I know it's not an issue of not liking men, all my daydreams surround a faceless one. I want a partner, I want romance and Hecate knows I want a physical relationship.

"I house the coven's gardens, making all the herbs and plants that we need. I'm also quite good at water and fire manipulation. Where did you move from before you joined the Walker Pack?"

"Pretty much everywhere. Never found a pack that had the same ideals until now. It feels nice to finally set roots down somewhere," he says.

We drink and eat; the conversation is easy and I wonder why I can't make myself want him. Why can't I have a nice thing?

"I'm going to go to the restroom. I'll be right back," I tell him with a tight smile.

He gives me an easygoing nod as I head toward the back of the restaurant, only I go out back to get fresh air. The door creaks loudly as I let the cooler night air hit my face and I press my back against the bricks. It's dark back here, the main street light is and the next one is a good fifty feet away, glowing over the restaurant dumpster.

I turn to go back inside, but the door apparently automatically locks.

"Fuck," I hiss, about to pull out my wand, as someone grabs me by the hair.

"God, I know you're going to taste good," the voice says, but as quickly as they say it, their hand disappears from my hair and a thud smacks against the concrete behind me.

My wand is fully in my hand now as I turn around. The gasp that slips out of me is heavy as I look down at the body with a stake protruding from its back. With a flick of my wand, it glows and I can see the black veins creeping around the body as it slowly withers. It shrinks and shrivels like a raisin, pooling in its own blood.

All that's left is a pile of goop, a stake, and his clothes…and whoever staked it is still out here watching me.

I keep my wand up as I walk backwards, using magic to open the door as I rush back to the table. I'm clearly flustered as Bobby looks at me with wide eyes.

"Is that blood on your dress?" he asks.

Shit.

"I'm actually not feeling so great. I'm sorry, Bobby. Thank you so much for taking me out tonight."

"Do you need a ride home?" he asks.

"No…no, thank you." I take out forty dollars and place it on the table so he understands my intentions as I head out of the restaurant and down an alley where I can teleport home.

My skills still aren't top tier in this department, but if there's one place I can easily get to, it's home. With a deep breath, I portal myself right outside the gates.

Only, I don't even touch the wrought iron as three large men in suits wait for me.

I keep my voice even.

"Is there something I can help you gentlemen with?" I ask sweetly.

"You're being brought in by the parish deputy vampire for the murder of a member of our nest. Come willingly or you will be subdued."

I weigh my options, and I choose violence as I lift my wand.

Before I can even say a single incantation, my wand is out of my hands and my wrists are tied before me. Fear prickles up my spine and I wonder what the hell I just got myself into.

Chapter 3

I swirl the lowball glass, hating the warmed up blood in it. Nothing has tasted good in years. The only reason I still drink blood is so I don't succumb to bloodlust and ravage a town, or let myself fall apart, it's completely lost its luster.

"Sometimes I think about staking myself so I don't have to watch you mope around anymore," Samantha says, as she twirls a knife in her hand. "The last decade has been rather depressing, father."

I glare at her, hating when she uses that term. I'm her sire, and I wonder if I made the right decision to change her every day. She was dying, young, and begging for her life. I never wanted to be responsible for a progeny, yet here she is, still with me for nearly a decade.

"You've only been a vampire for nine," I say back and she sighs.

"The statement still stands. Come on, I'm bored. Let's go travel. Forget about this place."

I glare at her. "You know we can't leave."

"No, you. You can't leave," she says and I look away.

I'm selfish. Always have been.

By now, most vampires would have removed the sire bond, and let their progeny go nomad and find themselves. Maybe I'm sentimental, or maybe I'm so afraid of being alone that I can't seem to let her go. I'm tethering Samantha to this life I built, one she never asked for.

She never outright asks me to break the bond either, and maybe that's why I haven't. Our relationship is truly a familial one. In some ways, she feels like my child and in others like a sibling I squabble with. Either way, she's the only person I feel some sort of tenderness towards. Well, the only person I can openly have some degree of affection for.

The person I want to show my true affections for is the one I can't have. If I have her, I'll ruin her. Though it doesn't stop me from meddling in her affairs or assuring that she doesn't have romantic encounters with anyone else.

See? Selfish.

"We can't leave, not until everything with Oz settles," I lie.

There's always some vampire who's going to want what I have and willing to take it by any means. Then there are the other threats that have been nothing but a nuisance as of late. Like the vampire slayer that killed my sire. Don't get me wrong, I didn't mourn for a single second when I saw what was left of him. But having a slayer in town will cause nothing but mayhem. If other vampires in the nest go missing, we're going to have a serious problem on our hands.

"I can't believe a slayer took Oz out," she says wistfully, sipping on her own crystal of blood.

"Me either," I agree.

Oz was always larger than life, he seemed indestructible to me. He was also possessive, and ran the nest like a dictatorship. He's the reason I never allowed myself anything good, knowing he would simply take it away to teach me a lesson. He's only been dead for four days, but it's been the greatest relief of my life…except the fact that there's now an active, strong vampire slayer on the loose. Oz was old and strong, if this slayer could take him out, there's no telling what they're capable of.

"If only we had…I don't know a witch to help us with this little problem," Samantha says, placing the bloodstained decanter on the table. "Oz is dead. You should go talk to her, go see her."

I turn away, and she taps her nails against my desk.

"I know you've been sending Betty to spy on her." I sharply turn to face her and she gives me a wicked smile. "Betty and Fitz talk. They're little gossips."

My phone rings and I answer it immediately, my glare not disappearing as I listen to the voice on the other end.

"Sir. Baptiste is dead, looks like another slaying, but didn't catch the killer on tape, just a witch outside with him. How would you like to proceed?"

I groan. Fucking vampire slayers.

"Send me the footage," I say, and my phone chimes. I pull it away and click on the video.

My heart stills when I see *her*. Baptiste threads his hands in her hair and tugs her back. She has her hand on her wand, but doesn't get a moment to use it as a stake flies right through Baptiste's heart and he crumbles to the floor.

Baptiste should be grateful for that stake. How dare he touch her? He nearly fucking sunk his greedy, filthy fangs into her perfect, delicate throat.

"Retrieve the stake and the witch," I reply.

"Sir."

"Oh, and there is to be no harm done to the witch. If someone so much as looks thirsty around her, I'll rip out their fangs."

Conner clears his throat on the other end. "Yes, sir."

"Bring her directly to my office, along with the stake."

"Immediately, sir."

I end the call and glance up at Samantha, who's rolling her eyes.

"What?" I snap.

"I don't want to speak out of turn and have my poor fangs ripped out," she says, flicking her dark hair and placing a hand on her hip. "It wouldn't happen to be a witch with perfect tits and big red hair, would it?"

"Her hair's pink now," I reply, looking back down at my phone and watching her fear-riddled face. She grabbed her wand at least, but she was no contender for the speed of a vampire. I need her to be able to protect herself better, what if one day I'm not around to do it?

If I had a heart, it would be pumping in my chest. This rage simmering inside of me is nearly boiling over at the thought of her being hurt. I've done my best over the last eight years to ensure her safety, that Oz never found out my little secret and how important she was to me.

My precious little secret.

Only Samantha knows about her, and I regret giving her this knowledge as she snorts and stares at me with an arched brow.

"I know it doesn't seem like it, War, but you deserve to be happy. Stop this self-inflicted deprivation of happiness and celibacy. Oz is dead. You're one of the strongest vampires in Louisiana. Why are you denying yourself?"

I blink at her and whatever she reads on my face has her torn. Her playfulness disappears as her eyes flick to mine.

"Do you know why I haven't asked you to break the bond, to let me go?"

I sit still as ice as she rounds my desk, looking out the large window of my office. It's nighttime, but they're the best money can buy with suppressing UV light. Though my skin can never touch the sun, at least I get small glimpses of what daylight feels like.

"You're the only real family I've ever had, the only person who ever really saw me. You gave me this gift of eternal night. I'm in your debt forever for that, but beyond that, I worry that if I left, I'd come back to find you gone. I selfishly stay because I know I'm the only thing keeping you here. I can't be your reason anymore," she says, turning around to face me. "You already know what she is to you. Don't deny yourself this."

"What are you saying?" I ask, standing to my full height looking down at her.

"I'm saying that you need more than this empire you've built. You need a life outside of your obligation to me and our house, that you shouldn't live in fear of what Oz will do to her. That she's your—"

I cut her off, grabbing her arm.

"Are you saying you don't want the sire bond anymore?"

She tilts her chin defiantly at me. "There's no way I would leave you right now to fuck this all up. Try with her, is what I'm asking."

"If I don't?"

"Then I want to be released from the sire bond immediately," she says.

If I had a beating heart, I think it may have fractured into millions of pieces.

"And if I try with her?"

"Then I'll stay until I'm no longer your reason." She takes a step toward me, straightening out my suit jacket. "Despite what you think, you're not evil, Warin, I think someone like her could show you that."

She pats my chest, taking the two glasses with her. She glances back at me from the door.

"It's not like you can outrun the prophecy forever, father," she says with a sharp click of my office door.

I fall back into my desk chair, rubbing the bridge of my nose, wondering how I can possibly make this work.

I don't want Samantha to leave. I also want my witch, but I can't have her—I don't deserve her.

My intention all those years ago was to one day make her mine, once I figured out a way to get rid of Oz, so until I could have her, I watched her.

She's so inherently good it's sickening. Someone like that shouldn't be in my orbit. I'd just destroy her.

But even then, I couldn't let her go. I'd watch her from the shadows and manipulate her mind to make her not want any other man.

I'm a sick, selfish, calculating fuck to my core. I'm like a child who hoards toys at a playground even though I'm not playing with them.

I could have my team turn around and send Ember home, knowing full well she didn't kill Baptiste, which would mean I would need to release Samantha tonight. If I try to get Ember to like me, does that mean I'm taking off my progeny's shackles and placing them on her?

I lose too much time contemplating my choices as my office door opens and a wide-eyed, beautiful as ever, Ember is brought into my office.

"Her wand," I say, holding out my hand. Conner places the cool metal in my hand without a question, also handing me the stake.

"Untie her and leave," I say and, like a good little minion, he does what he's told and leaves.

Ember shifts in her chair, her pulse pounding, nearly deafening me as I lick my lips. She holds her finger subconsciously, the one where I tasted her blood. Does some part of her memory remember that night?

The thought is too alluring. Years of restraint are about to be tossed out of the window over the way she touches the place I tasted her for the first time.

She changed her hair, which must have been when she went into her friend's shop earlier. It's more pink than red now, and it suits her. Her dress is a light blue, tight around her full breasts and flares out at her hips.

I round my desk, leaning against it as I take her in. She's not as timid as the night she came into my bar, but I knew that before tonight; I watch her more often than I'd like to admit. She might be disgustingly kind, but she still has a fire within her.

"Hello," I say with a smile, and her pupils dilate.

"I did not kill that vampire," she blurts out. "He was going to bite me and as soon as I turned around, he was dead."

"Mmm. Would you like a drink?" I ask her and she blinks her large green eyes at me.

"No. I would like my wand back and to be taken back home," she says, folding her arms across her chest.

It doesn't have the effect she hopes because now I'm staring at her large, full breasts, thinking about how delicious it would be to bite her there.

She snaps her fingers at me, and I'm taken aback as I blink at her.

"My face is up here," she says, pointing at her heart-shaped

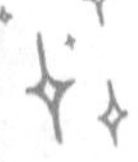

face that houses seductive green eyes and plush pink lips.

"Can you blame me for the distraction? Tell me, why were you at Howl at the Moon tonight?"

Her lips part at my slight flirtation.

"I was on a date."

My brows furrow. A date? Betty didn't tell me she was going on a fucking date. She and I are going to have words later tonight.

"Was he ugly, or boring? Is that why you found yourself suspiciously outside the back of the restaurant where a member of my house was found dead?"

"He was fine, handsome, nice, a shifter."

I rise too quickly from the desk and enter her space. Her spine goes ramrod straight in the chair, but her gaze doesn't look away from mine. I can't help but to smile at her ferocity and strength.

She might be good, but she isn't weak. Good…very good.

I tilt my head as I grab the arms of her chair.

"Then what was it? What did he do that made you want to run away?"

Her heart is racing, and she can't stop moving in her seat, even though she doesn't break our staring contest.

"I don't see how that's any of your business."

I click my tongue. "I don't know, a dead vampire found on Pack Moon Walker property with a Celestial Coven witch as the only witness. It's rather suspicious, wouldn't you agree?"

She narrows her eyes at me.

"I didn't do anything."

"I fear the vampire council won't agree," I reply, feeling like a bastard for making her sweat and lying.

She swallows thickly and I can sense true fear now.

"Perhaps more alliances will fall apart, maybe even an all out supernatural war for this transgression."

She narrows her eyes at me. "I'll show you my memories."

I make a tsking noise and grab her chin. Fuck, her skin is so soft and warm, I missed it. I lean forward, inhaling her sunshine and floral scent for a moment before getting closer to her.

"You think I would take a Celestial witch's memories at face value? Where is it that your old High Priestess got sent to for fucking around with memories? Toledo was it?"

Her bravado falls, and a deep sense of unfamiliar guilt hits me. The last time I felt true guilt was when I made the decision to change Samantha, but even then, it was short-lived when I saw how suited she was to the immortal night.

"I could save you from the council," I tell her, the lie easily falls off my tongue. She's not on council radar and never will be. As long as I roam this earth, Ember will be safe. I've protected her from the shadows, and now I can help her protect herself whether or not I can slither my way into her heart.

"Why?"

"Purely selfish reasons. I find myself in need of a witch as of late."

Her hand grips my wrist, but she doesn't tug me away from her face.

"I won't do anything illegal for you," she says and I smile so hard I can feel it around my eyes.

"Rather rude to suggest I'd have you do something illegal. I mean, you are the one who just staked a vampire," I whisper the last part, slightly covering my mouth like it's a dirty secret. That's when she pulls my hand away and I let her.

"If I refuse?"

"Then you hedge your bets with the vampire council. They're very into punishing witches."

What the fuck am I doing? Throwing eight years of restraint

down the drain and letting my obsession and some ridiculous prophecy win. I shake the thought away. It's not a prophecy, it's a fact. I knew it the moment I tasted her blood all those years ago.

I peek at the column of her throat, wondering if she tastes any different with age. I make a promise right then and there I won't taste until she offers it to me. The delicious thrill of a challenge has me fighting down excitement I haven't felt in decades

Her chest rises and falls. It's only a moment, maybe a figment of my imagination, but I swear I can scent her arousal.

"How long would you need my help?" she asks, and it takes me a second to get back to the conversation.

"Six months," I reply, throwing out an arbitrary number, hoping that it's enough time to make her like me. If that delusion isn't a possibility, at least it will give me enough time to give her the skills she needs to protect herself from my kind.

"I won't hurt anyone. I won't use dark magic. I'm not one of your lap dogs doing your bidding."

Have I smiled this much in the last century? I'm unsure.

"Alright."

"Alright?" she questions, shocked that I won't have her do evil deeds for me.

"I won't use you for nefarious purposes," I tell her, and she looks skeptical. If I can get her to agree to this arrangement, I can kill two birds with one stone. "In fact, I hope that I can help you elevate your magic. I've come across a great deal of artifacts that most witches would kill to get their hands on."

Take the bait, let the promise of stronger magic entice her.

"Why should I trust you?"

"I'm the better choice over the vampire council, and I'll agree to all your terms of what you aren't willing to do."

"I won't harm anyone," she says.

"What if they are trying to harm you or someone you care about?"

She purses her lips and adjusts in her seat. "I suppose that would be a different situation. I won't do anything that would endanger my coven, either."

"I think it's best if your coven isn't involved at all. You know, the punishment for staking a vampire is vast. I think the last witch who did it was nearly drained," I say, another lie. They keep falling out of me so fucking easily. Whatever I need to do to get her to agree, I will.

"I'm not at your beck and call like one of your undead minions, either," she says.

This…this one part doesn't sit right for me.

"Your nights will be mine if I choose so. The daylight is yours."

"Right, you can't come out in the sun," she says, and I just give her a small smile with a fang, letting her believe that part. While my skin can't touch the sun, it doesn't mean that money and science haven't gone a long way to help me walk during the daytime.

"So you agree, your nights are mine."

"Except full moons and rituals with my coven."

"Well then, should we seal the agreement with magic?" I ask, grabbing her wand and handing it to her. I need her to agree before she asks me for any more stipulations I can't possibly agree to.

She looks at me like I'm unhinged, but she might just match my crazy. Maybe the old homage of opposites attract could be true.

Darkness and sunshine, walking together into the pits of hell to see where we end up.

She shouldn't agree to my proposition, and I wonder if she feels the same magic between us as I do. Maybe she might fall right into my palm. I'll protect her, even if I have to trick her in the process.

"I need your name for the spell."

"Warin Auclair and yours?" I ask, like I don't know everything about her.

"Ember...Ember Hallow."

I make a vow of my own that somehow, someway, I'll get this witch, *my witch*, to fall for me.

Chapter 4

His name sounds like a caress as my magic surrounds us, binding our agreement.

I'm not sure if it's fear of being made a martyr by his vampire council or if it's something else…like this desperate ache and desire for adventure I haven't been able to put my finger on for so long.

His touch ignites a spark in me that I can't deny. Something that's been simmering under the surface is awakened in his presence. I should be terrified, screaming out the door and running for my coven's help.

Then there's the promise of learning new magic. Maybe this is what I need to become the witch I've always wanted to be.

Even if it's probably the stupidest thing I've ever done, the magic slithers up both of our wrists, connecting us to this vow. I'll help him for the next six months, and he'll offer me protection for a crime I didn't even commit.

Part of that promise is that I won't have to do anything illegal or anything harmful.

It will be fine, right?

The man—vampire—tilts his head at me. He's strikingly handsome. I'm not even sure how to put it into words. Looking at him does more for me than all the men I've come across in my life times one-hundred. How can this be possible? How is it that he excites something inside of me when no other man has.

His eyes look like a frozen glacial lake as he assesses me. He licks his lips as the vow seals itself and I pull my hand away from his colder one.

I wonder if manipulation is a power he possesses and maybe I'm not of sound mind as he appraises me. Maybe he hypnotized me with how hot he is, how rich and enchanting his voice is. This vampire is dangerous, not only because of how he could break me in half like a toothpick, but because when I look at him I feel something I've never felt before.

Hecate, Ember. Did you really get yourself into a complete cluster fuck over a hot vampire? Just because he's good looking and has butterflies flapping in my stomach doesn't mean he isn't potentially evil.

"What exactly is it you need help with?" I say, realizing I should have read the fine print before slipping into an agreement with a vampire.

His eyes search mine, and he doesn't clear his throat or make any human-like sounds. Instead, he stands to his full height, straightening out his suit jacket.

"I need a few items created, old magic. I have some grimoires for you to take home."

My brows furrow. "What? Like protection items?"

"Yes, something of that sort. I may also need your assistance with some vampires that I need to deal with."

"How would I help you deal with vampires?" I ask, thinking he has the wrong witch to help him with his problems.

I'm an elemental witch. If he wanted his gardens to win awards, that I could do. Maybe he needs me to set something on fire? That's also something I'm rather good at. But protection spells? Offensive or defensive magic? I'm probably below average in both of those departments and it has me adjusting in my seat, hoping that he can't tell how insecure I feel about his request.

He smirks, leaning against his desk. Each of his movements is graceful and effortless. He has a southern accent. It's subtle, but it's there. Maybe he comes from a prestigious family where you learn ten different types of forks and to never put your elbows on the table when you eat.

"Vampires live incredibly long lives. Lives that are built around keeping our secrets and protecting ourselves. I mentioned the grimoires. There are other spells to help…handle…a vampire if necessary."

"Listen. I didn't kill that vampire. I think you have the wrong witch."

"No. I most certainly have the right one. Here, we'll start with the first item and spell," he says, striding over toward the book-case, his finger trailing along spines that look like first editions, some of which could be ancient. "Ah, here we go."

The grimoire is small, a brown leather book, clearly made by hand. It's fraying around the edges as he opens up a page.

"One moment," he says, and as soon as I blink he's gone, and just as quickly, the door to his office shuts and closes. My hair whips around from the movement, and he stands before me like he never left.

I swallow thickly. I mean, the lore the humans spew about vampires is all over the place. I'd assumed the speed part was true, but I didn't realize they'd be this fast.

"This will be a perfect conduit. I believe the spell specifically says to wear it on your ring finger," he says, handing me the piece of jewelry.

"It's obscene," I say, the words slipping out of me before I can filter myself. But truly, it's a massive ring, clearly antique. It's reminiscent of an art déco design with slender diamonds stacked next to each other, shaped almost like a tiara. "I don't need something this fancy." I try to save my insult.

He doesn't shake his head, just tilts it to the left side once, a clear no.

"The gold in that ring belonged to a witch I knew a long time ago. She made the ring itself. The spell calls for a coven gifted ring," he says.

I've barely even had a moment to read the damn thing with how fast he moves, and I glance down at the handwritten pages. The spell is in a looped cursive and sure enough it mentions that the piece of jewelry must have been forged by a magical being.

Warin watches me with stillness that makes me feel uncomfortable. I try to ignore his presence, which is next to impossible, as I read on.

My brows furrow as I reach the point in the passage where the witch explains the use of the spell.

"You're giving me a grimoire with a spell that will protect me from vampires?" I ask, and blink as it sets in. "Wait, did you manipulate me into agreeing to help you for six months?"

He grins, his fangs shining next to the rest of his white, straight teeth. What it would feel like to have those fangs—no, bad. Very bad. This vampire is trapping us into a corner, not pushing us against the wall and ravishing us like some bodice ripper novel.

Something is absolutely wrong with me and I need to have my head checked immediately.

"No, darling. I fear you can't blame me for this predicament you've gotten yourself in."

"Why? Why would you give me this?" I ask.

He crowds my space, his arms grabbing the armrest of my chair, and I'm sure he can hear the way my pulse is beating like a war drum.

"Don't worry, sunshine, I don't bite." He leans in, the ridge of his nose barely touching my ear. "Unless you ask me to."

I swallow thickly, hoping he doesn't notice that my heart is racing or that I'm turned on by his presumptive words. He pulls away from the chair quickly, almost like he's collecting himself. He fiddles with his cufflinks that are perfectly in place and his tie that's already flat.

"I hope you find this first task stimulating. You have till the end of the week. I will have Conner drive you home," he says, his playful tone gone, as he rounds his desk and sits down in his chair.

"What if I…"

"What if you what?" he asks and I curse at myself.

Was I really about to ask this vampire—who clearly conned me—how to contact him if I needed him? I've officially lost it. Maybe Iris' new potion to change my hair color made me lose all my brain cells.

"Nothing." I grip the grimoire and slide the ring on my finger.

Warin watches the motion with an almost analytical gaze.

"I'll be in touch. Conner," he calls the man's name in a low voice and the same man who dragged me here is standing at the door. I give him a shitty look, but he doesn't even look at me. "Ensure that Miss Hallow returns home safely. She's under my protection. Do you understand?"

I look between the two men, feeling like they're speaking in some sort of code. How in the hell did I get here? What have I gotten myself into?

"Miss Hallow, follow me," Conner says.

I give Warin one last glance, but he doesn't look up from his paperwork. I'm not sure what his motives are or what he wants from me. All I know is none of this makes sense, and I plan on getting to the bottom of it and avoiding the vampire council at all costs.

Conner ushers me through the hallways of what I'm assuming is Warin's home. I was too flustered when we came in here originally. Too worried about what my fate was going to be, but now that I look around, it's clear that Warin is fuck-you rich.

His home isn't an ancient swamp mansion, by any means. The place is new, modern, and sleek. The design and decor would probably make a true southern belle scoff and roll her eyes at the egregious display of contemporary decor. The walls are rich woods and deep blacks, a massive window down the stairs Conner is walking me down overlooks a lake with magnificent gardens.

"Isn't it a little risky to have a window this big in your house when you're a vampire?" I blurt out.

Conner doesn't even look at me, just keeps walking a few steps behind me.

"It's the best laminated glass that money can buy. No UV rays can pass through," he says in a rather monotone voice.

"Huh," I speculate, looking out at the window one more time and click my tongue as I notice a particular part of his garden where ivy is choking out a few of the trees on the property. My fingertips itch against my wand, wanting to fix it, but I leave it be.

Part of me wants to ask Conner a million questions, but something tells me prying into his employer's business wouldn't be met with easy answers and anything I say would be regurgitated right back to Warin.

Vampires are the most complicated of all the main supernatural beings. They are more than likely the largest group of supernatural beings, which makes their lore harder to understand. Mortals have been spreading rumors and tales about vampires for centuries and while some of it may be true, others are clearly a work of fiction.

I wonder if Warin Auclair is even his real name? How old is he really? Does this home have a deed?

I keep these thoughts to myself and make a plan to figure out exactly what kind of man I'm dealing with the moment I get home.

The rest of his home that I'm able to see is clean with sharp lines and a mix of moody and bright textures as Conner opens up one of the massive wooden doors, leading me outside to the same black SUV that picked me up.

The cicadas are screaming their heads off, along with frogs croaking as we follow the solar paneled lights down the driveway and he opens the back door for me. When I slide in, I glance down at the grimoire and the ring on my finger.

What the fuck kind of arrangement did I just agree to with this vampire?

As soon as I open the door to my cottage, Gus is screaming into my mind.

"Where the fuck have you been? Who were those dickweeds and what did they want?"

He's scurrying around, more frantic than I've ever seen him, as I enter the living room and plop down on my second hand couch.

"*Answer me, witch,*" Gus says, waving his small raccoon hand in my face.

I lick my lips and clutch the book of spells against my chest and blink a few times before looking into Gus' dark, beady eyes.

"Vampires," I whisper softly.

"*Oh fuck. We're dead. We're fucking dead. They're going to come back here and drink us all dry.*"

I'm still staring at the wall where I have a painting of wisteria flowers hanging as Gus grabs my chin. He's nearly baring his teeth at me.

"*You stupid fucking witch! What did you do?*"

I have absolutely no idea, but it can't be good.

Chapter 5

The curtain in my bedroom rattles as the gossamer material shifts to the side, and sunshine floods my room as Gus rustles around.

I can tell he hasn't slept with the way he's shifting back and forth, his small paws clicking the aged floor.

"Gus, what?" I groan as I pull the patchwork quilt up to my face.

"You need to get to work on the spell he sent you home with immediately," he says in a sharp tone.

"I will. I don't need to get started at sunrise."

He jumps on the bed and I'm not sure how it's possible for a raccoon to frown, but that's what he's doing as he grabs the quilt away from my face.

"Did you even bother reading the whole thing? Or did you just go into this completely blind, just like you did when you made an unbreakable vow with a vampire you know nothing about?"

I want to tell my familiar to get off my back, but there's also this guilt in my stomach that knows he's right.

I messed up big time and I have no idea why I did it. There's no logical reason, besides what would happen if I face the vampire council. It's almost like I was under some sort of haze the entire night when I agreed to this stupid arrangement.

"The spell must be conducted with the sun high in the sky. I'm hoping you have some moon water at the ready?" he asks, irritation and urgency clear in his tone, even as he speaks to me telepathically. *"I don't know why this vampire is offering you a spell to protect yourself from other vampires, but you'd be an absolute fucking idiot not to take it. The quicker you have some protection, the safer you'll be."*

I've never seen Gus afraid of anything, while he's always been protective of me in his own way, this is beyond anything I've seen from him. Familiars are still a bit of an anomaly in the magical community. I don't know how old he is or where he came from. Just that one day, he scratched on my door and told me we were magically connected and that he wanted a bowl of ramen. We've been stuck together ever since, and not even at my lowest have I seen him this frantic.

"What do you know about vampires?" I ask.

A small chuffing noise leaves his throat as he hops off the bed and heads for the door.

"Never invite them in. And never trust them," he says with an eerie finality as he scurries to the kitchen.

None of it makes sense, but Gus' worry has me on edge. Have I put us in that much danger?

I groan, pulling myself out of the bed. With my wand in my hand, I flick my wrist, my hair braiding itself and a T-shirt and pair of jeans flutter across the room and land on my bed.

Hecate, I love magic.

My magic may be the reason I'm in a bit of a pickle right now, but something tells me if I was a human I'd find myself in sticky situations too. But I can't imagine life without magic, without a coven. It's who I am, and if anything, I'm on a quest to become even better at it.

Maybe I agreed to be Warin's on-call-witch because he sees potential beyond my elemental magic, or maybe I'm an idiot like Gus says. Or maybe it has something to do with this magnetic pull I'm trying to ignore that I feel toward the manipulative vampire.

I grab a quick breakfast, the grimoire under my arm as I head outside, ready to hopefully master this spell.

I shouldn't be surprised when I head outside that all the garden fairies know what happened last night. But I'm currently surrounded by magically grown flowers, a pissed off raccoon, and a mob of garden fairies that look like they want to start a riot.

"Are we even safe here? I heard vampires love to drain fairies dry. We'll be the first targets," Tabitha whines in her high-pitched fairy voice.

"My protection spell of the garden will keep you safe."

"Yeah, what about at night?" Domingo questions.

"You all can sleep in the cottage at night," I suggest, trying to save myself from a mutiny.

"*The fuck you mean they can sleep inside the cottage?*" Gus seethes.

A frustrated sound slips out of me as I rub the back of my neck.

"I need to work on this spell. You're all still safe here, and well, if you don't think you are, you can try to find somewhere better," I say, standing up straight and immediately feeling guilty right after. I should turn around and apologize, but Gus nips at my ankle, making me jump.

"Forget about the winged freeloaders. You have a spell to master."

"Right," I say, sitting on the old worn bench, surrounded by my rose garden. I open the grimoire.

Gus sits next to me, though he looks like he's about to doze off by the way he's slumped against the armrest.

With each delicate turn of the page, I read the looped words. I'm not sure if it's because she was powerful, but as I read it's almost like I can feel her presence around me as I go through her spell. It seems simple enough, the incantation, the time of day, the swish of your wand. The only thing that complicates everything is the last line.

Vampire blood is essential for the spell to take. It doesn't matter if it was taken or willingly given.

The object you wish to bless protection on must be submerged in a mixture of moon-blessed water and diluted vampire blood before the spell can even be cast.

Why give me the ring or spell at all? Unless he was setting me up to fail. Stubbornness rises up in my chest. There's this constant need to prove myself, and I don't like the idea of him having the upper hand on me.

Wait…

I open the book back up and re-read the page. It doesn't need to be willingly given! I jump off the bench, startling Gus awake as I run back into my cottage and grab the dress from last night. There were just enough spots of vampire blood on the dress from when the vampire was staked. The vampire who got me into this whole fucking mess—that I absolutely did not kill.

When I'm back outside with the dress unscrewing the lid of moon water, Gus is rubbing over his eyes and snout.

"What's this?"

"Vampire blood. It's the last thing I needed," I tell him, feeling almost manic as I drop the edges of my dress into the moon-blessed water and watch as a small tendril of blood spreads throughout.

"Will it be enough?" Gus asks, and I give him a shrug as I put different patches of the dress in the water, trying to get as much blood as possible.

I take off the ring, and plop it into the now slightly pink tinted jar, and watch as the water makes it look larger than it actually is, until it finally settles on the bottom. Based on the witch's instructions, the jar needs to be in direct contact with the sun, so I scoop it up and make my way to the meadow until I reach an outcropping and place the jar on a stack of rocks and take a deep breath.

It's serene in the meadow, quiet minus Gus' panted breaths and the buzzing of the pollinators in the meadow.

My wand is firmly in my hand and I whisper the incantation to myself one last time before getting down on my knees and staring at the jar.

"Okay. Here goes nothing." Deep breath. "Protect thee who wears this ring. Shield them from the demons of night. Strengthen their mind from evil delusions and protect them from an unwanted bite."

I flick my wrist one last time, the end of my silver wand pointing at the jar and I watch in fascination as the jar turns a shade of deep red, nearly black, before shifting back to clear.

The exhale I let out is dramatic and Gus looks at me suspiciously as I unscrew the top and dig out the ring. It looks and feels the same. Even when I slide it back on my finger, nothing changes and I wonder if I fucked the spell up.

"Do you think it worked?" I ask Gus.

"*Let's fucking hope so. Judge Judy is on and I need lunch,*" he complains, rushing back to the house.

The sun winks against my ring and hope fills me. Maybe I really did this right on the first try, all by myself. Or, I've made a fool out of myself and I've disappointed the very witch who came up with the spell to ward herself against vampires.

I guess only time will tell.

Chapter 6

I groan as I tap my fingers against the center console of the vehicle, sliding my phone into my pocket. Achille is driving us back from handling another possible slaying. I should contact the council, let them know one is in my area, but I don't truly want to deal with those pompous fucks.

I'll handle this all myself; the last thing I need is for them snooping around when I'm trying to get closer to Ember.

"I want to make a pit stop," I say, realizing Samantha is right, might as well own how desperate I am.

"The witch's cottage?" he asks. He was one of my men who picked her up that night, so I don't immediately question how he knows this information.

Paranoid, I chant to myself. Outside of Samantha, he's the only other vampire I would ever consider trusting with the truth. I knew Achille when he was human, he was Oz's driver before he was turned and kept the same station in the nest.

He's loyal, dependable, and if I'm not mistaken, he seems more at ease after Oz's death as well.

"Yes."

He doesn't ask me any further questions like Conner does, and he doesn't get on my case like Samantha. But he shocks me as we get closer to Ember's home and he breaks our usual silence.

"You don't plan on changing her, do you?" he asks.

I arch a brow at him, wondering why the fuck it's any of his business.

"I don't know," I answer him honestly, though I try to tamper down my irritation.

He taps his finger on his steering wheel a few times. "If you were to go back all those years ago, can you honestly say you would choose this?"

"I'm not sure if I would or not," I say and he nods.

When we approach her house, it's the same as the last time I saw it. A wrought-iron gate that could use some maintenance surrounds the parameter. Her yard is filled with flowers, the greenery is overabundant, nearly taking your eye away from the small home nestled along the entry way path.

"Should I stay?"

"No. Thank you, Achille."

When I'm out of the car, he drives off and I stare at her home. I've spent many nights out by this tree just staring at what I couldn't have. I'd watch her through the windows as she used her magic to braid her hair, or cook a meal. She often sits on her couch and speaks with her overly large raccoon familiar.

It's a peculiar familiar to have, but I suppose Ember is no ordinary witch.

Watching her has become habitual, a type of indulgence that I always edged myself with. Never once did I consider knocking on her door or approaching her. Distance was best for her, safest.

If Oz knew what she was to me, he would have killed her.

Now that Oz is dead, I still have to worry about her safety, but I'm done waiting. I'm probably still selfish for wedging my way into her life, but fate was always determined to bring us together, even if she doesn't have a clue. I'll protect her and give her the tools to protect herself. Even if this magic between us is only one-sided, I'll keep her safe until I'm no longer walking this earth.

The gate creaks as I open it, and it clunks against the lock as it shuts behind me.

"Ah! Everyone fly for your lives, he's going to drain us dry," a high-pitched voice screams and I roll my eyes.

Of course the witch has a penchant for saving homeless little fairies. I'd seen them from afar, the way they bitch and complain about every single thing. Yet, Ember is patient with them, providing them with everything they need.

My witch enjoys caring for things, nurturing them. It's a ridiculous concept. The moment the little shits bitched about the type of flowers she planted on the west-end of the property, I probably would have eaten them like Tootsie Rolls. My mouth waters when I think of the candy I haven't had in over a century, though I know of something that's far sweeter than any candy I've ever had. She's tucked away in a pretty pink cottage, in need of my assistance to complete her spell.

"Do you know how much blood is in a fairy?" I shout, with my hands in the air. "I'd have to rip off all your heads and only get a drop of blood. Not worth it, though I do hear fairies are quite delicious," I jest, not able to help myself.

There are more high-pitched screams as I watch the fairies all fly onto the porch of Ember's cottage. A small wooden door opening that the human eye wouldn't spot slams shut.

The steps to Ember's porch creak as I walk up them. I never dared to actually go on her property. I never let myself get too close, worried about how I'd react. The first time I tasted her, I knew what she was to me, what power she held over me. It was decades of restraint, self-hatred, and fear that kept me in check.

I'm a weak immortal being for giving in, for dooming her to be tethered to me. Yet, I can't seem to give a fuck as I hold up my hand and lightly tap against her door frame.

She swings the door open quickly; the speed whipping her wild pinkish hair behind her. She looks me up and down with her soft green eyes, like she's unimpressed and it has me grinning.

"So you're why the fairies are being frantic," she says, one hand on the handle of her door and the other on her hip.

I glance inside her home, not able to pass the threshold. There are areas I haven't been able to see from my typical lurking spots.

Her hefty raccoon comes to the door, a chittering noise escaping him, and I can only imagine what the ancient creature has to say to his bonded witch.

Ember purses her full lips and I stare at them a moment. They're full and pouty and absolutely turned down with my presence.

"May I come in?" I ask.

"Absolutely not. What do you want?"

I shove my hands in my pockets and shrug. "Was just here to see how you were coming along on the first spell. Perhaps you needed some assistance."

"Perhaps not. I got it working just fine on my own, thank you very much," she says, wiggling her fingers, showing me the sparkling ring that sits on her ring finger.

Little does she know the significance to me, that every time I see that ring on her finger I picture it as my claim on her. It suddenly dawns on me that if she completed the spell that she had the help of another vampire.

There's no fucking way.

There isn't a vampire in a hundred miles who would dare help a witch with something like this.

Unbridled rage fills me as I grab the frame of her door with both hands, making myself larger.

"And who might I ask gave you what you needed?"

Her eyes narrow at me. Maybe it's because she knows I can't come into her home. There's also our vow that I'll never cause her harm. Little does she know she's cast it twice now and there was never a vow necessary. I'd never dare to harm her.

"Me. I handled it. Did you just come here to check on my progress, or is there something else you need?"

"Whose blood was it, Ember?"

She arches a brow at me, unimpressed with my line of questioning.

"Does it matter?"

"What did they look like? Who the fuck gave you their blood? Did you drink it?" I question, my rage ratcheting up too quickly.

"Hmm, you know, I didn't get a good look at him. I think he was maybe taller than you."

"What was his name, witch?" I ask, my anger festering.

I never thought I'd be anything like Oz, but I am considering hunting down this vampire and staking him right in the heart for even approaching her.

"I didn't catch his name, it was all rather quick," she says with an arch of her brow.

Without even realizing it, my grip on her door frame tightens. It splinters and cracks under my palms as chips of wood fall to the ground between us.

She looks down at the mess on her porch, then back up at me before clicking her tongue and slamming the door in my face.

I blink at the door, not remembering the last time anyone dared to disrespect me in that way.

"Don't come back until you fix the frame!" she shouts from behind the door.

"Open the door, Ember!" I shout back.

She doesn't answer me or open the door and I stand there dumbfounded; she truly just slammed the door in my face and all but told me to fuck off.

I stare at the closed door a while longer, along with the mess I made with my tantrum. I pull out my phone, scrolling with unbelievable speed as I place an order at the home improvement store.

As I'm checking out, a nagging voice interrupts my thoughts, a voice I know all too well.

"Really fucked that up, didn't you, War?"

I pinch my nose, and glare at the shutters next to the door where my bat familiar is all but snickering at me in her head. Humans got some things right, but assuming we turned into bats was pretty far from the truth. Just like witches, vampires have their own familiar, with some significant differences. One being that vampire familiars only ever bond with one vampire, when their vampire meets their death, so do they. The other is the way we're able to communicate, it's all telepathic.

It's another way I've been able to keep tabs on Ember all these years.

"Mind your business, Betty," I tell her through the mind connection we have.

"Oh, shall I unfurl myself out of this shutter and go about my day then? Do you know how insufferable these fairies are? I guess I'll also keep the very vital information of whose blood it was too."

"Don't be petty, Betty."

"I should be. You're being a dick. Apparently, I'm not the only one who feels this way, either."

"You can have the next three nights off, do whatever you please," I tell her.

I see her small beady black eyes through the slats, and I swear I can sense a smile cross her features.

"She's a smart one, your Ember. She used the blood on her dress from the night Baptiste was slain."

Her words click then, that she didn't catch his name, that it was fast. Though she still toyed with me, making me think a living vampire gave her their blood.

"You're free to go."

With a high-pitched squeak, she squeezes herself through the slats and flies away.

"Good luck, you're going to need it," she chimes in before flying completely out of viewing distance.

I finally place my order, an involuntary smile taking over my face as I stare at my witch's door.

Maybe my sweet, caring Ember will survive me yet.

Chapter 7

I wake with a jolt, my breathing heavy as the dream fades away. I've had this dream plenty of times, a faceless man, his teeth in my neck as he holds me against his chest. But this time? This time he had a face, Warin's handsome face to be precise. It felt natural, like it's been him all along in my fantasies and I'm not sure what to do with that realization.

Why did it feel so right? He's secretive, he broke my fucking doorframe last night. Though, I think it was over the idea of another vampire being around me. Still, he can't be trusted and I absolutely should not be having wet dreams about the vampire who's basically blackmailed me into an arrangement.

It must be because I'm tired. I spent the entire night consoling crying fairies and dealing with Gus berating me about getting involved with vampires. I hardly got any rest, that must be why my mind is playing tricks on me.

Disassociation is the only way to handle a wake up call like this, the fairies and Gus must still be asleep, instead of sitting over here stewing over what I've come to believe is a century old vampire, based on my limited Google research.

So instead of thinking too hard about the dream or how I'm going to get myself out of this mess, I gather up the supplies Violet requested for her clinic and head to Main Street.

After I drop off the herbs with Violet, I chastise myself for not telling her about Warin. But as I watched her rushing around her clinic helping a set of twin sisters and talking about what's going on in the pack along with all the coven drama—most of which is centered around my grandma and other elders who hate change—I know I need to handle this myself.

I glance down at my protection ring and pride fills me. I did that. First try, with a workaround that I figured out. I'm capable. I just need the chance to prove myself.

I'm so caught up in my thoughts that I startle as I bump into a man standing outside of Iris' shop.

"I'm so sorry," I say, tilting my head back to see the man, he's extremely tall.

He's scowling, his dark eyebrows pinched together as he looks down his nose at me. He's dressed in simple jeans and a T-shirt, but his arms are covered in strange geometrical tattoos.

Suddenly, and almost animal-like, he tilts his head at me, his pupils dilating quickly, almost so black and large I think I'm imagining it.

"Do you shop here?" he says, pointing at Goddess Apothecary.

"Yes, it's one of my best friends' shops. Are you looking for something in particular?"

"Best friend?" he asks and I look around the street.

"Uh yeah," I reply, a tingling sensation shooting up my spine, and my pointer finger kinda throbs, so I squeeze it tight.

Who the fuck is this guy and why is he asking a million questions?

He looks down at my hand, his eyes dilating again.

"Interesting. You're Married?" he asks.

He stares at my ring and then looks over my shoulder, his pupils dilating. I glance over at where his gaze hits, and all I see is an umbrella swiftly shifting behind a building. His behavior is odd, but I shrug it off and cover my ring with my other hand.

I'm absolutely disillusioning this bitch the moment I get home.

"No. Uh. Sorry again for bumping into you."

"Right. Stay safe," he says, and I swear he looks back over at the building.

I'm sure I'm looking at him like he's crazy. There's no controlling my face at his weird words.

"Um, sure. You too," I say, picking up speed, getting the hell out of there.

Well, that was fucking strange. Despite the weirdness in town, I make my way home, while sending a quick text to Iris.

> **Me:** The guy out front of your shop is a little creepy.

> **Iris:** There isn't anyone there?

> **Me:** Okay good.

I let out a sigh of relief, knowing that he isn't bothering her. But when I finally open the gate to my house, that relief falls away. My grandmother and mother are on my porch, and I already know it's going to be a shitty visit. Wonderful, just what I needed at the end of a very weird day.

The fairies are in the garden, and I swear to Hecate, if they mentioned anything about my little vampire situation, I'll disown all of them.

My grandmother sits on a rocking chair, her red hair graying, her green eyes just like mine as she looks at me with disapproval.

My mother leans against the wall, her arms crossed, but she looks down at the porch floor boards, not at me. I spent so much of my life wishing she would grow a spine and stick up to her mother, but she never has.

"What in the hell did you do to your hair?" my grandmother asks and I sigh, running my fingers through the strands.

"Felt like a change."

She rocks in the chair, looking unimpressed. I immediately shove my hand in my pocket, remembering the ring. The old witch is too perceptive and I don't need her asking questions.

"Seems like that's the whole coven these days. Aster did so much for this coven and they set her aside for an alliance with a shifter. Our High Priestess is married to one, created that abom—"

"It's time for you to leave," I say, cutting her off. There's no way I'm going to let her talk about Violet or her parents that way.

"You're going down a dark path, granddaughter. I can feel it. The Hallows have been a part of Celestial Coven since our ancestors left Ireland. We need to fix this coven before it's irreparable."

"Do you have anything to add?" I ask my mother, who shakes her head, not even looking at me.

My grandmother rises from the rocking chair slowly, hands on her hips. She glances at the broken door frame.

"What happened there?" she asks and I try to quickly come up with a lie.

"I don't know."

My grandmother scoffs. "That's the problem isn't it. That head of yours never knows what's going on. So lost in your plants and your daydreams. This is serious. I know you're one of the weakest witches in the coven, but you need to pick a side."

I want to tell my grandma off, I want to tell her that I'm not weak, that I perfected a spell on my first go that I'm sure no one in the coven even knew existed. She'd be mortified to learn about my deal with Warin. She'd just say it proves what an idiot I am that I got myself into this mess. It's exactly why I need to prove myself.

"I'm sorry you feel that way, grandmother. But I think the coven is in a better place than it's ever been. I hope you have a good night," I say, passing her on the porch.

She grabs my arm, squeezing too tight.

"Whatever it is that you've gotten yourself into, I'll fix it, like I always do. Just make the right decision, the one that benefits the coven. No more outsiders, we need to repair our coven," she says.

I glare down at her, and it feels like she can see right through me, like she knows the trouble I've gotten myself into, and that it was inevitable that I'd be a disappointment.

"I think I'll be just fine without you," I tell her, and for the first time, I think I truly mean it.

There's no way I'd ever betray my coven. Blood doesn't determine the people who are most important to you, my grandmother has proven this point time and time again.

I tug myself from her grasp, and don't look back as I slide into my cottage. The altercation made it even more clear that I need to handle this Warin situation on my own. I don't need my grandmother telling me she told me so, and I don't need the potential blow back from my coven.

I can do this…I think.

It's just after dark, Gus is watching *The Incredibles*, and I'm

attempting to read more spells in the grimoire Warin gave me, when a car door slams in the distance. We both pause what we're doing and stare at each other.

"I swear if my grandmother came back to try and talk some sense into me," I groan.

"Do you want me to bite the old bitch?" Gus asks and I snort.

I'm about to get off the couch and peek through the windows, until suddenly, there's banging noises against the house.

"Holy shit. The vampire is fixing the door frame," Gus says.

"Holy shit is right."

He doesn't knock on the door, doesn't say a word. Gus turns down his movie as we listen while he works. It definitely sounds like a saw, and hammering at different points.

"How long is it going to take him to fix?" I ask Gus.

"Long enough to give me indigestion. I need the Tums."

I sigh, walking to the bathroom, where I grab him two Tums and hand them to him. As he's chomping on the tablets, there's a firm knock on the door.

"Do I answer it?" I whisper.

"I can hear you. Come to the door, Ember," Warin says from the other side of the door and I wince.

"Do you think he heard everything I said earlier?" I ask Gus.

"Yes," Warin confirms.

"Fuck."

I consider not opening the door, just talking to him through the walls, but then he knocks again.

"I'm not leaving until you open the door, witch."

"Ugh. Fine," I groan, walking over to the door and swinging it open.

My mouth parts and I quickly shut it.

He's lost his dress shirt and suit jacket. Just his undershirt on, combined with a ridiculously expensive belt, dress pants, and leather shoes. Despite all the effort he put in my doorframe, he doesn't have a bead of sweat on him.

Why is he so devastatingly handsome? And why despite myself do I find it charming that he actually fixed the doorframe? Did he do it because he wanted to see me again?

No, can't be it right, he needs me for nefarious reasons. I need to stop staring at the hot vampire on my porch and remember that I've entered into some messed-up agreement with said vampire who broke my doorframe in the first place.

"I fixed the door frame," he says.

"I can see that."

He stands perfectly still, his light eyes meeting mine. "Why don't you invite me in?" he says, his pupils dilating.

I hold up my hand, pointing to the ring. "Remember, protection spell."

He smirks, his fang digging into his bottom lip, and I can't help but openly stare, wondering how exactly that fang would feel deep inside of my neck. Does he know what he's doing to me?

I shake away the image and glance back at his eyes; he's smiling now, caught me in the act, which has me putting my guard back up.

"Was just double checking. I had no doubt about your capabilities."

"You're that sure that I'm the witch that you need?" I ask.

He leans against the door again, not able to enter, and the shirt stretches over his chest. I almost let out a wistful sigh as I openly stare at him.

"My eyes are up here, Ember," he says.

I clear my throat, crossing my arms over my chest. "I wasn't…"

"You weren't what? Checking me out? Look away, witch, whatever piece of me you want you can have."

I gape at him, not sure how to handle this open flirting. "I thought you were mad at the whole vampire blood thing?" I say, raising my eyebrow.

He's just as suspicious as he is attractive, which is a dangerous combo.

"Maybe I overacted," he says.

"You broke my doorframe."

"Yes, only because I was under the impression that some other vampire thought he could touch what is m—"

He doesn't finish his sentence as he turns sharply as he looks at something in the woods lining my property.

"Get in the house. Do not open this door, do you hear me?" His tone is firm, honestly the scariest I've ever heard him.

Instead of listening I peek my head out the door, and Warin grabs my chin now that I'm outside of the property.

"Ember. Do not leave this fucking house," he says sharply, before pushing my face lightly back into the house.

I swallow thickly and do as he says, shutting the door and grabbing Gus around the armpits, and hefting him close to my chest.

The fairies are screaming about how they're all going to die, and I wonder if they're right.

Chapter 8

As soon as Ember is in her house, I tilt my head, listening for the sound I heard. It wasn't a vampire, dead silent, but it wasn't a typical human heartbeat, either.

Ember lives far enough off the main road that there's no reason a human would be roaming near her property at night. Plus, I would hear the whooshing of their blood, this is something wholly different.

Did I miss their presence when I was working on her door frame? Or are they just now purposefully making themselves known?

I muffle out the other sounds surrounding me, the fairies crying inside of the house, Ember's breathing, along with the bugs and frogs outside. My head snaps to the left sharply as a wooden stake comes careening toward my chest.

I catch it in my hand with a growl. It doesn't shatter in my palm and when I glance down; it has the same carvings in it that Baptiste's did.

Is this slayer hunting my witch? Or worse, is he using her to get to me?

Fuck.

With unparalleled speed, I run around her property, searching for the piece of shit whose dared to step foot on Ember's property, who had the fucking gall to try and kill me on her doorstep.

This bastard is tricky. They always are.

A branch snaps to my right, and I adjust quickly, moving my body, right before another stake comes whistling next to my head and embedding itself into a tree.

"Show your face, Slayer," I growl.

"You're braver than most," a voice says, and I turn, trying to find his location. His voice is deep and otherworldly. "You'll need to be taken care of so I can take what I want."

"I'm going to rip your fucking heart out," I bellow.

The Slayer laughs, deep and hearty.

"It will be hard for you to do that when you're dead. I'm rather fond of this meat suit. So will she."

She? My Ember?

It's almost as if I see red. Every second of anger and sadness in my life has accumulated to this moment of rage. I nearly have the one thing I desire and he thinks he can steal it from me?

She isn't his. She's mine.

I run, searching, hunting, before I'm hunted myself. Wisps of green flashing around me as I find the being that thinks he can best me. There's a flash of white, and I don't hesitate as I tackle him to the ground, my hands wrapping around his neck.

His eyes are solid black, his sclera completely gone. A feral grin spreads across his face as the veins in his neck bulge. I realize then that he's the man I saw Ember speaking with in town today. He asked her if she was married, but his eyes were different, he seemed more human.

None of that matters, all that matters is that Ember is safe.

He's beyond human strength, we're a near match in strength, holding him down is exerting every ounce of strength I have. I hit him repeatedly in the face as I hold him to the ground by his throat.

He might not be human, but the human he's possessed is. He can be killed. The thought of what I'm about to do disgusts me, as I turn his head, sinking my teeth into his jugular. His blood tastes like shit, like charcoal against my tongue.

I can feel his odd heartbeat slowing, his fight leaving him. Until the sharpest tinge of pain buries itself into my stomach, making me release his throat. He rolls away clumsily, his hands covering his gushing wound, as he slowly stumbles out of the forest. He must be out of stakes, or worried he can't win.

A frustrated roar escapes me when I can't move right away, glancing at the stake in my stomach.

"This isn't over, Slayer!" I scream.

"Never is," he gargles back.

I lie there for a long minute, staring up at the branches above me. This can't happen again. I can't be cornered and unaware. I can't leave Ember here in the daytime for that prick to just stroll up and take her.

With a blood-soaked hand, I shove it in my pocket, taking out my phone.

I call Samantha.

"Hey old man, how did fixing her door go?" she asks.

"The fucking Slayer attacked."

"Where do you need me?"

"Prepare a room for Ember at the house, have the kitchen stocked by the human employees, and hire a chef. Tell everyone in the nest to be on guard. I want round-the-clock security detail on the house, humans during the day, vampires at night. I injured him, but I don't know how fast he'll heal or if he'll heal."

"Why do you sound like you're in pain?" she asks, as I try to muffle a wheeze.

"Fucker staked me in the stomach," I groan.

"I'll be right there," she says, and I let the frustration flow through me.

"No. Do as you're told. Send Achille with the car."

"But—"

"But nothing. Do what I said. I'll be home shortly," I say, ending the call and groaning as I look down at the stake.

I grab it at the base, trying to pull it out of myself with no give.

"Fucking wonderful," I mutter to myself.

That must be the inscriptions he has on the stakes. Some old magic that prevents vampires from being able to rip the wood out of their own flesh. Must be why he left me here and didn't put up much of a fight even though I ripped out his throat.

I don't feel pain like a human does, but as I roll on to my front, my hands and knees covered in dirt, it's the most intense pain I've felt in decades. With a ridiculous amount of effort I'm able to get on my knees and I rip my shirt down the front, watching where my skin is darkening around the stake.

If it was in the heart, I would have been dead immediately. Whatever magic is imbued in the stake is powerful. If I don't get it out soon, it might actually kill me.

I can't die now, not now that my witch needs me.

I'm glad no one is here to watch my embarrassing show of getting to my feet as I trudge my way back to Ember's home. Walking up the four porch steps is nearly enough to make me fall over. I press my forehead against the wood of her door, using my foot to knock.

"Ember," I rasp her name. "Open the door."

"How do I know it's you?"

"Open the fucking door," I say too sharply.

"Yeah, that's one way to know it's you," she says.

She's slow with opening the door, my body leaning against an invisible barrier since I haven't been invited in.

I need her to invite me in. More than anything, I need her to rip this stake out of my stomach.

She gasps as she takes in my appearance. Blood smeared on my chin, my shirt ripped in half, and a stake protruding out of my gut.

"I guess you weren't lying about killing Baptiste, sunshine. Slayer said he's after you," I tell her.

"What? Oh shit. Are you going to die?" she asks, looking me up and down as her hand goes to her mouth.

"Invite me in. The Slayer is injured and I need to be at full strength if he comes back."

This stake in my stomach makes me feel nauseous as I hope she lets me in. I can't decide if it's because the Slayer is out there or because I get a thrill from the idea of her inviting me into her home.

I can tell her raccoon is mouthing off, but I don't really have time for this shit.

"I'll protect you. I already vowed it. I promise not to harm your raccoon or the annoying fucking fairies either. Just invite me in and I'll keep you safe."

A truth, the most honest thing I've ever said.

She bites her lip, her eyes wide as she grapples over her decision. The witch is too caring, too sweet for her own good as the words, "Warin, won't you come in?" spill from her lips.

I stumble into the house. The raccoon is tugging on his fur, pacing in the small kitchen as I fall to the floor on my hands and knees and roll onto my back.

"Gus. Shut up. What was I supposed to do?" she shouts at her familiar.

My hands tremble, gripping the stake, as I attempt to tug again with no movement.

"Fuck," I groan as Ember comes to sit on her knees next to me.

No matter how much the wound aches, I can't help but notice the way her overabundant breasts spill out of the top she's wearing.

"Really? You're injured and staring at my boobs?"

"One last spectacular view before I perish," I say, attempting a smile that turns into a wince.

Ember's eyes are wide as she stares at my chest and examines where I'm impaled with the stake.

"Can't you just rip it out?"

"There are runes engraved in the wood. I don't think a vampire can remove it," I say, blinking at her, hoping with everything I have, this witch will take pity on me, and that I'm right about the runes.

She brings her wand over my abdomen and stops, turning to face her familiar.

"I can't just let him die," she says, and I nod my head in agreement.

The raccoon doesn't agree, making me glare at the small beast and he bares his teeth at me.

"What if I let him die and he's right? It's too many coincidences, plus what if the vampire council thinks I did this too?"

"You're a clever witch. You should take it out."

She tries to flick her wrist, using magic to remove the stake, and it doesn't work.

"I suppose the runes on the wood prevent magic as well," I

surmise, and a pained sort of whine leaves her.

"You mean, I have to physically pull it out?" she says, her complexion paling, showcasing a broad constellation of freckles on her face.

"Afraid so, sunshine."

"There's no one else?"

Not in this world or the next.

"No one else. See those pesky little black lines taking over my torso? I'd guess I have only a matter of minutes." I don't know anyone who's survived a slayer stake, the runes would be why. Who knows how much time I have?

"This is so gross." She sharply turns to her familiar and then glances back at me. "If I save you, I want out of the deal."

Ah. Too fucking smart for her own good.

"No."

She inhales sharply, like it almost pains her to negotiate and not help me on the spot. Her hands are shaking as they hover over my body.

"Then…then I can't help you," she says, though it doesn't hold as much bravado as she thinks.

The deal doesn't completely matter; it was a way to get her close, to protect her and maybe hope that she somehow found some sort of affection toward me.

It appears that I'll just have to be more conniving to get what I want.

"You'll let me die then? Just when things were getting interesting? I meant it Ember, I will protect you from the Slayer, from vampires. I'll even give you the tools you need to protect yourself," I tell her.

She makes a small huffing noise, glancing down at the ring I gave her and then back over at her familiar, and then she sighs with defeat.

"You better not make me regret this," she says quickly, her familiar making screeches of protest as her warm hand flattens on my chest.

A life altering set of shivers rip through my body as her skin touches mine. The pain momentarily gone as I take in her gentle touch.

Her other hand holds the stake close to my wound, and with a loud grunt, she tugs it out. I groan as it leaves my body. The wound is disgusting and takes far longer than normal to knit back together, the black lines slithering away from my veins.

Ember's skin looks green as she stares at the area, before she promptly passes out.

I catch her, holding her close to me, loving the way her hair smells like roses and sunshine.

A car door slams in the distance, and I sigh. Standing with Ember in my arms, the raccoon immediately comes up to me, biting my ankle.

"Little beast, do you wish to come with your mistress or should I leave you here? She's safe with me, and so will you be."

The vermin makes a hissing noise at me, before grabbing Ember's wand, and following me out the house.

Achille waits for us there, his dark eyebrow raised as he takes in Ember's lulled head.

"Poor thing passed out when she removed the stake from my gut. She'll be staying with us from now on. Alert the others that she's mine and if they value their life, they won't harm her in any way. It's probably best that they don't even look at her."

"The Slayer?" he asks, not even questioning my orders.

"Injured or dead, hopefully dead."

Achille opens the back door and I place Ember in the back.

Her familiar scurries up the back, guarding her. I'd send Achille in to gather her things so I don't have to leave her, but I don't like the idea of another vampire touching her belongings, plus he hasn't been invited in.

"I'll be back with her things shortly," I say, using my speed to rush into her home, collecting her clothes and things of importance.

The fairies are quivering somewhere near the floorboards. Maybe they'll learn how to treat their gracious host better now that she's gone.

Once the vehicle is filled with her things, I take the passenger's seat and hope she doesn't wake until she's safely nestled away in her new home.

A ridiculous grin spreads across my face. As big of a menace as this Slayer may be, he sure has helped me exponentially with pushing Ember right into my desperate, immortal arms.

Chapter 9

My head pounds as I shift on my bed.

Wait…

I tap around the bed, feeling way more pillows than I usually have, not to mention the linens feel like butter under my fingertips.

I blink open my eyes, staring at the blush pink comforter. This isn't my bed, it's far too opulent. I scratch my cheek and the last thing I remember is pulling the stake out of Warin's stomach.

"Yup. You really fucked up big this time," Gus says, and I turn on my side. My familiar is lounging on a deep green chaise, his hand deep into a Pringles can.

"What happened?"

Gus laughs, but it's not humorous at all. *"Oh, what happened after you saved the vampire who has you in this shitty ass predicament? I told you to negotiate, to get out of the arrangement, and yet, you still saved him. Guess what, witch? He's kidnapped you. We're at the dead man's house."*

"What?" I sputter, blinking at Gus.

"You just had to do the right thing and couldn't let him die. Now

we're stuck here. He has your wand. He'll probably drain you dry and make a Davy Crockett hat out of me."

"He vowed not to harm us," I tell him, mostly to get rid of some of this guilt weighing on my chest.

But I couldn't just let him die. Not just because he promised to protect me, but I couldn't be the reason he lost his life, the thought of it felt abhorrent to me.

Maybe if he hadn't crawled his way into my cabin begging for help, he would have died in the woods…but even that's a lie. Something keeps pulling me toward Warin, something I can't even describe.

The thought of him dying felt like a piece of me dying too, and I'm not sure how to come to terms with that thought. I barely know him, but there's something there, something I've never felt with anyone else.

If I'm being honest, it's the reason I haven't told anyone about him. I don't know how to explain this feeling or if anyone would ever understand it.

Gus crunches loudly on a few chips, staring me down.

"I'll get everything set straight. We'll be home in no time."

He rolls his eyes at me, grabbing a remote and putting on *Courage the Cowardly Dog.* I have to swallow down my irritation as I lie in bed.

I can't believe I passed out. My plan is to find Warin, and what? Give him a piece of my mind when a vampire Slayer is stalking me and nearly killed him? Run with my tail between my legs and tell my coven how bad I fucked up?

Maybe I'll just stay in this bed forever and not deal with my problems. But when there's a knock on the door, I have no other choice but to open it. With tentative hands, I grip the golden handle and open the door.

"Goodie, you're awake," the ridiculously pretty and young woman says.

"Who are you?" I say, maybe too harshly. So what if Warin has a super hot vampire girlfriend, besides the fact that she would definitely not want me here? Not with the way Warin salaciously flirts with me and stares at my breasts.

It's not like I have a right to care what Warin does. He's the bad guy right? The guy who kidnapped me?

The words feel like a lie, and so I push them out of my head.

"Right. Forgot about that. I'm Samantha. I'm here to show you around the house," she says, her tone kind, not one of an irritated lover.

"Where's Warin?"

The woman smiles, her fangs prominent as her nose crinkles. "Daddy dearest is a little tied up trying to find the Slayer that keeps trying to harm *his* witch," she says plainly.

"I'm not his witch," I quickly say. "Also, daddy?"

This amuses Samantha endlessly, as I say that word.

"Yes, he's my sire, the vampire who changed me. He's not a huge fan of the term, so I use it as often as I can."

"Listen, Samantha. I need my wand and phone back and I need to speak with Warin."

Samantha turns around from where she leads me down the hall, her big eyes blinking at me.

"In due time."

"I can't just be locked up in this house without my things," I respond, she raises an eyebrow at me like she's unimpressed.

"You're safe from the Slayer here, and you'll get your things in due time."

"I'm not a vampire, I still don't understand what he would want from me."

"Obviously. You don't have enough self-preservation to be a vampire. That said, Slayer knows where you live, what you look like. A Slayer so powerful, he took out the oldest vampire I've ever met."

"Right, he knows where I live," I say, holding my hands tightly together.

"Slayers are summoned by humans. Did you know that?" Samantha says changing the conversation.

She turns back, walking down the hall, her straight black hair swishing behind her, and I quickly follow.

"What do you mean?"

"Come with me to the kitchens to get something to eat and I'll tell you," she bargains and I roll my eyes, but continue to follow her. She's absolutely related to Warin in some twisted way with her easy manipulation, or maybe that's a vampire thing.

When we reach the kitchen downstairs, a woman with buzz cut hair is cooking, a wide spread of food placed on the island.

"You have a chef?" I say out loud, with confusion.

"Now we do," Samantha supplies. "Cecile, this is Ember, who you'll be cooking for."

I clear my throat. "Just me?"

"Welcome, miss Ember, if you have any allergies or preferences just let me know. I've made a wide variety for you to try and see what you like," she says with a thick cajun accent.

"Uh. Thank you," I tell her, not wanting to be rude. She's made all this food. "Wait. Did Warin hire a chef just for me?" I ask, turning to Samantha.

She looks at me like I'm stupid. "No, we really love the aroma of food that we can no longer eat," she deadpans and I bite my lip before grabbing a plate and filling it with chicken cajun pasta, etouffee, and shrimp. "Cecile, take the rest of the night off in your quarters," Samantha says to the chef.

Cecile nods, leaving the kitchen right away as I pop a shrimp in my mouth.

"Does she know she's working for a house of vampires?" I whisper, wondering if I need to figure out a way to free her.

"Cecile is paid well to do her job. She's allowed to come and go as she pleases. She knows we're different, but she's compelled to never share our secrets, as are all the humans who work for us."

I hum under my breath, not knowing how I feel about the ethics of all of this.

Samantha seems irritated by my judgment. "She's paid ten thousand dollars every week that she works here. Please, tell me how many chefs are making that type of income?"

"I suppose not many," I say sheepishly.

"No. I suppose not," Samantha says, tapping her black nails against the countertop. "Fuck, I miss food."

"Uh sorry?" I reply, shrugging my shoulders and stuffing my face. I can't even really dwell on the fact that they compelled Cecile to some degree, because damn, can she cook. I clear my throat. "The Slayer?"

"Right. Who knows when the first slayer was created, thousands of years ago, probably? The magic is old, ancient, only passed down to small communities over time. I would imagine now that the rituals of making slayers are mostly lost in time. Only a few select families would know how to summon one, create one."

"Create one?" I question.

"The slayers themselves are so old, just jumping from human body to human body endlessly. We don't know if they are demons, spirits, or what. What we do know is they're dangerous and only care about one mission, what they've been made for, protecting humans. While vampires have always been the biggest threat because of our bloodlust, and vampires that lack control. But that doesn't mean other supernaturals aren't on the table. If the Slayer sees you as a threat, you're a target."

"So, the Slayer has a human host, and even if you kill the host?" I question, fear churning in my gut.

This could mean that I'm endlessly in danger, that I'll have to run from this beast for the rest of my life.

"This is the first slayer we've seen in years. Like I said, there are very few humans who know how to summon one. All we can do is take out the host and hope that they don't get brought back."

I take a sip of the water bottle that was placed in front of my food; I don't even know when it got there.

"What about my coven? Are they in danger?"

"I don't know. Have they been moonlighting with any vampires?" Samantha says, and I glare at her. Meanwhile, her expression doesn't change.

"No. Not that I know of."

"Then your coven should be perfectly safe. The Slayer is injured, Warin and the rest of the nest are out looking for him. You're here because he wants you safe."

"But why does he want me safe?" I push her.

"I dunno, witch, maybe because you have great tits, or he needs you for a spell. How would I know?" Her response is quick and irritated as she stands up.

Something tells me she knows more than that, but she just won't tell me.

"Have you had enough to eat? Let me show you around the rest of the house."

My stomach is full of delicious food as I nod.

"Shouldn't I contact my coven and let them know that I'm

safe?" I ask Samantha as I scratch my cheek. Her hand quickly swats away my hand from my face.

"Don't do that to your face. The noise is grating. No, not yet. Wait until Warin is back."

I take a sigh of relief; I didn't truly want to have to call my friends up, or heaven forbid, my family, and tell them about the complete clusterfuck I've gotten myself into. Asking for help? I think I'd rather die.

Maybe Warin will take out the Slayer tonight and it will be a non-issue. I'll just spend a night or two here, eating Cecile's food, and getting a much needed break from the fairies.

Samantha shows me all around the massive house, telling me nothing is off limits besides her quarters. She also shows me the gardens and tells me that Warin said I could do whatever I wanted out here.

Part of me wants to grow a bunch of bushes that look like middle fingers or phallic-like, but the grounds are too pretty for such a petty retaliation. Plus, what am I retaliating? Him somewhat kidnapping me for my own good?

It's so late, I can barely keep my eyes open and Samantha brings me back to my suite.

"There will be day time security. Do not leave the house. Roam around as you please on the grounds and Cecile is there to make anything you wish."

"Thank you," I tell her, as she stands at the door frame.

She tilts her head before speaking again. "I know Warin can seem…"

"Rude? Manipulative? Scheming?" I suggest.

She shrugs. "Yes, all of those things. But I promise there is also far more to him than that. Just…just know that you're safe here," she says, shutting the door behind her.

"*You better not go soft on me and trust any of these bloodsuckers,*" Gus says and I sigh, climbing into bed.

He follows suit as I rest my head against the pillow.

"Don't worry, I won't," I tell him.

I can't lose sight of who I am, or what I'm supposed to do, even if sleeping in this bed, this house, is the most comfortable I've ever felt in my life.

Dreams flutter behind my eyes as I sleep. It almost feels real as cool hands push my hair off my face.

"Sweet dreams, my beautiful witch," the husky voice says, and I know it's Warin.

I'm not even mad as he infiltrates my subconscious, pressing lips against my forehead.

Disappointment floods me as my dreams shift away to something less interesting, but I sleep soundly.

More soundly than I ever should be in a vampire's home who's holding a magical contract over my head.

Chapter 10

"See, this is what happens when I'm not around," Betty chirps in my mind as she flies around town, trying to find the Slayer.

Most of my nest is out hunting for him, while a trusted few are back in the house, making sure that Ember is safe. Samantha, being the most trusted of all of them, that is, as long as she doesn't expose any of my secrets to the witch.

That's another problem for another day.

At least Ember is safe in my house. Her floral scent is soaking into those ridiculously expensive sheets Samantha purchased.

I smirk when I think about her pissed off expression when she realizes where she is, that I've taken her.

It's better this way, at least for me.

I can go days without rest, and with her in my home, I'll be able to speed the entire process up. She'll have the skills to protect herself from my kind and she'll fall effortlessly in love with me.

She's already saved my life. She couldn't help herself, or maybe she already holds affectionate feelings toward me.

My phone chimes in my pocket as I pull it out.

I smile to myself again. Maybe this will be easier than I thought. Very Stockholm of me to have her fall for me this way, but I don't feel bad about it.

My face falls from that second message. Okay, so we have more work to do. She didn't call me ugly, or that she disliked me. Also, manipulative and scheming, I accept fully. Rude?

Maybe to others, but never Ember.

Well, besides breaking her door frame and making demands of her. I'll work on it.

For now, I need to push Ember from my forethoughts as we hunt down this bastard.

Though…him not being found immediately would be of more benefit to me. Or at least, I could not tell Ember that he's dead when I do kill him, so she'll stay in my home without putting up a fight.

That would be the manipulation she's talking about.

Hmm. Perhaps she can come to love my wit and realize it for what it is. I'm just smarter than everyone else and I like to get the things I want.

"Boss," Conner says, taking me out of my thoughts.

"What?" I snap.

"We've lost his trail. He's lost a lot of blood, but it still smells vibrant. He isn't dead, but we can't figure out where he's hiding."

"Any information on the human host?" I ask.

I'm not sure if it could be described as a possession. Most vampires don't survive a slayer to tell the tale. Most of what we do know is hearsay. But when I think about his completely black eyes, there's no doubt in my mind now about the demon aspect possibly being true.

"Not yet, sir," Conner says, and I stare at him.

"Don't bother me again until you have something useful."

"Yes, sir," he says quickly, running off into the woods.

I should have done more to subdue him, to make sure he didn't walk away from our fight at all. A low growl hums in my throat as I turn in place and make my way back to my home, back to my witch.

Before I can even saunter up to her room, Samantha greets me in the foyer with an unamused expression on her face.

"She's asleep. Have they found the Slayer?"

"No. We lost his trail."

She hums looking me up and down. "Are you sure you lost the trail?"

"What are you insinuating?"

"Warin, please. You'll do whatever it takes to keep your witch in her perfect little tower. She won't like you if you keep trying to trick her."

"I'm not—"

"Please," she says, holding her hand up. "I know part of you was hoping you wouldn't find the Slayer, so you have a reason to keep her here. She's not like us. She cares about things, she wants to be a good person. You know, her first concern, besides not being your captive, was if her coven was safe?"

"And?" I say, bored with the conversation.

"If you want a shot of her actually caring about you, you need to stop orchestrating everything. Maybe, just maybe, give her the pieces of you that no one else sees that I know are there. If you keep up all this scheming, you'll lose her."

"If I don't engineer her needing to spend time with me, how do I get her to want to be around me?"

"You're so stupid sometimes it hurts," she says, lightly tapping my face twice before walking away.

Samantha is out of the room before I can even reply.

How to get this witch to like me without coercion?

I laugh at the thought, heading to my office and sitting on the massive leather chair. A soft tap against the glass has me opening the window, as Betty flies in and hangs upside down from her perch.

"Are gifts manipulative?" I ask Betty.

"Well, are you hoping that in exchange for the gift she gives you something in return?"

"Her affections for me, perhaps."

"It would need to be a very good gift. Your witch doesn't seem like someone who is persuaded by money."

"I knew it, I'm fucked."

"But…her figuring out the protection spell on her own was one of the happiest moments I've seen her."

"So you're saying I should give her a new spell to crack? Maybe rip out a page so that she'll need to come to me for help?"

"You would think all your time on this earth would make you less stupid. No, give her another spell, knowing that it will make her happy, that is all."

"But then, why does she have any reason to speak to me?"

Betty sighs, making a high-pitched squeaking noise.

"You must stop with the selfishness or you'll never win her over."

"So you're saying I should prioritize Ember's happiness and perhaps my own happiness will follow?" I ask her, tapping my finger on my desk.

"Yeah, let's just go with that. The sun will be rising soon. I need

my rest and you're giving me a headache," she says, adjusting her wings, and cutting the conversation off.

I round my desk and look at the bookshelves before me. Some of them bring me sadness, knowing why I have them. If Ember knew how I came upon these grimoires, she probably wouldn't want anything to do with me. I suppose that's no different from how she feels now.

My finger trails the spine of the dark green journal and I pull it out, flipping to the page I had in mind. I'll never forget the first time I felt the pain of a witch scrambling my brains.

I bring it to my desk and write a note to Ember.

Beautiful Ember,
My home is your home.
You'll be safe here, that I can promise.
This spell is a difficult one to master, but I'm around any time you need a test subject.
P.S. Thanks for removing the stake.
Yours,
Warin.

I grab her wand, phone, the note, and the grimoire and head to her bedroom.

She's asleep, her pink hair splattered around pink linens. Her lips are parted as she rests, and her soft lashes rest against her cheekbones. The raccoon familiar is snoring in the corner as I place everything on the nightstand.

I'm not able to resist myself as I move a curl out of her face.

"Sweet dreams, my beautiful witch," I tell her, being selfish and greedy, as I lean forward and place a delicate kiss against her forehead.

She makes a soft sound of contentment before falling asleep

again.

"I'll do whatever it takes for you to want to be mine, Ember Hallow," I whisper as a pledge to myself.

Now I just have to figure out how to get this sunshiny witch to fall in love with a jaded wretch like myself.

Chapter 11

I sleep way better than I should in Warin's guest room. I should have been tossing and turning in an unknown bed. Yet, here I am, fresh as a daisy as I wake up with a smile on my face.

Gus doesn't seem too put out either as he crunches on a piece of bacon, a massive food cart in front of his chair.

"I'm still mad at you, but the room service is incredible," he grumbles.

I make myself a plate as I sense my wand. My brows furrow as I glance at the nightstand. My wand, phone, and a note sit there and I grab the note first.

Warin's note is short and I'm even more confused when he mentions practicing, and then I flip open the new grimoire that was just underneath the note. The handwriting is the same as the one with the protection spell.

"What ass backwards spell is he wanting you to learn now?" Gus says as he bites into a pastry.

I clear my throat. "On rendering a vampire immobile," I rasp out.

Gus moves quickly out of his chair, rounding the food cart,

danish still in hand as he glances over my shoulder and confirms what I just said.

"Hmm…this dead man makes no sense."

"You're telling me," I say, reading over the spell and making sure that Gus doesn't get any crumbs on the book.

"Well, if it takes you a few days to figure it out, it's not a big deal," Gus says, moving back to his chair and turning on the TV.

"What happened to me getting us killed and being the stupidest witch on the planet?" I say to my familiar with an arched brow.

He shrugs his furry little shoulders. *"That was before I realized the level of our accommodations. You're still walking around with all your blood, and he's teaching you how to protect yourself from his kind. Don't get me wrong, we shouldn't trust him, but have you tasted the beignets?"*

I sigh, tuning Gus out as I read over the spell. This one has a lot more to do with practiced skill versus doing the right incantation and having the right items like the last spell.

To immobilize a vampire, you're basically sending them a high-pitched frequency into their mind, almost like a dog whistle, rendering them unable to function.

In the margins, the witch mentions what has and hasn't worked. That the older the vampire, the more difficult it is to use this magic.

How old is old in vampire years, anyway?

"I'm going to go out to the gardens and practice," I tell Gus, and he waves me off as he slouches, a beignet perched on his stomach as he watches his show.

I get turned around in the house a few times, but finally make it out the back door. The house is so quiet that you could hear a pin drop. I wonder if Warin and Samantha are resting. Do vampires actually use coffins?

When I get outside, I'm able to appreciate just how beautiful his gardens are. They're filled with colorful roses, lush bushes, and ancient trees.

There are a few plants that need pruning and a little love. I take care of that easily as I find a small patch of grass that's covered in shade. I toss the blanket down, resting on my stomach as I read through the entirety of this journal.

I meditate, I practice clearing my mind and being more intentional with my magic. But I realize that there is no practicing this spell without a vampire. The last bit of his note makes sense. However, I don't really feel like talking to the vampire who is keeping me in this very serene prison.

It's been a whole day, and I haven't seen a single soul, besides the chef, Cecile.

So I'm shocked when Conner approaches me in the kitchen as I'm eating dinner.

I glance around. "Uh, isn't the sun still up?" I ask as he blinks at me.

"It is," he says simply.

"Doesn't that mean you should be sleeping or something?"

"Oh, we don't—"

"Conner," Warin's voice cuts through whatever Conner was going to say like a sharp knife. "Don't you have other things you need to be doing? Like not standing in the kitchen," he says, not looking at me, only staring at Conner.

"Right. Yup. Loads to do. See ya later," Conner directs at me, and Warin glares at him further.

I take a sip of my red wine and Warin faces me, his face unreadable as he watches me drink. I clear my throat and I'm thankful that I was almost done eating my meal or else this would be even more awkward.

"Did you find where I left your wand?" he asks.

"I did," I reply, taking another sip.

"Hmm. I see," he says, glancing at the stool across from mine.

"It's your house. If you want to sit down, you can."

"Right," he says, quickly taking his seat across from me. He's more casual tonight and dare I say, he looks nervous.

I make this super rich, ridiculously attractive vampire anxious?

"Do you sleep?" I blurt out, and Warin blinks at me with his serene eyes.

"Sometimes."

"Because you need to?" I inquire, trying to get more of a story out of him than his usual riddles.

"Vampires who rest more frequently tend to not go mad. It's a way to cure boredom, but it isn't completely necessary. A vampire who doesn't rest for a long time may have symptoms of sluggishness or irritability. Same as if we don't feed for a while, we usually need more rest."

I'm shocked he answers my question so easily and without snark.

"Interesting. Do you sleep in a coffin?"

His lips twitch. "If you wish to see my private quarters, all you need to do is ask."

I click my tongue. "Yup, now I remember why I don't ask you questions," I say.

"No, I don't sleep in a coffin," he says, backpedaling. "Did you sleep well in your new accommodations?"

"I can't deny that the bed is probably the best one I've ever slept in. Keep sending food up to the room and Gus will never want to leave."

"What about you? What would it take for you to want to not leave?"

I blink at him a few times, taken completely off guard. "I'm just here until the Slayer is out of the picture. I have a coven, responsibilities," I say, and even as I do I can feel heat rising to my cheeks.

"Hmm. I see. I don't know how long it will take to find the Slayer."

"But there is a time limit on our arrangement," I remind him and he hums again. "An arrangement that didn't involve me living here."

"We could amend that, you know."

"I don't think that's necessary. I appreciate you keeping me safe here until we figure out the Slayer situation, but once it's taken care of, I'll have to get back to my life," I tell him.

What was my life before Warin crashed into it? Rather boring, I was doubting myself, having these feelings I couldn't express to anyone. It doesn't matter though, even if I did let myself indulge in what I want, it would never work anyway.

Something tells me if I let myself even get a taste of the fantasy I've been thinking about, I'd never be able to let it go.

I stare at Warin's fang and he tilts his head at me.

"Right. Until the Slayer is handled," he reiterates.

I clear my throat. No indulgence, we'll ride this wave out, get the hell out of here and get out of this arrangement or finish it up. So far he's asked nothing nefarious of me, only giving me new spells to protect myself.

"So how old are you anyway?" I ask.

"I was born in 1898," he says and I whistle. "Are you afraid of an older gentlemen?" he asks and I nearly choke on my wine.

"What? No. I mean, that's just a long time to be alive, you've probably seen a lot of things."

"Nothing as pretty as the witch in my kitchen right now."

Okay, that has me squirming in my seat. My freaking pointer finger is on fire for some stupid reason and I squeeze it. Am I sweating? No way.

"Is that why you're giving me spells to protect myself against vampires, because you think I'm pretty?" I flirt back.

I fucking flirt back with the vampire and I like it. There's no way this ends well, I'm already in a cauldron load of trouble, but as I sit at the counter with him, both of us leaning closer I can't help myself.

"Because I want you safe. Being beautiful is just a bonus," he says simply, like that was the easiest answer.

"Why do you want me safe?"

"For so many reasons, I'll explain in due time," he says, and I cross my arms against my chest.

This only makes Warin stare at my breasts for a moment, before they slowly slip back to my face. One moment he's flirting with me and then the next he's being secretive and pushing away.

What does this vampire want from me? And am I open to indulging him?

"In the meantime, I suppose I will need to do a better job of showing you that I very much care about you being alive."

"You know, I'm not a fan of secrets. I'd much prefer your honesty."

"Honesty?" he asks, clearing his throat, like it's a confusing concept.

"Yes, honestly. Like not hiding secrets, being forthcoming with information. I'm sure you've heard of it."

"I'll have to look this word up. Honesty."

I take a sip of my wine and Warin watches me intently, like I'm the most fascinating thing he's ever seen. It's nice being desired, even if I don't know what he truly wants from me, it's fun how openly he desires me, I've never felt that before.

"You do that," I tell him.

"You haven't brought up my note," he says, changing the conversation, which he is especially good at.

"No, I haven't."

"Why haven't you asked me to help you?"

What do I say, that I am feeling stubborn? Or that I don't want to be embarrassed if I can't do it right?

"I've been working up to it, plus I thought you'd much rather me torture one of your minions instead of you."

"No. I'd very much enjoy you torturing me. You're already so good at it," he says with a smirk. "Tonight. In the gardens, we'll practice."

"I…no, we can do another night."

"Tonight, in the gardens," he repeats. "You have about four hours until the sun sets. I'll see you then."

He's out of the kitchen before I can even retort. I breathe heavily through my nose, not even wanting to eat the rest of the fish Cecile prepared.

I'm not sure what's more dangerous. Spending alone time with Warin, or the potential that I might completely fail at this spell.

The moon is high, nearly full. I'm going to have to figure out something with Warin so that I don't miss my coven's ritual. If I don't show up, Violet and Iris would be concerned. Hell, I should probably be more concerned by the fact I'm basically being held hostage by a vampire—one I'm embarrassingly lusting after.

He's hiding something from me, there's a deeper reason why he has me in his house, why he tangled me up in this agreement, and I have to put that over my stupid hormones that need to get under control.

Like he knows I was thinking of him, he appears in front of me; I clutch my hand at my chest.

"Fuck. Can you make a little more sound when you stalk around?"

Warin clears his throat and sits next to me on the blanket without an invitation.

"I'll work on making a little more noise next time," he says sheepishly. "How is the spell coming?"

I blow my hair out of my face, holding the journal open.

"I didn't know witches could specialize in magic that affected vampires so much."

Warin nods. "Yes, well, I'm pretty sure a lot of vampires destroyed any evidence of this type of magic over the years. There were times vampires and witches loathed each other, especially in large cities. A lot of vampires are the reason witches were hunted. In the last fifty years or so, tensions between the two have turned into more of surviving the mass population of humans over fighting each other."

"Why haven't you destroyed these spells, then?" I question him.

"Maybe I'm more sentimental than you think," he says with a wink and I shake my head.

"No, I don't think that's it."

He sighs. "These grimoires. They belonged to a friend," he says it like he didn't want to be honest with me, like it pained him to tell me a truth about himself.

Why do I crave him being honest with me? It's like I crave

these small little secrets he's willing to share, like it makes me special. It's rather pathetic and I chastise myself.

"A witch was your friend?" I ask, and he barks out a laugh, making me jump, and I can't help but smile. He's got one of those laughs that makes you want to laugh along with him.

"I suppose friend is a strong word. She wanted them preserved, and so I preserved them."

My cheeks heat. Did he used to date a witch? Why does it irritate me?

"Pauline probably hated me, no she absolutely hated me. I had only met her that night, but I felt like I owed her."

"Why?"

"It was the least I could do."

"Always so cryptic."

"It's a story I'll tell you another day. When you don't hate me."

"I don't hate you," I say under my breath and he sits up straighter, adjusting his suit like he's nervous.

I might be confused about how I feel about the secretive vampire, but it's definitely not hate.

"You know a lot of…friendships"—I say friendships, because I'm not sure what other fucking word to use for the predicament I've found myself in—"start with sharing information about yourself. You know, honesty."

"Honesty…I think I looked it up on the internet earlier, it's an interesting concept."

I roll my eyes at him and stare down at the spell, changing the conversation. It's clear that Warin struggles with sharing information about himself. It makes me want to crack him open even more. What would it feel like for an immortal like Warin to trust me with his secrets?

"The basis of this spell reminds me a lot of memory retrieval, the way you're looking into someone's mind," I tell him and he makes a noise of agreement.

I glance up at the moon, wondering if I should bring up that I'll need to be with my coven in a few days. It's a gorgeous spring night, the sky with scattered stars. It's the type of night's sky that makes you feel insignificantly small.

When I turn back, Warin is staring at me. I blush against my will.

"Have you retrieved someone's memories before?"

"I've manipulated some memories," I say under my breath, his vampire hearing too damn good as he lets out a scandalous gasp.

"That's a very naughty witch thing to do," he says.

"In my defense, it was to protect my friend, my coven. As far as memory retrieval, I haven't been great at it. Iris is better."

He hums again, a gloved hand rubbing his chin.

"You could try it on me. This honesty you speak of. I could show you a memory."

I bite my lip and stare at him. Is this vampire so emotionally unwell that he doesn't even know how to have a conversation about himself? Would it really be that much easier to just have me slithering around in his mind"

"What kind of memory?" I ask him, again, my curiosity always wins out.

He's trusting me with something, and it feels like a big win, and I'm going to take it.

"Ask me what you would like to see and I'll consider it."

"How about when you were turned?" I ask. He makes a huff, falling onto his back, the moonlight glinting off of his too handsome face.

"Really going for the jugular with that one," he says.

This sends a little thrill down my spine. Would he really be that vulnerable with me, and why would he want to be.

"There's a chance I can't even do it, anyway," I say self-deprecatingly.

"Go on then, try it," he says, his arctic eyes feel like they're piercing through my soul.

I raise my wand, with no intention of hurting him like the spell warrants. Being able to look into his mind, gain access, is like the first stepping stone to being able to do what I want.

I take a deep breath, holding my wand, and gasp as I'm brought back to 1924 in Warin's mind.

Chapter 12

New Orleans

"Bonjou," Clement says, as he helps me load the gin into the back of the truck.

He's the best brewer within an hour of New Orleans, and business has been booming. Things taste so much sweeter when they're illegal.

"Hey, Clement," I say, as we check over our shoulders, making sure the cops or any unsavory types aren't watching our pick up.

"Have you spoken to Achille or seen him lately?" he asks about his grandson.

"No, sir, I haven't," I tell him honestly and the man nods with frustration.

"You hear anything? You'll let me know? That boy never fucking listens or checks in."

"Yes, sir. Speaking of next week, the boss wants to double our order for the week," I tell him.

He takes a deep inhale, taking off his flat cap, running a towel over his sweaty head before putting the cap back on.

"I'll see what I can do. You tell him daytime crew only now, ya hear? I don't care how much money Mr. Oz wants to throw at me. I'll brew his gin, but I ain't dealing with his night crew and if I hear anything about Achille joining the night crew I'm done. I don't care about the consequences."

I furrow my brow, placing the produce boxes overtop of the crates of gin.

"I was hoping to join the night crew," I tell him honestly.

That's the next step.

Oz's daytime rum runners make a decent enough living. But the night time crew is bona fide, the entire town respects and fears them. They stroll around New Orleans in their tailored suits with money to burn like there's no tomorrow. I know it'll mean getting my hands dirty, they're considered gangsters to most, but I'm tired of having just enough to get me and my ma by.

I want it all.

"You listen to me. You don't want nothing to do with that night crew," Clement says, and I give him a nod, though I don't agree. Clement might be a wiz at what he does, making hand over fist selling illegal gin. He's a wise man, but he's wrong about this.

"I'll see you again next week," I tell him, and he arches a dark brow at me.

"Yeah, I'll see ya, and it better be in the fucking sunlight," he says, pointing to me before getting into his Chevrolet Superior.

He's probably had a bad encounter with one of the night guys. They're tough, rougher around the edges. It's how we keep the operation running. People need to pay up on time and they need to keep their mouth shut if we don't want to get shut down. The last thing we need is someone spilling their guts during another fucking raid.

Oz keeps his circle tight because he's a smart man. Though I haven't met him, I report directly to Eugene. But from what I've heard, and the talk around town is that you don't fuck with Oz.

I think about all the times my pa hit me and my ma, how I never did nothing and now we live in a shit hole that barely has running water. I wasn't the man I needed to be then, but with him out of the picture, I could be.

I'm gonna prove myself. I'm gonna get on the night crew and get us a real house. Maybe I could make enough that she could open a storefront, she could tailor the suits and dresses for the rich in New Orleans, no more of the odd jobs that pay next to nothing. In fact, maybe I could make so much on night crew that Ma wouldn't even have to work anymore.

The sun is beaming; the air feels like fucking soup against my face as I make the drive back to town.

How am I gonna prove myself? What's it going to take to even get on Oz's radar to prove I can be the man that he needs me to be?

It was avaricious what I wanted.

My pa would've told me God would've been disappointed by my greed, but he wasn't alive anymore and we were better for it.

Once he died, we moved out of the fucking swamp and made things work in New Orleans. It wasn't easy, but when I fell in with Oz's crew, things got better. Maybe having clean clothes and not worrying about my next meal went to my head because all I wanted was more.

I wanted respect, along with the lifestyle that came with being in Oz's inner circle.

I'm so lost in thought that I'm startled by the man standing off on the side of the road. He's clutching his stomach and waving me down. I glance around, seeing no one else besides the man. The brakes creak as I stop the vehicle and look out the window toward him.

"You alright?" I ask.

He's still hunched over, grabbing his stomach before suddenly standing up straight, a gun in his hand as he points it at me.

"Yeah, I'll be alright as soon as you get out of the truck," he says.

In my peripheral vision, I see another man coming out of the field. He has a knife and not a gun.

"Listen, I don't want any trouble. I don't think my boss will take kindly to you stealing his produce," I lie. The one thing you don't do when you're smuggling liquor is let anyone know what you have in the back of the truck.

He barks out a laugh. "You can tell Oz exactly who stole his gin. We're Henry's crew."

Fuck.

"Henry can't source his own liquor?" I say, slowly grabbing the switchblade out of my pocket.

"Enough chit chat. Get the fuck out of the car or I'll shoot you right there. Which would be a huge pain in the ass to clean."

"Go on and get out of the truck and we'll let you live so you can tell the mythical Oz who stole from him." The other man laughs.

Neither of them are dressed nicely, both of their shirts a tacky off-white covered in sweat stains. Their suspenders are stretched out and their trousers all seem one size too big. I turn the vehicle off, taking the keys out of the ignition.

I open the door, the second man glaring at me.

"Look at this, Clint, he's got a real pretty boy working for him," he jokes.

"Shut the fuck up, Dale, go look in the back," the other man says, pointing his gun toward the back.

It makes me wonder if he actually has bullets, and it has me feeling bold. Not only am I not going to let these two men steal Oz's liquor, but this is the opportunity I needed to prove myself. Maybe I can subdue him and get in my truck and get the hell out of here quick enough that they can't chase, I don't see a car nearby.

"Give me those keys, boy," Clint says and I take a few steps toward him, my hands in the air and the switchblade in my sleeve, the keys looped around my finger.

"I'm sure we can come to an agreement," I say, getting a little closer to the man.

"Sure. The agreement being we take your shit and we let you live. You can walk all the way back to New Orleans."

"Oz will retaliate," I say.

Clint laughs. "We're plannin' on it," he says, taking one hand off the gun, no longer holding it straight as he holds out his palm to take his keys.

"This could have ended differently," I say, moving as fast as I can, smacking the gun to the side with my left hand, and sinking the switchblade into his kidney with my right. He nearly collapses on top of me. He goes for the gun, his fingertips nearly reaching for it when he goes limp underneath me.

I climb off him, grabbing the gun, and staring at him for a long moment. What have I done? I'm covered in blood as I grab the gun and my heart races in my chest.

"Oh, hell yeah. We're about to have one fucking payday!" Dale screams from the back of the truck, startling me.

Clint's dead on the side of the road, one press of my knife is all it took. My hand shakes as I open the chamber of the gun, It's loaded, three bullets. He would've shot me, there's no doubt about it. Knowing I was defending myself and Oz's product doesn't make the realization of what I did any easier.

I hold the weight of the metal in my hand, knowing that if I let Dale leave I'll be arrested or worse. Fuck, am I really going to do this?

I round the back of the vehicle. Dale is climbing out, a big ass grin on his face, until he sees me covered in blood. His face goes shock white, and he goes to hold his hands to surrender, but I don't even give him the option. I fire the weapon; the kickback is fierce and my ears ring from the pop.

It was a clean shot, killing him instantly as blood pools beneath him, darkening the dirt. The sun beats down against my skin. I'm covered in sweat and blood as I look at the man I just killed. The second man I killed.

I should feel more, right?

My body is filled with adrenaline as I grab his ankles and drag his body into the nearby soybean field. It won't offer much protection, but maybe enough for me to get back to town.

The only person I saw on my way here is Clement, and he won't say shit. I just need to get to the warehouse and make sure no one sees me covered in blood.

I'm panting, overexerted as I nearly toss Dale into the field, only to have to do the same with Clint.

By the time I hide their bodies the best I can, I'm so tired I can barely stand. I'm filthy and thirsty as I get back into the driver's seat and drive away from my crime with only one thought in my mind.

This could change everything, but at what cost?

I've been sitting in the same clothes I killed Dale and Clint with for the last five hours, tied to a chair. I thought when I arrived at the warehouse and told my tale to Eugene I'd be rewarded, honored for protecting Oz's supply.

Now I'm wondering if I've just destroyed my whole life.

I've held my piss for a ridiculous amount of time and I smell so fucking bad I consider vomiting on myself.

My neck aches as it hangs low and I stare down at the warehouse floor, when suddenly and quietly, a pair of leather shoes is all I see. How didn't I hear anyone walking in? The man grips my chin with his ice-cold fingers as he stares at me with a cool expression.

"Handsome this one. You killed those men who tried to steal from me?" he asks.

I admire him for a moment. His suit is crisp and expensive, his face harsh and stern as he digs his fingers in my cheeks.

"Yes, sir."

"How did you do it?" he asks, not letting go of my face.

"I stabbed one with a switchblade and shot the other."

"How did it feel?" he asks, his face getting closer to mine. He's single-handedly the most intimidating person I've ever met.

"It felt good," I say, feeling like I can't lie to him, almost like I'm under some sort of hypnosis.

"Would you like to feel this good every day…" He tilts his head and I assume he's searching for my name.

"Warin."

"Do you want to feel that all the time?"

I look around the room, there are a few more men here, but I can't make out their faces.

"Yes, sir. I promise if you let me join your night crew, I won't let you down."

"I know you won't."

"I can change him," a deep voice says from the shadows and Oz clicks his tongue.

"No, I think I might take him for myself. He'll be better than the last one," Oz says and I swallow thickly. What the fuck does that mean? "You'll leave your old life behind. Whatever family you had is gone, you're dead to them. But you, young Warin, as long as you listen to me, you'll have everything."

Everything. Money, respect, and maybe one day I'll be as powerful as this man.

"I sure hope you enjoyed the sun today," Oz says with a feral grin and my brows furrow as he leans forward. I try to shuffle away from him, but it's no use as something sharp digs into the side of my neck, making me gasp.

There's no moving, there's no getting away. All I can do is sit here and slowly feel my consciousness drift away. My head feels light and my throat is stinging as I blink.

Oz is holding my face.

"You must drink for the transformation," he says, holding his wrist to my mouth.

What the fuck?

The coppery taste fills my mouth and I find…it's not so bad.

The man pets my hair in a nearly affectionate way. "Now you are a son of darkness," he whispers.

Looking back, if I would have known that was the last time I'd ever feel the sun against my skin, I would have spent it more wisely.

Chapter 13

I pull out of Warin's memory, blinking wildly at him.

The memory felt so real. Like I could feel the humid summer air, like I could scent the blood of the men Warin killed before he was even a vampire.

I know my heart rate is up, that I'm doing a shit job of hiding my expression. I knew Warin was dangerous, but seeing what I saw shed him in a more complicated light. He did something wrong, but he also never knew what he was getting into, what being on night crew meant.

I reiterate in my mind he's made a vow to never cause harm to me or those I care about.

"It is not a pretty story. Most of my existence isn't. I'm not a good man."

I take a deep breath, trying to really take in everything he showed me. He was greedy, proud, and he hurt people. But he was also young, naive, and hopeful.

"I meant what I said. I'd never hurt you, Ember."

"What about other people?" I ask softly.

I believe that he won't hurt me, even if he won't tell me why, but I have to know what kind of man I'm dealing with.

He closes his eyes, his hands resting on his chest, almost like he can't bear to face me. Why should he give a single shit about what I think of him?

"Those men that I killed. They would have killed me. There's no doubt in my mind. It was kill or be killed in that situation."

"And what about now?" I ask, a little too sharply.

"Who do you think I am? Do I seem like a blood thirsty monster to you?" he asks with a husky laugh. "I won't deny that I've done wrong things, that I've been selfish and destructive, most of it never of my own will. But I don't go around killing humans, that's not my thing."

I adjust how I'm sitting on the blanket, curiosity getting the best of me. I think back on the vampire that changed him in his memories and I wonder if Warin will be even more honest with me.

"Oz was like what you are to Samantha?" I ask and he hums. He still hasn't opened his eyes to look at me.

"Yes, he was my sire. He was very possessive of me in that regard. Even when he released me from the sire bond, he was always near, always wanting some control over my life."

I clear my throat. "Were you lovers?" I ask.

That has him cracking his eye open to glare at me. "No, probably to Oz's chagrin."

"You can't just blame another person, though, for doing bad things."

"I know that. He's just a part of it. But he's dead now and there's no excuse."

"He's dead?" I ask, lightly rubbing my throat. Did Warin kill him?

"Don't worry, sunshine, I didn't kill him. Pretty sure our little slayer friend did, didn't leave much behind either. That's why I'm taking this all so seriously. Oz was centuries old, strong, and one slippery motherfucker."

Since he's in such an honest mood, I ask the question that I know is wholly inappropriate.

"Are you glad he's dead?"

Warin sits up quickly, his hand on his jaw.

"Yes."

"He was that horrible?"

"He kept me away from what I wanted most." He stands, holding out a gloved hand, almost like some sort of trauma dump olive branch. "I think that's enough for tonight. We can practice more tomorrow."

I take his hand, mostly because I'm not sure what else to do. He tugs me to my feet, grabbing my blanket and folding it at a light speed as we walk into his mansion.

"Will you be hunting the Slayer tonight?"

"Yes. I know you don't trust me, Ember Hallow, and I don't blame you. I know that my past is irredeemable, but I'm hoping that perhaps you would consider gifting me with some of that delicious kindness you hand out to other pathetic creatures. I was quite hoping you'd like to be my friend."

I pause our trek to the house. Lighting bugs glitter the sky and frogs bellow as I stare at the vampire before me.

"Warin, I literally just watched you kill someone in your memories," I say plainly.

"Yes, but that was a hundred years ago," he says, like that makes so much sense in his mind.

I suppose that makes sense, for him it feels like multiple lifetimes ago. I rub the bridge of my nose. He was honest, he did what I asked, I can give him some leeway too.

"What does being friends mean to you?"

"Well…we would hang out. We would talk to each other. I don't know, do stuff," he says, like he's making it up as he speaks.

"Do stuff?" I repeat.

Warin holds his hands up in the air, exacerbated. "Yes, like go places and talk or laugh."

"Go where, Warin? A day trip to get beignets and a cup of coffee?" I say it, and it feels rude even as I do, guilt churning as the words slip out of me.

"Is that what it would take?"

My brows furrow as I stare at him. "That was rude—"

"No. If being your friend means being able to take you out during the day then I'll work on it," he says with a smirk.

I place a hand on my hip. "Warin, you're a vampire."

"Yes. A very rich one," he replies, placing his hand on my shoulder.

The touch sends a tingle down my spine, and it's impossible to ignore.

"But you are a witch. Which means you need around six to eight hours of sleep a night. I wouldn't be against you going nocturnal, but as it stands, you need your rest and I have a slayer to track down."

"Uh, okay?"

He walks me all the way to my room, not entering the doorway.

"Have a wonderful night, Ember. I'll work on our friendship date," he says, not allowing me to answer as he shuts the door.

I blink at the wood, before gripping the handle and swinging the door open, but of course, he's long gone.

"What the actual fuck?" I whisper to myself as I turn around in the room.

Gus is eating popcorn, nodding his small head.

"I say the same thing every time you go off and do something stupid. What did you do now?" he asks.

"I think I just agreed to be friends with a vampire."

"At least he has good snacks."

I walk over to him and touch his forehead, which he swats away. "Oh my gods, Gus. Did they Stockholm Syndrome you with food alone?"

"The chef made this popcorn on the stove, Ember. Then she poured Isigny Ste Mère butter on top. It's honestly about time I started being treated like a king. Plus, not a single fairy in sight. These vampires are deathly quiet." He laughs maniacally for a moment at his own joke.

His laughter quickly ends as I grab a fistful of popcorn and shove it in my mouth.

"Oh, this is really good," I mumble as I swallow, grabbing another fistful.

"Get your own, witch. And go suck up to that vampire so I can have a rich step daddy."

"Gus," I chastise. "You hated him. You told me how stupid I was for letting him in the house, how we were all going to die."

"I'm a confident enough familiar to admit when I was wrong. I was wrong. This is the life," he sighs, relaxing more into his chaise as he lounges deeper into the chair.

I consider telling him what I saw in Warin's memories, but something stops me. It was a private moment, one filled with insecurity, and Warin showed it to me. Telling Gus would be an invasion of that trust and I just can't do it.

Could I truly be friends with Warin? Could I truly trust him to be honest with me?

I think back on all my interactions with him. He's been rude and demanding, sure. But he's never been pointlessly cruel. He's never tried to harm me. Manipulate me, sure. But something tells me that the reason Warin manipulates people is because he thinks he knows best.

No matter how much good he's done, though, I think back

to the memory and how he took both men's lives. I do think he believes he was in a do or die moment, but it still gives me pause.

Even if I'm drawn to him, I need to be smart about this. If he wants to be friends, he needs to earn it, with actions and being truthful.

The house is extremely quiet during the daytime. The only sounds are when Gus is eating or when I go down to the kitchen.

I realize then that I'm almost aching for it to be nighttime, so I have someone to talk to. Which is embarrassing.

I'm almost missing the fairies bitching and complaining about every single thing. It makes me wonder if I'm incapable of being alone or if I'm just endlessly lonely?

How could I be lonely when I'm surrounded by an ornery raccoon, catty fairies, or my amazing friends?

I tap my fingernails against the countertop, hating the realization, not understanding what it means about me. I have everything that a witch could ask for, yet I don't feel fulfilled.

With frustration, I wipe a rogue, unwanted tear from my face.

"Are you alright?" A voice startles me and I nearly jump out of the stool.

These sneaky fucking vampires need to learn to make sound when they pop out of nowhere. I was hopeful that it was Warin, but his voice isn't anywhere near as rich.

When I turn, Conner is standing there. There are no windows in the kitchen, and even if they were, Conner already told me that they don't let any UV light in. It's nearly sunset, but I'm pretty sure if he were to go outside right now he would burst into flame or something else extremely graphic.

"I'm fine. It's a bit early for you to be up, isn't it?" I question him.

Cecile is back in the guest house and it's just the two of us, which makes me slightly uncomfortable.

"Younger vampires need less rest. We aren't on the verge of losing our minds like the ancient ones," he says it like a joke, but there seems to be some malice in it.

"You think Warin has lost his mind?" I ask.

"Keeping a witch inside his home surrounded by vampires, I'd say so," he says, coming to sit next to me. I scooch away from him, not wanting to be too close. It's night and day to how I felt last night when Warin was in the same seat.

Conner's words have me on edge, and I'm not sure why.

"Why would that make him crazy?"

Conner's green eyes glance down to my throat and I swallow. Quickly holding up my left hand, I showcase the ring I never bothered to hide since I've been at the mansion.

"I have protection," I say. It's a stupid and arrogant thing to do.

"Magical blood is the most wanted on the market, you know?" he says, hand quickly grabbing my own. Too fast for me to even think as his cold fingers pull the ring off my own.

He holds it between two fingers, holding it up in the air.

"Looks like your cute little protection spell doesn't help if a vampire physically takes it off."

My hand is wrapped firmly around my wand, and I try to remember everything I've been studying in the new grimoire. I think about last night, how I infiltrated Warin's memories and how I need to use similar magic to slip into this vampire's mind and subdue him.

"I'm under Warin's protection."

Conner rolls his eyes. "He isn't half the vampire Oz was. We've all gone soft since he took over the parishes. I was supposed to be moving up the ranks, not doing grunt work, driving witches back to their fucking cottages."

I have no clue if Warin is home, awake, or how deeply vampires sleep. All I know is that I need his help to handle this situation right now.

"You're making a mistake."

"It's alright, I'll treat you nice. I mean, I will have you locked up and drain you as much as I can daily to keep you alive, but by that point, you'll be so delirious you won't feel a thing."

Conner looks down at my neck. I'm sure my pulse is throbbing.

"Don't worry, little witch, it won't hurt…much."

"Warin!" I shout his name and Conner tsks.

"He's been starving himself. He won't wake until the sun sets. He isn't strong enough to fight me and neither are you," he whispers, a sinister grin spreading across his face.

Alright, Ember, it's do or fucking die.

I pull out my wand as quickly as I can and focus, pouring every ounce of energy I can into the spell. I slip into his mind, a jumbled mess of memories, as I finally find what I need, sending the high-pitched signal right into his mind.

He grabs his head, crashing to the floor, as I run as quickly as I can.

Right into my sleeping captor's bedroom.

Chapter 14

I stir in my slumber, which is unusual. My mouth waters as her scent hits me in my dream, making me pull her even closer against my body. Ember, my sweet Ember, in my bed.

What a selfish, delicious thought.

There's no other reason my sunshine would be in my bed right now, other than some sick manifestation I came up with in my comatose state.

She hates me. She hates that I'm a killer, that I'm not a good man.

She'll never love me, yet, I'll never stop trying to convince her.

A good man would walk away and understand that she's too good for them. Maybe it's because I'm not a man, in the sense that I'm immortal and tied to the night. Or maybe it's because my pull to her is so visceral that there's no other option.

Even if Ember never agrees to be mine, she always will be. I'll lurk in the shadows, protecting her and coveting every moment she gives me.

I take a deep inhale of her hair, nuzzling close. I wonder if I could taste her in my dreams. If I could sink my teeth into her freckled throat, or her full breasts and taste what I've denied myself for nearly a decade.

Even in my sleep, I can't do it. It must be the hunger talking, but I can't drink from another. I won't.

Ember may not realize I'm fully hers, but I am. The idea of drinking from someone else while she sleeps in my home, while I feed her and keep her safe, is abhorrent.

It doesn't help that no one's blood will ever compare to hers. Maybe she'll never grant me access to her sweet nectar. Maybe I'll die from starvation.

In the dream, my cock can get hard, a true surprise when I haven't consumed blood in days. It's a testament to what this witch does to me.

Her body is so warm and soft. Her curves are full, and I just want to knead every inch of her soft flesh.

She's perfect, my witch, in my dreams and in the waking hours.

Even if she hates me, thinks I'm deplorable. Fuck, I want her sweetness. Her delicate smiles, and tender sweetness. I want to wrap her kindness around me like cotton candy.

"So fucking perfect, witch," I say, squeezing her breast.

God, her fucking tits are enough to make me start a religion about her. I'd go door to door selling scripture over their beauty and fullness. Then again, maybe I wouldn't, because then they would be looking at my witch's chest and I'd have to rip their hearts out.

It would be a religion of one, on which I would get down on my knees and worship daily.

"Warin!" she shouts my name and I shiver. What I wouldn't give to have her shouting my name as her blunt pink nails trail down my back while my cock and teeth are sunken inside of her.

This dream is the best I've ever had. I'm not sure I've dreamt in over a century. I don't hate it.

"Warin. Wake up," she says, trying to wiggle out of my arms. I only hold her harder. She can't escape me, not in my subconscious. "Wake the fuck up," she growls.

I hold her tightly, absently rubbing myself against her as her nails dig into my forearms. Her ass is soft and round against me and I can't help but to moan in her ear before dragging my teeth against her throat. Her pulse is pounding and the dream feels so real, so perfect.

"Oh Hecate," she rasps out. "No. We can't be doing this right now. I need you to wake up."

"Always so bossy," I mumble against her hair. She smells more like the sun there. I wish she was making more sense and telling me to fuck her instead of waking up from this heavenly dream.

"Warin, Conner was trying to kidnap me. Wake up. Please wake up." Her tone is pleading and I groan as I come out of a daze.

It takes me too long to get my faculties. I'm too hungry, I realize, if I wasn't starving myself I'd wake up more clear-headed. Fuck, I probably would have risen as soon as I heard Conner speak to Ember if I was more aware.

I'm finally rising from my bed and Ember looks at me with wide eyes.

"What did you say?" I ask her. My unexpected rousing has me disoriented.

"Conner…h-he said he was going to take me and sell my blood."

I see red, but I do my best to not startle Ember. She already thinks I'm a monster, but I don't need her to know the true extent.

"As soon as I leave this room, you will lock yourself in with magic. Do not come out until I get you. Do you understand?" I tell her as calmly as I can.

As much as I want to find Conner and dismember him, placing his body parts on stakes outside of the property so everyone gets the memo to not betray me, I have to be delicate with Ember.

My darkness scares her, and I have to shield her from it, that's the only way I stand a chance of ever earning a sliver of her affection.

"Sunshine, do you understand?" I ask her.

She nods quickly, and I'm out of the room in a flash, trusting that she'll do as she's told.

"Conner!" I shout the name with such torment and anger that I think the foundation rattles.

It's not long before Samantha is in the kitchen with me, still ruffled from sleep. I glance around the kitchen and spot Ember's ring on the floor and I pocket it.

Rage simmers under my skin. He tricked her into taking it off, or physically removed it from her fucking finger so he could manipulate her.

"Conner tried to abduct Ember. I want him brought to me. Alive," I tell her, my teeth nearly clenched so I don't shout the words.

Samantha doesn't question me as we search the house, both of us pausing as we get to the front door that's slightly ajar.

A sliver of sunlight reflects on the floor, not allowing Samantha or I to pass without the proper gear on. There's only a half-hour before nightfall.

"Contact everyone. Conner and the Slayer are to be dealt with tonight," I say, the words dripping with malice as I seek retribution.

"You need to feed," Samantha interjects, and I look down at her.

She isn't wrong; I do need to feed. The hungrier I am, the more reckless and bloodthirsty. But I need to be stronger than that. If I want to capture Ember's heart, then I need to prove my devotion in every way.

"Just do as you're told," I tell her, and as her sire, she can't question me. Her brows pitch in as she goes back to her room to contact everyone in the nest.

Tonight we hunt.

Tonight I kill the beings who dared to put my witch in harm's way. I'll rip both of their hearts out and dip them in gold, using them as door knockers so everyone knows that fucking with what's mine is a one-way ticket to their final resting place.

Chapter 15

BETTY

Being a vampire's familiar is such bullshit.

The only perk I get for the endless torment of being at Warin's beck and call is having found my own love in Fitz, Samantha's familiar.

We're hanging upside down in our bat house on the side of the property. It's cozy and warm as we nestle next to each other.

Just a lovely night relaxing with the love of my life. We've been working endlessly trying to find the Slayer and sometimes a girl just needs a break.

Working for a man has been taxing on me over the last century. It's about time I finally got some R&R.

There's a tap on the bat house, and I groan.

Fitz grumbles his irritation as I slide down the box.

Lennox, a vampire familiar of Chester, who lives multiple parishes over.

"What?" I ask in an irritated tone.

"The vampire council. They're headed here tonight. Warn your people."

"Fuck," I hiss. "Thank you for the warning."

As soon as Lennox flies away, a rage-filled summoning comes from my master and I groan internally.

Tonight is going to be a mess.

"Let's go," I tell Fitz, who immediately follows my direction. By this point, I have him trained to be a very good boy.

We fly through Warin's office.

Fitz goes to Samantha's shoulder, and I do the same to Warin. The vampires are discussing the betrayal of Conner and how to handle the Slayer.

Great, Warin is going to be in an extra shitty mood now.

"Hate to make your day even worse, boss. Vampire council is headed here as soon as the sun sets," I tell him.

Warin pinches the bridge of his nose. "Fuck!" he nearly roars out loud.

"How do you have this information?" he asks me with no one else in the room knowing.

"Lennox, Chester's familiar."

"Change of plans. The Slayer will need to be ignored for the night. Addison, Michael, Luke, Henry, and Daisy, you all will be hunting for Conner tonight. I want him kept alive. Use the warehouse until the council leaves. Samantha and Achille will stay here with me to deal with the council."

"And your witch?" I question and a frustrated noise slips out of Warin's throat as he looks through the heavily tinted window, watching as the sun sets.

"Not enough time. Alert me as soon as you sense them in the area," he tells me and without another word, me and the rest of the familiars are slipping out of the small bat window off to do our respective jobs.

I glance over at the other familiars and wonder if they would be open to the idea of unionizing.

Chapter 16

As soon as I lock myself in Warin's room, I realize Gus is still passed out in the guest room.

"Dammit," I hiss as I bang my head against the door, considering what to do.

Do I listen to Warin and keep myself locked in this room until he comes back? Or do I go get Gus and make sure he's safe?

What if Conner took Gus? What if Gus was passed out and had no idea what was going on?

I'm safe in here, at least for now. I'm not so sure about when Warin gets back. The way he was holding me and speaking to me before he woke up was…something.

I'm still flushed thinking about it. I've never been touched quite like that. But he was in a deep sleep, nothing else.

With a shake of my head, I make a decision. Gus is my familiar, his job is to guide me through my life filled with magic, and I owe him the same respect.

My hand is high in the air as I release the spell locking me in the room. When I swing the door open, a very pissed off Warin is standing before me.

I don't think as I slam the door shut in his face.

"Did you just slam the door in my face, again?" he says through the wood and I wince.

"If I told you I could sense you were on the other side of the door, would you believe me?"

"No," he replies sharply. "Open the door," he says.

I'm not sure why he doesn't open it. I've lifted the spell, and it is his room, after all. But against my better judgment, I open the door and look into his hypnotizing eyes.

He digs in his pocket. "Put this back on and for the love of fuck, cast a quick illusion spell or something," he says a little too sharply, and I wince. "Sorry," he mumbles and I squirm a little bit.

"I need to make sure Gus is okay," I say, needing to know my familiar is safe.

"Your small beast is still passed out on your bed, none the wiser to what's going on right now. The ring, Ember, now," he says.

I slide the insanely opulent ring on my finger and take a deep breath as I hold my wand against the jewelry, shielding the ring from anyone's view except mine and Warin's.

"You need to hide it. Other vampires can't be aware of it," Warin says, and I want to roll my eyes. One moment he's telling me I'm perfect and the next he's being a demanding dick.

"It is. Only you and I can see it," I tell him.

Something crosses his face far too fast and fleeting for me to decipher the emotion.

"We have bigger problems than Conner right now."

"What do you mean?"

"I'm so sorry," he says, and I blink at him. Warin apologizing, twice in one night? "The vampire council. They're on their way here right now."

My eyes widen, and I can feel adrenaline coursing through my veins.

"Are they here for me?" I ask, pointing at myself.

"I don't know why they're coming here, but I will protect you. I just need you to play along."

"Play along?"

He rubs his chin, his bare hands gliding against his throat. Without the gloves on, I can't help but to actually notice how long his fingers are, as well as the red veins hiding beneath the surface.

"The vampire council is full of old vampires who have nothing better to do than dictate the lives of others. While they do hold a lot of authority, I'm in charge of all of Eastern Louisiana. They can only really do anything if a true law has been broken."

My swallow is near cartoonish with how loud it is.

"What laws?"

"Killing a vampire, an egregious amount of human murders, along with some other stupid rules. Basically, they like to swing their dicks around, but I know better how to deal with them."

"Will they come after me because they think I killed Baptiste? That was the fucking Slayer and we all know it." I'm raising my voice now and Warin takes a deep frustrated breath.

"No, but there will be concerns about why I have a witch living in my home. I've already hid the contraband."

"Contraband?" I parrot, my voice getting squeaky.

"Yes, what do you think all these grimoires I keep giving you about protecting yourself against vampires are? You'll get them back when they leave, don't worry."

I rub my head, just even more confused by this vampire. He mentioned that vampires wouldn't be happy knowing he has this material, let alone giving it to me, but if it's that serious. Why in the world would he take that risk?

"I don't understand. What do you need me to do?"

"I need you to play the part of my obedient, magical, little pet," he says in a too seductive tone.

"Your what?" I sputter.

His hand comes to my mouth, his body pressing close to mine as his lips press against my ear. Goosebumps cover my flesh as he holds me like this. My body having another involuntary response to his skin touching mine.

"They are almost here. They will hear every word you say, everything you do. This is what has to be done to keep you safe. Make them believe you aren't a threat. As soon as they leave, everything will go back to normal."

I glare at him, and he doesn't let go of my mouth.

"If it's ever too much, just say you're tired and I'll figure out a way to get you out of the situation. These vampires will test you, try to get under your skin. I need you to trust that I'll protect you above all else. Can you do that for me?"

Can I trust him? It's such a loaded question. When it comes to my protection, though? Somehow, there isn't a doubt in my mind.

Despite what any sane witch would do, I nod, and he gives me a wide grin, his fangs sharp and bright.

"Go put on one of your pink dresses, and make sure your familiar stays asleep," he says. "This is the last time we will speak plainly till they leave. It's all just a game," he says.

"A game, right."

I take a deep breath, bypassing him in the doorway as I go to my room and do as he said.

What's another day of me getting tied up in dangerous vampire bullshit?

I change into a maroon summer dress with a tight bodice that flares at my waist along with simple ballet flats. Then I put a slumber charm on Gus, so he shouldn't wake up as a light tap sounds at my door.

I can do this. I can act like I'm Warin's little play thing until these vampires leave.

Don't smack him, don't be rude to him, just nod and look at him like I don't have a brain cell in my head. Those are the things I chant to myself as Warin comes to my door.

He's back in his usual attire, a suit that's firmly in place, though no gloves. I'm irritated with myself when I can't stop thinking about his veiny hands or how good his cool palm felt against my lips.

Bad Ember. Very bad.

"You look delicious tonight, darling," he says and my lips part.

A quick retort is on my tongue, but I lick my lips instead.

"I always aim to please."

Warin grins at my reply, placing a hand on my waist as he leads me down the stairs and we wait in the foyer.

There are a million questions on my tongue. Who makes up the council? What kind of punishments can they dish out? Are they more powerful than Warin, older than him? Do all the vampires hold an election? Now that would be something.

I keep a long list in my head to ask him later as a sharp thwack of a door knocker hits his front door, sending shivers rolling down my spine.

What if Warin can't protect me from these people?

"Don't be nervous, pet," he says, kissing my hair, before leaving me standing alone by the banister.

I try to slow down my breathing from his quick affection. He said it was a game, but yet he also said he wants me to trust him. It has me questioning how real all of this is.

His smile is a farce as he greets the vampires at the door.

"What a wonderful surprise. Please come in," he says as five

vampires stroll into the foyer.

The five of them are all different in age and looks, minus their attire, which is strangely extremely business casual, like they all just left their day jobs in corporate America. The three men are wearing long sleeve button up shirts and black dress pants, while the two women are wearing modest black dresses with tights and flats.

"What's the meaning of this impromptu visit?" Warin asks.

The vampire with a pinched expression, her dark hair in a chignon, with minimal makeup on her face arches an eyebrow at his attitude. Her posture is unreal with how straight she stands as she looks down her nose at me.

"War, aren't you going to invite us in for a drink?" she says, looking me up and down.

Ew, they're on a nickname basis is my first thought, until I realize that she's looking at me like I'm the appetizer for the evening.

Oh fuck no, there's no way I can do this.

"Of course. Samantha, go fetch the AB negative from the warmer, would you?"

"I'll be right back," Samantha says in the most docile voice I've heard her use.

"I suppose it would be too much to ask for straight from the tap on such late notice?" the rude-ass-bitch I already hate asks.

Who does she think she is, showing up at Warin's house and asking if they can pass me around like a midnight snack?

"Ah, I don't share this one, Joyce," Warin says, his hand firmly on my hip, his thumb rubbing comforting circles on my flesh.

"It is a bit odd having a witch at your disposal. Are you sure you aren't open to sharing?" the tallest man of the council asks.

"Envy looks absolutely disgusting on you, Magnus. Now, shall we head to my parlor to discuss what exactly it is you're here for?" Warin says.

The massive vampire known as Magnus looks simply irritated at Warin's words, but doesn't reply.

Warin holds out a hand, the vampire that works for him leading the way. I can't remember the guy's name, but Warin makes sure that we're the last to follow, that none of the council members are behind us.

I haven't been in this room, it's moodier than the rest of his house, little light and tons of dark wooden accents. The hearth is blazing with a fire and all of the council members sit on the chairs furthest away from the flame.

Warin takes a seat at the largest leather chair, grabbing my hips and placing me on his lap.

It takes everything in me to not gasp out in shock. It's fine, totally cool. I'm sitting on the lap of the extremely attractive vampire who kidnapped me. No big deal, not at all, not the way he holds me like I belong there, or how confident he is in showing me off to his council.

This is all totally normal.

His arm spans my middle, his hand splayed on my stomach as he presses my body against his. It shouldn't feel this good.

"How pestiferous," Joyce says, her chin high in the air.

What an old immortal bitch? It has my body relaxing further against Warin's large chest. Hatred for this judgmental vampire fueling my willingness to play along, it's not that I'm also enjoying this. No way do I like how strong his thighs feel under mine, or how comforting his touch is around my waist.

It would be wrong to love this vampire's touch, especially with the given company.

"Now, Joyce, you didn't simply come here, into my home, to be an absolutely horrific cunt to my guest of honor, now did you?" Warin asks.

I shouldn't like him calling her that word. It shouldn't give me a sick satisfaction. I definitely shouldn't be smirking at this extremely pompous woman, but here I am.

Her jaw clenches before her cheeks hollow, a clear attempt at trying to keep her mouth shut.

The other woman stands, walking behind Joyce's chair.

"Excuse Joyce's manners. But we wouldn't be here if it was something minimal, you know this, Warin. You're the functionary of Eastern Louisiana since your sire's passing," she says in a thick English accent. "Your position is indeed in place to not only keep the vampires in your area in line but to also report back to the council if there is ever an issue against our greater good, is that correct?"

"That is correct," Warin says behind me. His body is tense, yet his fingers are gentle on my skin, reassuring even.

"Then please enlighten us on why a slayer is in your territory and you didn't deem it absolutely necessary for the council to know," she says, and all the council members stare at him.

I try not to let my relief show. They aren't here for me in any capacity; they want the Slayer.

"You mean why would I want my vengeance on the monster who killed my sire?" Warin says, and I wonder how he can so easily lie to their faces; I suppose I'm doing the same, though he seems way better at it.

Joyce snickers, but the other woman doesn't move an inch, almost like she's frozen in time.

"Please, we aren't fools, Warin. Your relationship with Oz was a complicated one. You had nothing but to gain after his demise," Joyce says.

"It's being handled," Warin states, and the balding vampire stands next.

I wonder if you can't grow hair once you're a vampire? Are you permanently frozen however you looked when you died? If so, it's honestly a shame for this man.

"You mean mismanaged? How long has the search been going for? We've only just gotten word that your sire's death was potentially a slayer, why didn't you alert the council?" the bald vampire says.

I swallow thickly, and Warin holds me closer.

"Justin, a displeasure as always to see you. We are hunting the Slayer nightly, which your arrival has set back extraordinarily. If you would like to add more soldiers into the fray of finding the Slayer, please, by all means. Or maybe you'd like to get your hands dirty for once and go out there yourself?"

Warin has a way of getting under these people's skin and I can't help but enjoy the show.

Cool lips press against my throat and I can't help but to let out a soft breath of air. Just the small touch sends a fresh set of shivers down my arms and I'm not sure if I should let the council see how he affects me, or if I should be unaffected by his touch?

I really needed more guidelines on how I'm supposed to act in front of these people. I probably need to figure out how to act around Warin in general. The conflicting feelings of all the dirty things I want to do with him and what secrets he's keeping are hard to navigate.

"Unlike the lot of you, I have delicious things to keep me busy. I'm sorry that you weren't notified but I promise it wasn't because of lack of respect for your prestigious council," Warin says, planting another kiss against my throat.

The bridge of his nose glides along my neck. The caress feels

wicked against my skin. A clear show of how ridiculous he finds these vampires coming into his home and demanding answers from him. Or maybe it's more?

He flirts with me endlessly, stares at my breasts like they might disappear. He's attracted to me, but is that all this is?

"Can I interest anyone in a glass?" Samantha says, and I blink. When the hell did she even get here?

The vampires make a mumbled noise of agreement. Warin does not.

"You won't be toasting with us?" Magnus asks, holding the cup up to his nose.

"It's like asking me to drink boxed wine. I've been spoiled as of late," Warin says, pushing my hair to the side, his tongue swiping out and licking my throat. This time I can't help but gasp and wiggle into his lap.

None of the council members drink their glasses, and they're all staring at us.

Why do I kind of want them to leave and see if Warin would do this without their presence? Oh, Hecate, what is wrong with me?

"Do you think I'd be petty enough to poison all of you?" Warin asks, and I can hear the humor in the way he says it. "Samantha, show them that it is safe," he says to his progeny and I wonder why he won't drink the blood.

Samantha takes the lowball glass and takes a big sip. Joyce raises a dark brow at her and Samantha looks like she's holding back an eye roll as she downs the rest of the blood.

Samantha clutches at her throat and makes a harrowing noise. All the council members are on their feet, before Samantha lets out a laugh, all choking noises stop.

"It's not poisoned, for fuck's sake," she says, putting the decanter on the coffee table.

"This lack of respect is abhorrent. We should take him and the witch for further questioning," Joyce suggests, motioning in our direction. "There's no way he actually wants her. She must have some other purpose. Just look at her."

In a single moment, I'm off Warin's lap, my ass falling into the leather cushion as Warin is on his feet.

A large crash startles me as the decanter goes tumbling to the floor, blood pooling on the ground.

My reflexes are too slow compared to a vampire. It takes me too long to realize that Warin has broken off a leg of the coffee table and fashioned it into a makeshift stake that is now protruding out of Joyce's stomach.

"Apologize," he growls in her face.

"This is ridiculous. You're threatening a member of the council," Magnus says, but no one intervenes.

Maybe even Joyce's co-workers hate her a little bit. From what I've seen, it tracks.

"She came into my home, disrespected me and my companion. The stake isn't in her heart. Though," he hums, his arms shifting and Joyce's eyes widening. "It would only take the slightest movement to poke at your wretched little heart, wouldn't it, Joyce? Apologize."

I shift in the chair, knowing that I should hate this. That I should be horrified by Warin's behavior. The act of violence should have me running for the hills. I should be passed out over the spilled blood on the floor and the threat these vampires pose.

Yet, I despicably feel something the opposite of disgust. Maybe it's part of the game we're playing, the show we're putting on for the council. But there's something so raw and unfiltered in Warin's gaze as he holds the coffee table leg deep in Joyce's gut, commanding her to apologize to me.

"You must be using her for some other purpose," Joyce says, doubling down.

He pushes the wood deeper into her gut and my nails dig into the arms of the chair as I watch his anger rise.

"Are you jealous because she can hold my attention? Because I want her? It's very pathetic, Joyce. Should I tell you how hard my cock gets when I feed from her? How I feel like I could come the moment my teeth sink into her perfect breasts?"

My heart is racing and I can tell it has the attention of every vampire in the room as I listen to Warin's words. I think about the things he said when he was asleep.

Do I actually have that much power over Warin's attention?

"You lie," she seethes.

A growling noise leaves him as he pulls the stake out. It's high above his head. He's about to fucking stake a vampire council member for disrespecting me.

The man who hasn't spoken grabs Warin's wrist. He looks endlessly bored. His dark black hair in a knot on the back of his head. I wonder if he was a pirate when he was turned, he's handsome, but nothing compared to Warin.

"That is enough. Joyce shut the fuck up and stop poking at him. Put the stake down and take a seat, War," the vampire says.

The stake comes clattering to the ground.

Warin looks at me quickly, then down at his bloodied hands. He wipes them on his suit jacket before grabbing me by the hips and placing me back down gently on his lap.

"My apologies, Sebastian. Continue," he says calmly. Like he didn't almost kill Joyce.

I think about using our safe word, of saying I'm tired, but my ridiculously curious nature keeps me firmly placed on Warin's

lap, which by some bizarre turn of events is somehow the safest place I could be right now.

Chapter 17

I tap a bloodstained hand on the arm of my chair as my other defiled hand wraps around my witch's body.

I've shown them too much. Joyce is smug as she sits there, her abdomen stitching back together.

"Samantha, dear. Please fetch Joyce some more blood so she can heal faster," Sebastian says.

Samantha nods, leaving the room. Achille hasn't moved an inch, just watching the madness unfold from where he stands against the wall.

Sebastian was the oldest and most dangerous out of the five here. Beatrix, I believe, was born in the forties, Joyce was turned before me, I think by a decade or so but I'm not entirely sure. Justin was only turned a decade ago. Magnus may be a century or two old, but Sebastian, I wouldn't be surprised if he is close to four hundred years old, nearly competing in age with Oz.

"Now is not the time for jealous petulance. It's clear that his witch means a great deal to him." He shifts his body, folding at the waist as he looks at Ember.

Fuck, I should have told her that she needs to answer all of his questions. If he tries to use his influence on her and it doesn't work they will know she has some sort of protective magic on her.

"What is your name?" he asks Ember.

My hand tightens around her waist, her ass shifting further against my lap and I hope that the small adjustment of my body tells her everything she needs to know.

"Ember, sir."

"Tell me, Ember, why would a witch want to be a vampire's pet?" he asks, a smirk spreading across his face.

Part of me thinks about picking up the coffee table leg and attempting to kill him, but I'd likely lose, and then I'd leave Ember unprotected.

"Are you blind?" Ember asks and I swear a squeak, a fucking squeak, almost leaves my chest.

"Pardon?" Sebastian says, just as surprised as he inches closer to Ember.

"Just look at him," Ember says, her fingertip drawing against my jaw as her deep green eyes clash with mine. "It's hard to find a man who can keep up with me, you know?" Her hand falls from my face, interlacing her fingers with the bloody ones spanning her waist. "I can't deny that I'm not entirely susceptible to his money and charm."

She's smooth as butter, but Sebastian's been around for a long time.

I want to close my eyes and wince as I watch his pupils dilate. He's putting Ember under his influence, but it won't work with the ring. The one that only I can see, the one I convinced her to wear on her wedding finger.

"What about your coven, witch?" he asks.

"I'm a nomad," she says quickly and evenly. If I didn't know any better, I would assume she's under his influence.

"Why?"

"I'm not a fan of their rules."

Sebastian laughs. "Then I suppose this unlikely pairing makes more sense."

He glares down at the mess of the blood on the floor before addressing everyone in the room. "No more bullshit. We're here to discuss the Slayer, not petty quarrels between former lovers," he says.

Ember stiffens on my lap, her hand falling from where it was interlaced with mine. Shit, and here I thought maybe we were getting somewhere the way she was melting against my body.

I should definitely kill Joyce.

"I can't deny that it does wonders for my ego that one single night could still cause so much enviousness." I say it for Ember's benefit; she needs to know that Joyce is nothing, less than nothing to me.

"You motherfu—" Joyce hisses.

"I said enough," Sebastian's voice booms.

Ember's breath hitches and she becomes more pliant in my lap again. Her body is warm, her hair is near my face, but I don't dare sneaking a sniff as the council surrounds us.

Part of me wants this frivolous meeting to last all night so that she'll stay perched against me. Yet, the deeper part of me wants her safe. That is the most important thing above all else.

"The Slayer is injured, last seen two nights ago. He's lost a lot of blood. He's compressed inside of a human male who is likely around thirty. Dark hair, brown eyes, above average height and build, black tattoos up and down the lengths of his arms." I give them as much information I can reveal without putting Ember in harm's way.

"How was he injured?" Justin questions.

I hate that prick so much. He was turned only a decade ago in his late forties and assumes because he appears physically older than all of us that he automatically deserves respect.

"I sunk my teeth in his neck."

"Then why is he not dead, drained dry, the Slayer being dragged back to hell or wherever they preside until they're summoned into another host?" Beatrix asks.

"Because I was staked."

Ember wiggles her ass in my lap and I hope she doesn't take offence at the fact that I'm not rock hard right now. If I wasn't so starved, I know it would be rubbing against her backside. Perhaps it's for the best.

Being hard and aching would likely be more embarrassing than anything else that happens this evening.

"Yet, you live to tell the tale?" Sebastian questions.

"In the stomach. Hurts like a bitch, doesn't it?" I say to Joyce.

Her lips purse, but Sebastian ignores it.

"He did not end you and you did not end him. I don't understand."

"His stakes, they're imbued with some sort of magic. A vampire can not remove their stakes. If it had been left in me, despite not being in the heart, I would have died," I state.

"Who removed the stake?"

"Ember did," I reply honestly.

He doesn't need to know that we were at her cottage, that she didn't really want to do it, but did it despite herself.

"Hmmm. I see. This Slayer is strong, a bigger problem than your nest can handle. We'll bring in more vampires and mortal alliances to help with this issue. I assume you have enough space to accommodate the council while we assess this issue?"

Fuck.

If I tell them to leave, it will make everything more suspicious. If I let them stay, then Ember will be in danger. As soon as the Slayer is dead, they'll leave.

Something clicks at that moment.

"How exactly did you hear about the Slayer's presence?" I ask Sebastian.

"That, of course, is private information," Sebastian replies.

Conner.

When I get my hands on that lying fuck, I'm going to chain him to a pole and watch as the sunrise licks at his feet, turning him to ash.

My grip on Ember must be too tight as she whispers.

"I'm tired."

Her green eyes meet mine, and I wish I could understand what she was trying to convey.

"Samantha, why don't you get everyone another round while I get Ember settled and we will discuss our plans further?"

Sebastian nods, and none of them question me as I usher Ember out of the room and up the stairs. We head to her room and as soon as the door is shut she looks at me, waving her hands in a haphazard sort of way.

Anything we say could be heard downstairs and I lick my lips, going to her nightstand and grabbing a pen and paper.

Grab the raccoon and anything else you need, you're moving to my room and you'll ward it.

Her brows furrow as she grabs the pen from my hand.

I can't stay here!!! They all looked like they wanted to kill me.

The exclamation points are excessive, I think as I take the pen from her.

I will keep you safe. There is no other option. You will be safe as

soon as we ward the bedroom.

She looks pissed off, and it might be the most beautiful she's ever looked as her cheeks redden and her breasts bounce as she snatches the pen out of my hand.

I'm not your fucking pet.

The underlining of the word pet is superfluous, yet cute. There's no way I'd let her leave this house with the Slayer out here, and there's absolutely no way that I'd let her out of my sight with the council here either.

Instead of communicating via scribbled messages, I just stare at her, hoping that my gaze tells her everything that she needs to know.

There's no arguing the matter, not when they can hear.

A slight growling noise slips from her throat as she grabs her raccoon like an oversized infant in her arms.

"Have one of your goons move my shit," she says, not caring if the council can hear or not.

There's a chance they are chatting amongst themselves and not paying attention to the rest of the house, but either way, they can't suspect she speaks to me like that.

"Go to our room and do as you're told, pet," I tell her, her eyes narrowing as she finally makes her way to my—*our*—bedroom.

The thought of her being in my chambers has me softening up to the council ever so slightly, forcing our hand in the matter.

I grab as many of her belongings as I can carry and follow her to the room.

She places her familiar on the lounge chair in the corner and I place her things near the closet door.

I pull the pen and paper from earlier out of my pocket.

A sound proofing spell? I'm assuming your warding of the bedroom is still intact?

"Of course it is," she snarks, a hushed whisper falling out of her as she moves her wand. "There. They won't be able to hear us now. What the actual fuck, Warin?"

She storms away from me, pacing the room, tugging at the wild pink strands of her hair. Her dress swishes with the motion, momentarily rendering me unable to focus as I catalog the way she moves. I'm not unfamiliar with watching Ember, I've been doing it for years. But watching her move in my bedroom? Hearing her say my name?

These were things I thought I'd never have. I'd denied myself, thinking I was keeping her safe, I probably was. Staying far away from me was the safest thing for Ember.

Yet, the sick satisfaction of having her in my space outweighs anything right now.

I'll keep her safe. It will just be more work.

"This is just fucking awesome. Fantastic really. Not only is there a vampire slayer who has a vendetta against me because I've accidentally been around vampires at the wrong time. I get kidnapped by one, and one of his lackeys wants to make a human juice box out of me. Now, some version of the vampire government strolled up, one of them you apparently used to fuck and wants to rip my head off—"

"It was one time. Many years ago, before I even knew you," I immediately add in.

I don't tell her that it was in 1932 or that I haven't been with another female since I learned what I did in 1933.

"Like that matters. They're staying here in your house, and now for my protection, I can't even leave your room. It's the full moon in three days. If I'm not there with my coven, they'll come looking for me and the last thing I want to do is put my coven in danger."

"We will figure something out. With the help of the council, we should be able to take the Slayer out and they will leave. None of this will fall back on your coven."

She pauses her pacing and stares at me.

"And then what, Warin? What happens after the Slayer is gone and the council leaves?"

"Then we continue our arrangement as we originally vowed."

She takes two steps toward me, her wand at my chest as she looks up at me without an ounce of fear.

She's gorgeous, and I'm not sure she knows how perfect she is. I'll have to work on telling her more often.

"The arrangement? The one we had to protect me against the vampire council?" she seethes. "All of this from the beginning has been a trick, getting me to agree to the six months, giving me these old spells. What is it that you want from me?"

My hand comes up to her face, the pad of my thumb caressing the warmth of her pink cheek.

"Everything, Ember Hollow. I want everything."

She blinks wildly as I drop my hand from her face and turn on my heel, leaving the room to deal with the council and before I slip and tell Ember everything.

Chapter 18

Vampires are dirty, no good liars, and it won't be soon enough to be rid of them all.

I can't believe the thoughts I had when I was sitting on Warin's lap earlier, the fact that I was sitting on his lap at all. It was a ploy to not be on the vampire council's radar, to protect myself and my coven, at least that's what I keep telling myself. Admitting I liked the way he defended me and held me would be…well it would be absolutely ridiculous.

Almost as ridiculous as the words that just slipped out of his mouth.

He wants everything from me. What, every ounce of dignity and blood I have to spare?

All I know is that he's tricked me into this entire situation. Everything that has transpired over the last few days is his fault.

Well, I suppose being in the back of the restaurant when that vampire was staked had nothing to do with him, but he has orchestrated every single moment since then.

I'm so angry that I can't help the frustrated tears that slip from my eyes. I feel like an idiot.

Gus is still asleep from the spell I cast on him, and I don't have the heart to wake him for my meltdown. I wish I had Iris or Violet to talk to. The idea of having one of them wrap their arms around me and giving me a hug has fresh tears falling down my face.

I'm not sure why I'm so emotional, but I chalk it up to being a prisoner and having no clue when I'll see my coven again. I get ready for bed and stare at my crestfallen expression in the mirror. My cheeks are blotchy, and I try splashing some water on my face after brushing my teeth.

When I go back into the room, I wonder if Warin will come back here tonight and I hate that I'm at war with myself on whether I want him to or not.

With the combination of having the room warded, and mental exhaustion, I fall asleep quicker than I could've imagined.

When I crack my eyes open, the room is still dark and I have no concept of what time it is.

What I do know is that Warin's face is nearly nuzzled against my breasts, an arm slung over my waist, and his leg wrapped around my own.

I take a deep breath, and he doesn't stir at all. With another breath, I realize that my abdomen aches.

Fuck. My period. I started my period while being surrounded by vampires. I almost laugh at the horror of it all. And here I thought things were as bad as they could get when a vampire was staked next to me.

I don't have any of the things I need to help my period pass quickly and I don't know if Warin could even get them for me, at least not until night falls.

With a heavy sigh, I grab my wand on his nightstand, flicking it in the air to see that it's nearly noon. I can't remember the last time I slept in that late. It must be how dark his room is. Unlike his office or the room I was staying in, his bedroom is devoid of windows.

Warin is so still it's almost creepy. I start by shifting his leg off of my body; he doesn't startle at all. Then I move his arm, unceremoniously plopping it on his own sleeping form. That has him stirring, gliding his nose against my breasts before I hiss with annoyance and slip out of the bed.

Gus is still asleep and I rub the bridge of my nose with my thumb and forefinger, knowing the moment I wake him up, he's going to have a lot to say.

I decide that his berating of my choices can wait. Maybe a hot shower and another good cry will make this all better.

Of course, I don't have any of the hygiene products I need. I'm about five seconds away from a total breakdown when there's a knock on the door.

With as delicate of footsteps I can manage, I tiptoe to the door and press my ear against the door.

"It's Samantha," the voice beyond the door says.

I almost contemplate not answering it, but even if the door is open, as long as I don't step outside of the room I'm safe.

When I open the door, Samantha is standing in front of me, looking more casual than I've ever seen her. A man's T-shirt hits her at the knee and her hair is in a bun.

"Mind your business and I'll mind mine," she says, tossing a box of tampons at me.

"Do I want to ask how you knew I needed these?"

Samantha snorts. "What, do you think I could smell your period all the way down the hall? Please. Warin texted me that you might need something," she says casually.

Meanwhile, I know my cheeks are flushed and I'm filled with mortification. The other vampires in the house thankfully can't scent my current situation, but Warin did.

"Don't be embarrassed. That's like eating a day-old hot dog when you could have a prime rib steak, ya know?"

She shrugs her shoulders and walks away and I stand there dumbfounded. Did she just compare period blood to hot dogs?

I shut the door, my brow furrowed from the conversation I just had with Warin's daughter, progeny, whatever the fuck. When I look at the sleeping vampire on the bed, I allow myself to do some ogling.

In his sleep, he looks softer, like a prince taking a little nap at his leisure. Warin Auclair is quite the conundrum. One moment he's playing puppet master with me, telling me what's best for me and tricking me into agreements. Then the next moment he's thoughtful, making sure I'm comfortable, defending my honor, and promising to keep me safe.

I feel lost, which is a feeling I'm all too familiar with. When I think about the last week, though, when I was working on spells that have been forgotten with time, I felt powerful.

Warin gave me that feeling.

He's also gifted me with a sense of hopelessness. I have no clue when I'll see my coven again or when I'll leave this room. Even if I do leave, will I have any of my life back? Or will I be in hiding forever?

I stare down at him one more time, wishing there were more moments like this. I can't decide if it's because he can't talk or because without him ruining the moment, I get to appreciate how handsome he is.

All I know is there's no way in hell I should care about my captor's looks or that he can be charming and an asshole in the same conversation. I need to focus on how I get the hell out of here and back to my life.

Even if I let myself see Warin as anything beyond the vampire who conned me, he's still a vampire. Something I would never be. There's no way I could give up my coven or the sun, and from what I've seen of vampire life, it's not something that I could ever become. Vampires and witches don't mix, and that's the reality of the situation, there's no point in even thinking about an alternative.

Whatever my stay is at Warin's mansion, I'm just a blip in Warin's very long life. As soon as the Slayer is handled, I can finish out the rest of our "arrangement" from the comfort of my small, no-chef-having cottage.

The day feels like it's never going to fucking end. Is this what prisoners in solitary confinement feel like?

"You need to learn the art of being lazy. Ring the chef again for some more of that popcorn," Gus says.

He's taking our captivity far better than I am. He even said that Warin's room had a cozier feel and a larger TV.

"I don't know how to just do nothing," I complain, and Gus makes a chittering noise.

"Snoop around his room," he says.

"You want me to snoop around in the sleeping vampire's room? The one who basically kidnapped us?"

"*Yes, that's precisely what I fucking said. He hasn't so much as moved in his sleep, and to be honest, you're kind of ruining my movie.*"

"Oh, well, don't let me ruin your fun."

"*Thank you,*" he says as I roam around the room, cautiously snooping.

His drawers are organized to a level of neuroticism that I can't even compute. I'm not sure I've ever matched a pair of socks on my own in my life, that's what magic is for.

I'm even more quiet when I go through his nightstands. Again, nothing special, I'm not sure what I expected to find? Condoms?

Do vampires even need to worry about that sort of thing?

Once I go through most of his room, which doesn't have much to show for itself, I go to his closet. His suits are pressed and hung neatly on hangers, each of them a different shade of black.

I push a few of his suits apart, and I see a safe. I look back into the bedroom. There's a few hours until sunset, but I don't know if he will wake up earlier.

I pull my wand out of my hair and whisper an unlocking spell. The dial moves quickly as I watch the mechanism shift, swirling right and then left and right again.

My brows furrow as I realize the combination to his safe just so happens to be my twenty-first birthday. It's too big of a coincidence, but I ignore it as I open the heavy door.

The first few items in the safe are the grimoires he's hiding from the vampire council, which is no surprise. I'm delicate with them as I take one individually, rubbing my fingertips over the covers. I'm not sure what it is about these magical books, but something about them calls to me.

After they're safely on the floor, I grab the first black box. I glance over my shoulder to make sure that Warin hasn't stirred before flipping the lid open.

Inside are a variety of what appears to be fake identification documents, passports and birth certificates with different names, none of them with Warin Auclair. What takes me by surprise is that there are also falsified documents with my picture on them. I flip through them all, before putting them back in the same manner they were before. Something tells me that my snooping won't go unnoticed if he looks in his safe.

Beneath the black box is a pink one. If I thought I was confused by a fake passport of myself, I'm even more surprised by the keepsake box filled with items I've lost over the last decade, hair clips, gardening gloves, my favorite chapstick, along with what look like PI-like photos of myself wandering around town.

Who is Warin Auclair? What does he want from me? And most importantly, why am I not absolutely horrified by what I found in his safe?

Chapter 19

I only started dreaming when Ember joined my bed. Of course, her presence in my bed isn't in the capacity I wish it was. But as an eternal being, I have limitless patience with the witch who's fated to be mine.

Right now, my dream is a delectable sense of delirium. The scent of her blood is faint, nearly nonexistent, but just enough for my mouth to water. My tongue burns with the need to taste her, claim her, show her that she belongs to me.

In my sleep I reach for her, and she's nowhere to be found. Is she safe? She has to be safe in this room. In my room. But what if she isn't?

The lack of blood is making me slow, it's hard to wake from my sleep, but I persevere, groaning as I rise from the bed and blink at my surroundings.

"You're awake," her melodic voice says and I can't help the grin that takes over my face. My sweet Ember is safe, and that's all that matters.

"Did you miss our foreplay-like-banter all day long, sunshine?" I ask her.

The raccoon makes a snorting noise and Ember rolls her eyes.

"More like I was bored to death. I can't stay in this room forever," she says.

"No, unfortunately, you are far too bright to hide from the world forever. Hopefully we find the Slayer tonight and the merry band of the undead will fuck off out of my house."

"Then what, Warin?"

She asked me the same question last night, my answer is the same, but I know she doesn't want to hear it.

Her tone is deeply suspicious, and I tilt my head and assess her. She's had access to my quarters all day. What did the little witch find that has her on edge?

"Whatever you wish. Despite what you may think, I'm not your captor."

Her fist is under her chin as she blinks at me like I'm an idiot, before rolling her eyes. All I can do is smile at her as I lean back on the pillows.

"Are you still upset?" I ask.

Wrong fucking thing to say.

She stands, her hands on her hips as she laughs sardonically.

"Am I still upset? Which part, Warin? Am I upset that you tricked me into this arrangement, for reasons I don't understand? Or am I upset that I'm potentially being hunted by a vampire slayer? Oh! Or maybe it's the fact that I am, in fact, a prisoner in your house filled with vampires."

"Did Samantha give you the items you need for your condition? Is that what this is about?"

Again, the wrong fucking thing to say. Before I can even read her expression, her wand is out and items start flying right at my face.

I catch two books, before a metal globe hits me square in the fucking nose, breaking it, as blood gushes down my face.

"Fuck," I hiss, grabbing a pillow and placing it on my face.

"Oh, Hecate, I thought you'd catch everything," Ember says, coming to sit next to me on the bed.

It doesn't hurt, I can feel the cartilage and bone piecing back together, the loss of blood is an issue, but she doesn't need to know that.

She pulls the pillow back, glancing at the blood and swallowing thickly.

"Sorry," she whispers, holding my chin, and inspecting the wound. Her eyes are glassy and there's clear guilt on her face.

"I'm old enough to know the mention of a woman's period isn't something you bring up," I reply, taking the blame. I shouldn't bait her when she's already upset.

"Regardless, I didn't mean to hurt you," she says, her wand out and ready to heal my nose.

I place my hand over hers.

"No need. It's already healed."

She doesn't pull her hand away from me immediately, and I consider that progress.

"I'm not one to sit idle. I need to get out of this room, out of this house. I can't miss the full moon."

"I will make it happen. Whether we find the Slayer tonight or not, I promise you that you will not be trapped in here forever."

She looks skeptical, and I take a risk, touching her warm hand again, rubbing my thumb against her smooth soft skin.

"I promise, Ember. The last thing I want is for you to be displeased with me."

She looks at me curiously and sighs.

I stand, letting the sheets fall away from me. I'm slightly lightheaded, but ignore the feeling as I grab my shirt from the waist and tug it over my head.

"What are you doing?" she says in a choked voice, though she doesn't look away from my shirtless chest.

At least I know the witch is attracted to me; I don't think she would have been able to fake the night before if she wasn't.

"Showering. Would you like to join me?" I ask with a smile.

"I'm not showering with you," she says like she's scandalized, yet, her gaze doesn't leave my half-undressed form.

"Because of your period?"

She raises her wand again and I place my hands placatingly in the air.

"Please don't break my nose again."

"I won't if you stop bringing up my *condition*."

"Don't be embarrassed, Ember. I love being edged with what I can't have," I tell her, turning on my heel and heading into the shower.

After my shower, I throw on some sweatpants and consider going back to the room without a shirt on. Wanting to not piss Ember off anymore than I already have, I throw a shirt on.

When I'm back in the room, she's lying on the bed, bored, braiding a piece of her pink hair.

As an immortal being I know a thing or two about boredom.

"Is your nose okay?" she asks, and the sick part of me wants to pretend it hurts so she'll make it all better; she clearly feels guilty. I find her temper endlessly cute.

"It's fine, my own doing. How about some Gin Rummy before I have to go?" I ask her, grabbing the card deck out of the top drawer.

She sits up in the bed, skeptical but eager to do something other than sit around. "What are we going to bet with?" she questions and I smirk.

"What do you want if you win?"

She licks her lips, scooting on the bed, crossing her legs and I sit on the edge of the bed, shuffling the cards with speed.

"Another secret. What do you want if you win?" she asks.

I could be crass, could irritate her even more, but instead I ask for something I know she'd be willing to give. "I'd also like to know a secret."

She squints at me, but nods. "I can do that."

Her raccoon familiar is absolutely snooping the entire time we play, but he's quiet, letting us play our game. When it's my turn I grab from the discard pile and Ember curses under her breath.

"How do I know you aren't using your vampire speed to cheat?" she asks.

"How do I know you aren't using your magic," I retort and she clicks her tongue.

"A promise that neither of us will cheat." She holds out her hand and I take it in mine, squeezing her soft hand for a moment.

She looks down at where our skin touches and I rub my thumb over her skin.

"You feel it don't you?" I ask her.

Her breath hitches and she slowly tugs her hand away from mine, looking back down at her drawn hand.

We go back and forth, running through the deck until the end of the game and we have to lie down our cards and count points.

The witch wins.

"Yes," she hisses as we count the totals. Alright, so my witch is a little competitive, I like it.

"What secret would you like?" I ask her, hoping to fuck it's an easy one.

I hand her the cards for her to be the dealer and she shuffles them with magic, the cards floating in the air, leafing between one another.

"What did you want to be when you grew up?"

I blink at her. I was expecting something cutthroat, like how many people have I killed, or if I have bodies buried in the backyard, or even worse, why I tricked her into this arrangement in the first place.

I don't think she's ready for the truth and I can't risk losing her.

"Things were a little different when I was a boy. We didn't dream big, you know? Becoming a part of Oz's night crew was the first time I ever let myself think that I could be more than a farmer or a rum runner. But…"

"But what," she asks, leaning closer, the cards now in her hands.

"But I thought airplanes were fascinating. I think if I wasn't some poor boy from the swamps of Louisiana, I'd want to be a pilot."

Ember smiles at me, not saying anything about my dreams as a boy as she deals the cards. She seems lighter the more that we play. I win this round, and she seems irritated from losing but waves her hand in a way to show it's my turn to ask for a secret.

"What is the worst thing you got in trouble for while growing up?" I ask her.

Her cheeks tint and she bites her lip and shakes her head.

"I do believe a very beautiful, smart witch told me the pillar of friendship is honesty."

She gives me a look with no heat as she bites her lip.

"This stays between us?" she asks.

"I'll pinky swear it," I say, holding out my pinky finger. She laughs, but wraps her pinky in mine, before huffing a breath.

"I set the town church on fire," Ember says under her breath.

"I'm sorry, what was that?"

"I was twelve, and I didn't do it on purpose. Iris and I spent a lot of time around town escaping our homes, her mom had just passed and my mom and grandma aren't easy to deal with."

"Why are your mom and grandma difficult?" I ask.

"They just don't get me," she says sadly, shaking her head. "But that wasn't the secret you won. Anyway, we went to the church at night that everyone said was haunted. My elemental magic was pretty fickle then. I thought I saw a ghost orb and well, fire just kind of slipped out, lighting the drapes behind the pulpit on fire," she says with a grimace.

"Gorgeous and an arsonist, a woman after my own heart." She shoves my shoulder and I don't know what possesses me, but I poke her side and she immediately laughs.

"Oh no. No no no," she says and I tickle her side more, her head is thrown back, her laugh is wild and she looks free, happy even.

Our eyes lock, and it's almost like she can't believe she's having fun with me. The moment is broken with a knock on the door.

"Goon squad is ready to go, War. Hurry the fuck up," Samantha says.

I stare down at Ember and she looks up at me, not in disgust but in curiosity.

"I should go," I say, even though it's the last thing I want to do.

Ember's breaths are fast as she licks her lips, her gaze going to my mouth. Would the witch want to kiss me?

I can't help it as I place a finger on her bottom lip rubbing the

flesh. Her soft lips part and her pupils dilate as she looks at me. I can smell her arousal, and I'm so close to leaning down, kissing her and seeing what it feels like, when Samantha pounds on the door three more times. "Don't keep them waiting."

Ember shakes her head, like she's been broken out of a spell and my hand falls.

"Right, yeah. Thanks for playing," she says, gathering the cards acting shy.

"I'll be back as soon as I can."

"Just take care of the Slayer and get rid of the council," she says, sitting next to her raccoon, who I swear is raising an eyebrow at me as I leave the room.

"How was I supposed to know you were having a moment with your witch? Soundproof, remember?" Samantha hisses at me as we wait outside.

Sebastian seems on edge, like he wants this to be over with just as badly as I do. I don't know if the Slayer or the council is the bigger threat, but I want them both gone. What if once all the threats are to the wayside I can have more moments with Ember like I did tonight?

I crave it. The way she smiled, that she confided in me. Whatever I have to do to get more moments like that with her, I'll do it.

"Let's end this tonight. I need to feed and this town is dripping with other paranormals I have no interest in running into. I have no idea how you stand it, Warin," Sebastian complains.

"Did you not smell the witch through the walls this morning? I understand wholly. Are you sure you don't share? I'm willing to pay whatever price," Justin says.

I roll my eyes, acting indifferent, while deep down I want to pick up the largest rock in the forest and bash Justin's head in ten times over. Instead, I give him a glittering smile.

"I'm sure you find it very difficult to get any woman to willingly let you feed off of them."

He snarls at me, an unmanicured finger pointed in my face. "You little—"

His words are cut off by Joyce. "Are we sure Warin is feeding on the witch? I scented his blood this evening. What's to say it isn't the other way around, that the witch is using his blood."

I roll my eyes. "Just say you're boring in bed, Joyce."

She scoffs, looking like she wants to fight me as Magnus rolls his eyes.

"Enough, children. Let us find the Slayer and be done with this."

Sebastian pushes his hands in his pockets. "Samantha and I will search the main town. Magnus and Warin will search the perimeter of the home. Everyone else will have other areas to check."

I glance at Samantha, who doesn't seem to be put out about working with Sebastian. I don't like it one bit, but I bite my tongue as we dash through the woods, searching for the Slayer's scent.

Yet again, he goes undetected.

Chapter 20

I expect to wake up with Warin wrapped around my body again. It's embarrassing when I wake up disappointed that he's not there.

Hecate, am I really upset that I didn't wake up next to a vampire?

"Good, you're awake. I have breakfast," Warin says, and I startle, blinking to where he stands next to the bed.

"Shouldn't you be resting?" I ask.

"And give up the chance to entertain you all day, doubtful," he replies.

"You're staying awake to spend time with me?" I ask, grabbing a piece of toast and nibbling on the corner.

"I couldn't manage getting us out of the house today, but we should be set for tomorrow. So I figured I'd give you the next best thing. Quality time with your favorite vampire."

He grins, but despite his cheery words, I can swear he looks tired.

"Really? We're leaving the house tomorrow?"

"You said it would make you happy. In the meantime, I was

thinking you could work on some spells, we could play more card games, oh, and Samantha gave me this. I don't know how it works," he says, tossing a Nintendo Switch on the bed.

The smell of food must have woken up Gus, because his greedy little hands are grabbing everything he can. As he eats, he gets crumbs on the bed and Warin looks less than amused.

"So, you're staying up so that we can play cards and I can show you magic spells?" I ask.

"Exactly. Let me go grab the grimoires."

"Wait!" I say quickly, not wanting him to go into the safe just yet. I know without a doubt once he opens it, he'll know I snooped. "Let me wake up first, maybe we could watch a movie."

"Alright," he says, grabbing a remote from his nightstand and a massive projector comes out of the ceiling.

"You mean I could have been watching my shows on a projector this whole time?" Gus complains.

I ignore him as Warin looks down at his clothes.

"Just a moment," he says.

Again, with his vampire speed, one minute he's in a suit and the next he's shirtless and in sweatpants, and crawling into bed with me to watch a movie.

I glance over at him and clear my throat. He just smiles, and I can feel my cheeks heat.

Sure, we've slept in the same bed, but this feels different. It feels so easily domestic in a way that shouldn't be possible.

"What should we watch?" he asks, handing me the remote.

"Twilight?" I jokingly ask and he glares at me.

"Really?" he questions, his brows furrowed, like he'd really watch it if I wanted to. I can't help but to laugh, and his face transforms into something softer as he looks at me.

His gaze goes down to my lips and it's so similar to what happened the other night. I feel my walls crumbling, logic about our situation falling away.

As badly as I want to kiss him right now, I know I can't, not until he tells me the truth.

There's something more here, and I just can't put my finger on it.

Instead of leaning forward and kissing him, I plop back down on the pillows, flicking through the remote and finding a neutral show for us to watch.

Gus plays Animal Crossing on the Switch and the whole time we watch the movie, it's like my body is on fire. I keep getting closer and closer to him.

At some point, my side touches his, and neither of us says a word, watching the movie in silence. I want to reach out, interlace our fingers together to see what it would feel like, but when I look over at Warin, I realize he's fast asleep.

I shouldn't do it, but he doesn't move as I grip his cool hand in mine. My finger throbs and I make a promise to myself to figure out the truth.

Why does this vampire have such a visceral effect on me, and why do I love it so much?

Exhaustion fills me as I finally make it back into my room after another fruitless night of searching for the Slayer. It's truly like he disappeared out of thin air.

If I was fully fed I wouldn't feel this tired, but without sustenance I feel sluggish. Regardless, I have a plan for the day and I refuse to have my witch sad and displeased in my room another day.

I send a text to Samantha and Achille confirming that everything is organized for our day trip.

The council doesn't need to know what we do in the daytime and I may just ask another spell of my witch. I want to make her happy, and I know right now, the thing that would make her the happiest is getting out of the house.

She sleeps soundly as I enter the bedroom, and I don't disturb her as I go to my closet and open the safe.

The mechanism whirls, and when I slide the door open, I tilt my head. One of the spines of the grimoires is misaligned.

It seems Ember did more snooping than I realized. That means she knows, or at least suspects, that this obsession with her has lasted far longer than she ever imagined. She didn't confront me, either, even when we were exchanging secrets, or when I stayed up with her all day.

I've been sensing that maybe this magic between us isn't as one sided as it originally seemed. A vampire can dream.

With the grimoire I need in hand, I dress in one of my most expensive suits, grabbing gloves, glasses, a hat, and my largest umbrella on hand. All of them are the best money can buy.

I take the liberty of setting out a pink sundress for Ember and I sit on the bed, waiting for her to wake from her sleep.

Her lips are slightly parted as she sleeps, her raccoon next to her, a hand gripped in her hair, as he uses her breast for a pillow. I never thought I'd be more jealous of vermin.

She doesn't have her guard up. Even when she wants to let go around me, she doesn't fully let herself.

She said that she wants my honesty, that she wants to know the real me. I haven't been a particularly honest man in a very long time, but I suppose for Ember to potentially like me, for her to want to stay with me and not run away once there's no longer imminent danger, it's what I'll have to do.

The thought that there won't always be some danger is ridiculous. Ember is mortal, though her lifespan is longer than humans, it doesn't seem long enough. I will give her the tools to make herself more powerful. I'll protect her with my last breath—well, not breath I can't breathe—with my last moments on this earth I vow them to Ember's safety.

Now, to become a man she would entrust with her wellbeing.

I push a piece of her strawberry hair off her face, a smile taking over her face as she sleeps. I'm greedy with my touch, as I glide my fingertip over her freckle-covered cheekbones.

"I am yours, even if you never let me have you. You are everything to me," I whisper, and she doesn't stir.

However, her raccoon's beady eyes are staring right into my soul. I stare right back until Ember mumbles and blinks her eyes open.

My ego inflates tenfold when she doesn't startle at my presence on the bed.

"How does brunch sound?" I ask cheerfully and Ember drags a hand down her face.

"It's daytime and you don't eat food."

"I see no issue with either of those things."

She squints at me. "You can go out in the sun?"

I hand her my sunglasses. "The best money can buy."

She puts them on her face and moves her head around. "How can you even see with these on?"

"Vampire vision. The suit and umbrella are also made with anti-UV material."

"Like your windows?"

I tilt my head. "Who told you about the windows?"

She grimaces. "Conner."

I make a noise in the back of my throat. I haven't forgotten he needs to be murdered. It's definitely a setback in being a better man, but Ember doesn't need to know everything.

"Imported from Japan. There's a vampire there that's rumored to be from the Yamato period. Who knows how true that is, but he invented the material, so he could see the outdoors during the day and he makes a fortune selling his inventions to other vampires."

She rubs the material between her fingers. It's thicker than a usual suit, and would probably send a human in Louisiana right into heat stroke.

"Isn't it still dangerous?"

"Yes, but worth it. Now put on your pretty dress and I need you to cast a little spell so my unwelcome houseguests don't question our whereabouts."

I pull out the black leather grimoire and flip to the page for sleep paralysis in vampires. Granted if any of them are awake, this will be difficult.

"It's very odd that you keep giving me spells to hurt you," she says.

"Yet the only thing you've hurt me with are items from my own bookshelf."

She winces at the reminder and takes the grimoire into the bathroom to get changed.

The raccoon lies on my bed, arms crossed, staring at me like I owe him money.

"Can I help you with something? Perhaps I should have some popcorn brought up?"

He adjusts himself, no longer in a defensive position, as I take out my phone and text the chef.

"It's done. Don't worry, I won't let anything happen to your mistress. I'd rather die than ever see her harmed."

He seems to believe me as he grabs the remote and puts on a show, no longer interested in our one-sided conversation.

Ember comes out of the bathroom looking like a vision. If I burn in the sun, it would be worth it seeing the smile plastered on her face as she reads off the spell. I can feel it wash over me, and I'm nearly tempted to fall asleep myself.

"Do you think it worked?" she asks, nibbling on her lip.

"Undoubtedly, my talented little witch."

She doesn't bluster and I wonder if this is the turning point of her accepting my compliments.

Chapter 22

He's going into the fucking sun to make me happy and I can't decide if I should try to run away from him or let him seduce me.

This is all such a complete mess.

What I found in his safe should have me running for the hills, but instead, it's giving me pause. Warin understands actions, not words it seems, and when I look back at everything he's said and done for me, things are clicking into place.

His actions are louder than I want to admit. Giving me the grimoires and granting me access to spells that could cause him harm? Him protecting me from the council and staking Joyce? Not to mention all his little nicknames and sweet words he says to me. I've never had a man give me so much attention. It's clearly going to my head. Despite his actions, despite this rippling in my gut, I know I can't completely trust him—a vampire.

I sigh as I put on my makeup. Why couldn't I be a normal witch? Why am I so charmed by the idea of Warin taking care of me and why is him being possessive and protective such a turn on? The back and forth banter we have is fun, I like sparring with him as much as I liked playing cards and laughing.

Hell, I even like that he's a vampire, the idea of him sinking his teeth into me while he shoves his…No, those deviant thoughts are exactly what got me into this mess.

No man has ever interested me like Warin does. Somehow this scheming vampire has all my attention.

I groan at myself. This attraction for danger, this magnetic pull to Warin, it's confusing and I'm not sure it would ever work. Why couldn't I be into witches or short flings with human guys?

Nope, I had to be attracted to the hottest, richest, asshole vampire there is.

He's a vampire and I'm a witch. The two don't mix. Even if I have had very explicit dreams about what he would do to me. Or even more dangerous, the way I'm longing for more of his touch and sweet words.

I point at myself in the mirror, hating that I put the dress he wanted me to wear on. I don't speak out loud, knowing he can probably hear my heartbeat right now.

He isn't charming. This isn't some fucked-up romance between a vampire and a witch. He kidnapped you. He's very likely been stalking you for years. This isn't cute, Ember.

Even as I say the words in my head I feel like a fraud. He is charming, even when he's being an asshole.

Ugh. Enough. Back to the plan. I should run back to the coven with my tail in between my legs and tell them the mess I'm in. It won't be a surprise. They don't expect much from me.

Warin does. He told me I was talented, but it doesn't matter. I have to stick to the plan.

I leave the bathroom and stare at Warin in his UV protectant attire. He's risking the sun for me and I'm considering running out on him. It has my stomach sinking, guilt slithering around my gut as I look at him. My body is revolting against the idea of running away from him, but my mind knows what I need to do.

No matter what Warin promises, I can't stay here. It's not truly safe. Being locked away in his windowless room isn't the safest place for me, back with my coven is.

"Beautiful as always. Ready to go?" he asks.

"Ready as I'll ever be."

We go through the house, the windows not affecting him. None of the vampires in the house are milling about and I wonder if my spell was that potent, or maybe they're all just as heavy of sleepers as Warin is.

Just as we're about to reach the garage, Sebastian leans against the door, standing there in nothing but his underwear. He's attractive, I suppose, but nowhere near as good looking as Warin.

"Hmm, taking your pet out for a day stroll?" Sebastian questions.

"Yes, pets need water, food, and sunshine, Sebastian. Shouldn't you be resting?" Warin retorts, his hand on my lower back.

"Oddest thing, I wasn't tired at all, planning on getting some accounting done while the sun shackles me to this house, but a sudden sense of exhaustion hit me. Luckily, I'm no longer affected. Would you happen to know anything about that?" Sebastian directs the question to me.

"Can't say I do, I only just woke up myself. Still trying to get used to the nocturnal lifestyle."

Warin's thumb circles my back like he's giving me a sign of approval, and I love it. His cool fingertips are a gentle reassurance and I'm about to try and run from these feelings. But as I glance at this threatening vampire in front of us, I know I don't have a choice.

It isn't safe here, even if Warin thinks he can protect me.

"Very well. Maybe you'll have better luck finding our little

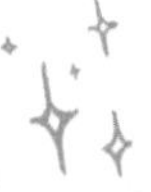

slayer problem during the day," Sebastian asks, a smirk on his face.

"Perhaps," Warin replies, but I can feel his irritation that dealing with the Slayer is the last thing he wants to do. "Let's go, Ember."

He directs me into the garage. Achille holds the back door open and I slide in, Warin behind me. Samantha is beaming in the front seat.

"Day time adventures are always exciting. Will I die? Will I find a human who will let me drink right from the source and they'll taste like the sun? The possibilities are endless."

Warin rolls his eyes. "You're here to be backup, Samantha."

"That doesn't mean that a handsome chef who eats clean and basks in the sun won't bare his neck to me and tell me to feed to my heart's content," Samantha retorts and Warin just sighs in response.

I shift in my seat a little, wondering if Warin feels the same way. Does he wish there was more than chicken and waffles on the menu for our little outing? Is he going to partake while I sip on my latte and eat French toast?

Warin taps my thigh.

"Don't worry Ember, we don't drink from those who aren't willing."

"I didn't ask," I reply, and he gives me a grin.

Achille plays some light jazz in the car, and there's no way that the glass in the vehicle is road legal.

It's only as we're driving that I realize that Samantha's and Achille's faces are both nearly covered up. Warin only has the sunglasses and I wonder if it's sufficient enough.

I shouldn't care so much about the manipulative vampire or his pretty face.

We pull into the back of the restaurant. There's barely enough space for Warin to open the door.

"Wait here. I'll call for you if there are any issues," Warin directs to Samantha, before holding out his gloved hand.

I take it and shimmy my way between the car door and the brick wall.

He's diligent with his umbrella, blocking us from any sunlight, and I'm slightly shrouded in the shadows as Warin shuts the door and confidently slides a hand down my back, directing me through the workers' entrance.

A man in bright chili pepper pants, an apron, and a black shirt opens the door.

"My old friend, it's good to see you again, and what stunning company. Come, I've reserved you the back table, and turned down the blinds," he says, leading the way through the bustling kitchen, tasting something on a spoon along the way. "Ramon, those grits shouldn't be wetter than when I'm touching your mom's pussy, thicken them up!" He shouts at his sous chef.

I cover my mouth to not burst out in laughter.

"My apologies, if you'll follow me."

The kitchen door swings open, and Warin has his umbrella in hand. A few beams of light slither through the shades and Warin avoids them, sliding into the cozy booth, and I follow suit.

The chef only hands me a menu and I look over at Warin.

"Thank you, Tony," Warin says to the chef, though he's blatantly staring at me.

"Of course. Veronica will be by shortly to take your order," the chef says, giving me a wink and walking away.

I turn to Warin, not even looking at the menu.

"He knows what you are?"

"Yes. All humans under my employ know what I am. They're

just unable to tell anyone else."

"Your compulsion?" I say, glancing down at my ring. The thing that protects me from him ever using it on me.

"Yes. It is necessary," he says, tapping a gloved finger against the table.

"How does the council feel about that?" I question.

"Dealing with humans is a part of our existence. As long as we protect our kind, it is not frowned upon, in fact it's typically encouraged."

I purse my lips and open the menu, trying to decide between savory and sweet. Though, what I should really be figuring out is how the hell I'm going to ditch this vampire in this booth.

"They seem pretty suspicious about me being in your house though, not the humans you employ."

"Well, I have given you access to spells that hurt our kind," he says with a smirk and I sigh.

"Why is that exactly?"

"I've been nothing but honest in that regard, Ember. I truly want to keep you safe."

"Even from you?" I ask with an arch of my brow.

His hand gently grips my wrist.

"Yes, Ember, even from me. Now, Tony is an amazing chef. Have you decided what you'd like?"

I hum under my breath and Warin clicks his tongue.

"Order as much as your heart desires."

For once, I actually listen to Warin, ordering more food than I know I'll be able to consume.

"What's your coven like?" he asks, taking me off guard as I bring a glass of water to my mouth.

I worry about how much I should tell him, giving him some insight into my grandmother and mother was probably already

too much information.

"I have no ulterior motive other than to get to know you, Ember."

"They're amazing, they mean everything to me, especially my best friends. I mentioned Iris who was there when I accidentally burnt the church down, and Violet came into our lives as teenagers. I can't imagine my life without them. The coven has its own issues, but we're working through them," I say honestly. I'm not sure why I want to be honest, maybe it's a bit of practicing what I preach.

"Things have changed since Aster was sent away. She was a bit of a bitch," he says and I snort into my water.

"You're not wrong. My grandmother is beside herself that Lavender is High Priestess, she's probably been the most vocal about it in the coven."

"This upsets you?" he asks and I shrug my shoulders.

I lick my lips. Should I tell him more information? Right now I'm supposed to be separating myself from Warin, not getting closer.

"She's disapproving of a lot of things, including me," I say the last part in a near whisper.

Warin reaches out, touching my wrist with a gloved hand and squeezing softly.

"Then she doesn't see what I see," he says as he stares at me.

Okay charming, sweet Warin is in this booth with me, and I'm not sure what to do with him when he's like this. It's easier when he's been demanding or scheming, but when he's like this, I can't help but to like him. So instead, like a coward, I pull my wrist away and change the subject.

"Do you like being a vampire?" I ask him, starting off easy.

"I do. I like being powerful, strong, and eternal. I miss the sun,

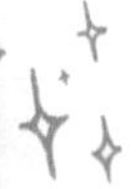

I miss my ma, but my human life wasn't much of a life."

"What about drinking blood?" I ask, with a thick swallow, wondering about his answer. I don't know why I need to know, but the idea of him sinking his teeth into someone else's throat bothers me.

What's wrong with me? My whole plan was to run away, but yet, here I am, endlessly fascinated with the vampire sitting across from me.

"At first, I loved it. Oz, despite his many faults, saw humans as a valuable resource. More than just food, he taught me restraint and how to contain my bloodlust." He clears his throat. "The only humans I've ever killed were the ones you saw in my memories."

I tilt my head at him, wondering how hard it was for him to indulge that little piece of him. I'm not sure why knowing that information helps me view him in a different light. I've seen Warin violent, but the fact that he isn't aggressive toward humans softens me even more.

He's been nothing but protective of me, and I can see that he's trying, he's doing what I asked of him.

I don't want to run away from him, and that thought is terrifying.

"And vampires?" I ask, wondering if his answer will change my mind.

He smirks, a bit of fang showing. "I wouldn't mind killing Joyce right about now."

"I can't believe you ever slept with her." The words slip out of my mouth before I can take them back.

"It was another life ago. I haven't…there's been no one in a very long time," he admits, and I swear there's a blush to his cheeks, maybe I'm seeing things. "What about you? Do you enjoy being a witch?"

I grin and nod while the server brings our food and I start in on the blueberry and peanut butter crepe.

"I can't imagine my life without magic. It feels like it's a part of me. I don't know anything else, but I wouldn't trade being a witch or my coven for the world. I might not be the best at it—"

"I think you're quite good at it. I think that your magic has been criminally underutilized. Clearly, you're talented with your earth magic, but I think defensive magic is your true calling. Not any witch could master the spells in those grimoires like you could."

My cheeks heat. My family never compliments my magic. Violet and Iris do, of course, but not as reverently as Warin does.

This vampire looks at me like no one else ever has, and despite my better instincts, I'm falling for it.

"I don't know about that," I say with a shrug.

"I do. You're talented, beautiful, generous, and too fucking hard on yourself. You're an exceptional witch and if someone has told you differently, I don't mind making a pit stop on the way home."

He looks dead serious, and I sigh.

"Are you really going to take out my grandma?" I snark.

He smirks at me, his elbows on the table as his gloved hands rest under his chin.

"Is that something that friends do for one another? Take out bitchy grandmas?"

I blink at him a few times and he grins.

"This is our friend date, and I have to say, it's going rather swimmingly. Maybe this honesty thing isn't so absolutely horrible. What else would you like to know?"

I have a bite of my omelet ready to go into my mouth when I pause at his question, bringing my fork back down onto the plate and wiping my mouth.

"You really want me to like you, don't you?"

"More than anything," he replies, his eyes searching mine.

It's pathetic how happy I am that he took the sunglasses off when we sat down. His eyes are far too pretty to be hidden away.

"You'll tell me anything I want to know, even the bad stuff?"

He nods, his nostrils flaring ever so slightly.

"Then you'll tell me why you wanted this arrangement with me and about why you've been stalking me for what appears to be the last decade?" I ask with an arch of my brow. It's the last piece I need to know, it's what will tip the scales on whether I stay and see what this connection is or if I run out this door kicking and screaming.

I'm staring him down. His lips part to speak when everything goes to absolute hell.

Chapter 23

It all happens so fast. One moment I'm staring at Warin, ready for him to come clean and finally explain everything to me, and then the window shatters in front of us and Warin is manhandling me under the table.

Endorphins are rushing through me, and my heart is raging in my chest as Warin groans. It's taking my mind a few moments to realize what's going on.

"Samantha!" Warin's voice roars.

His hand is on my back, and he's arched on the floor. I can't see his face.

Warin is hissing and panting when I finally see the stake protruding a few inches from where I was sitting. With trembling hands, I touch my face, deep-red blood drips on my fingertips and my hands tremble.

The pain finally radiates through me. There's definitely a shard of glass from the window in my thigh and I whimper.

"Are you hurt?" Warin's voice says, his hand on my hip, but he doesn't look at me. His voice sounds garbled, like he's wearing a mask.

"Some glass, and I think maybe the stake sliced my face," I say. "What about you?"

He shakes his head, still looking toward the floor.

"Warin?" I question, grabbing his shoulder.

"Samantha will be here soon. You go with her, she'll keep you safe."

"Warin, what's wrong?" I slide my hand further up his shoulder.

When he turns to face me, I gasp. He's no longer the charming vampire I was having brunch with. His face is nearly unrecognizable. It's almost like his face was pressed into a bonfire, and unlike the other time I saw him injured, he isn't healing.

I swallow thickly, my first instinct to reach out for him. "Warin, what do I do?"

He pulls away from me, looking back down at the ground.

"Just go with Samantha. I can't. I can't be around you right now."

"What? Warin, we have to get you somewhere safe. We need to get you healed. Is there a reason you aren't healing?"

"Yeah, the dumb motherfucker hasn't fed and has sustained two serious injuries," Samantha's voice says behind me.

She's covered head to toe in black, not a single inch of skin in sight as the sun beams behind her.

"Leave me. I'll figure it out. Take her to safety," Warin says.

"Mmm, the sire bond is feeling a little weak. Just so you know, this wasn't the Slayer," Samantha says.

That information has him turning, and I can't help but to wince when I see his burned face.

"Conner. That's why the aim was so shit," Samantha says, pointing a knife at me. "Now, are you done being difficult?"

"No," Warin grumbles, nearly falling to the floor.

Samantha sighs.

"Here," she says, handing me the umbrella. "I need you to guard him from the sun with this and take up his right side. I'll carry most of his left. Achille is dealing with Conner. We just need to get him to the car."

"I said leave me. Take her to safety."

Even with Samantha's eyes covered, I can sense her eye roll. "If I leave you here, will you feed?" she asks.

Warin is silent, and I glance over at Samantha.

"You're such a pain in my fucking ass. Just tell her, Warin, tell her or I fucking will," she seethes.

He doesn't move and I decide maybe a softer approach.

"Warin, please come with us. My healing magic is just okay, but I'd feel a lot better knowing how you were doing. I'm not leaving without you."

He looks over at me. His pretty eyes are hard to see.

"Are you manipulating me, witch?" he asks, and it sounds like he's trying to laugh, but it sounds more like a gargle.

"Maybe I am," I say proudly, popping open the umbrella. "Now, we're getting the hell out of here—together."

"My lot in life was to be surrounded by women who boss me around."

"Aren't you lucky then," I say.

He groans as Samantha picks up his one side, and she truly carries most of his weight. I'm mostly here to make sure I block out the sun with the umbrella.

Warin is stiff next to me and I think back to the time I pulled the stake out of him. He seemed perfectly fine the next time I saw him. Joyce also healed super quickly when he staked her with the coffee table leg.

"Blood will help?" I ask, mostly to Samantha.

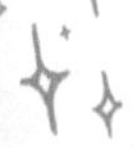

"It will more than help. It's exactly what he needs. The stupid fuck hasn't fed since—"

"Enough," Warin interrupts, even though it takes all of his strength.

I hold on to his waist, making sure that no more of the sun's rays touch his skin. I glance back, realizing exactly where the stake is embedded in the booth. If Warin didn't move me as fast as he did, if he didn't risk the sun exposure, I'd be dead right about now.

I hold him closer, and he moans, but I'm not sure if it's from the pain he's in or something else.

"You'll be okay, just keep moving," I say gently.

"Seriously, War, when did you get so fucking heavy? Take some bigger steps, fuck," Samantha complains.

Mostly because of her strength, we make it through the kitchen. The staff is somehow emptied out, no one in our way as we make it to the backdoor.

"Okay, it's a tight squeeze. Be super cautious with the umbrella," Samantha reminds me.

I give her a sharp nod. "I've got you, Warin. It's going to be okay."

With the utmost care, I make sure that the umbrella covers his skin as Samantha all but hefts his larger form into the backseat. He grumbles and makes pained sounds as he lies on the backseat. I have to basically crawl over him to take a seat next to him, placing his face on my lap.

"You torture me," he rasps out.

"You don't have to talk," I tell him, not knowing where to put my hands. I don't want to cause him any more pain.

Samantha gets in the driver's seat, pulling the balaclava off her face, her dark hair falling around her.

"Fuck this. He has the restraint of a fucking saint, you can't risk going into bloodlust with her bleeding like that. I'm barely holding it together."

"Samantha," he growls out her name.

"No. This is enough. He won't drink from anyone else but you. It's why he's weak, why he isn't healing. He's been starving himself. Maybe if he hadn't already taken a stake to the stomach he'd be fine, but he won't heal, not unless he drinks blood."

Samantha drops that bomb and turns to face the steering wheel, backing out of the alleyway like a bat out of hell.

"Is that true?" I ask softly to Warin.

"It's not your problem," he says plainly.

"You saved my life back there. I'm the reason you got burned," I say softly.

Without him, I wouldn't be here. If it's my blood he needs, that's an easy sacrifice. It's more than guilt over him saving me and being injured, there's this pull to him I've been denying myself and seeing him hurt is sending an ache through my chest.

"I can help you, I want to help you," I say, looking down at his poor face.

"Take us to the bunker," Warin whispers so softly, I'm almost positive I didn't hear him right.

"You'll need to be back before nightfall," Samantha says from the driver's seat.

Warin doesn't answer, and he noticeably doesn't respond to my offer or look at me. Not knowing what else to do, I place a hand on his chest, knowing that hasn't been burned. There's no heartbeat, no movement. But when his gloved hand covers mine, a sense of relief fills me.

My plan today was to run away from him, and instead I had to convince him to let us leave together. I'm not sure what's happening, why I feel this way, or why I can't stop it.

But as Warin holds my hand, as he sits there in pain, I'm start-ing to realize that there's no way I'm ever truly escaping Warin. What's more confusing is I don't think I want to.

The drive isn't long, the road is unpaved, rocks hitting the side of the vehicle as Samantha zooms down the dirt road. Warin is clearly in pain, but doesn't complain about Samantha's reckless driving.

We finally reach the end of the road. All I can see is a large hill. It would be easily climbable. Samantha puts her balaclava back on, and glances back at us, casting a worried glance.

"Ready to hold the umbrella again?" she asks, and I nod, grab-bing it, popping it open in the car as Samantha opens the door.

Moving Warin is harder, and it has my stomach filled with lead. I have my own injuries, but I don't even feel them as we round the hill. Samantha leans Warin against the grassy mound, opening up a panel.

She inputs a code and the mechanism whirls as a door slides open.

I was expecting a military bunker, but the space is actually rel-atively cozy. A red and brown Turkish rug takes up the majority of the space, along with a queen bed and a small kitchen area.

Samantha hefts Warin up on the bed, lying him down.

"I'll be just outside," she says, more to me than him.

She doesn't linger, rushing out the door, the harsh metal clanging in her wake.

I sit on the bed, pushing all my pinkish hair to the side of my neck. I'm sure he can hear how wild my heart rate is. I'm really about to do this, aren't I?

I'm offering myself on a platter for the vampire who's tricked me, lied to me, and stalked me. But he's also taught me, protected me, and saved me.

While I'm not sure those things completely cancel each other out, it feels significant.

"Drink, Warin," I tell him.

He doesn't stir, and I look down at him, trying not to have a reaction to how he looks.

"Is this the equivalent of a pity fuck?" he grates out and I can't help but to laugh.

"We're friends, right?"

"Mmm. Do friends let friends drink their sweet, magical blood?"

At least he seems to be getting a bit of himself back. Though he attempts to hide his burned face from me.

"In the same way, friends don't let friends get staked in the face."

"I'm going to kill that motherfucker," Warin whispers.

"Might be a little difficult if you aren't at full strength, wouldn't it?" I say, exposing my neck even further.

"You don't know what you're asking, angel."

"Warin. Drink," I say more sternly.

He leans forward and I look away, taking a deep breath. His gloved hand tenderly holds my hair as the heat of his face radiates against my neck.

"Where's your wand?" he asks.

"Here," I whisper, holding it in my hand with a white knuckle grip.

"If I go too far, if you feel faint, you stun the fuck out of me. It's…it's been a long time since I've fed from someone and I'm weak. I don't trust myself."

"I've been bleeding since the incident. If you were truly out of control, you would have lost it by now. I trust you."

The words feel right and wrong at the same time.

I do trust Warin with my safety. As far as other things go, I'm not sure. But deep in my bones, I know that Warin would never hurt me, never intentionally.

"You're so fucking perfect," he says, right before he sinks his teeth into my neck.

I expect pain, a sharp bite into my neck that stings. Instead, it's a tantalizing mix of pleasure and pain as he drinks from me. I'm writhing on the bed, but not from pain, only pleasure.

Never in my life have I been this aroused. No fantasy, no man, nothing has ever made me feel like this.

Every nerve ending feels like it's on fire, a flaming inferno that I don't want to be put out.

I can't help myself as I lean into Warin, his strong arm wrapping around my waist, as he holds me against his chest.

Masculine moans fall out of his mouth as he drinks me down, and I don't think I've ever felt so powerful.

It's like this sexual need and desire that I've never felt is finally blooming to life and I might just be addicted, I want more.

I'm consumed with greed and want.

No man has ever made me come, but something tells me I might just be able to finish from this alone.

Warin grips me harder, his thumb grazing the underside of my breast, and I can't help but to moan.

I want more, so much fucking more with this vampire and in this moment I don't feel shame. All I feel is unadulterated desire.

Chapter 24

She tastes like sunshine bottled up.

Like flowers and all things good wrapped up in a delicious, beautiful fucking package. The precious gift of her blood explodes on my tongue as I hold her.

Her body is soft, feminine, and an obsession. I don't know how I forgot just how deliciously sweet she was. How in the world could I ever forget?

Maybe it's because she only gave me a meager drop last time. Maybe it's because I tried to not think about what I was missing out on. All I know is that when I taste her, when I hold her, I'm the closest to heaven I'll ever be.

Despite my wicked past, my penchant for violence, this beautiful angel is in my arms gifting me her blood—gifting me her.

I take a heavy draw of her blood, the warm liquid trickling down my throat. I feel my strength returning tenfold.

My thumb is dangerously close to her breast and all I want to do is squeeze, touch, and press her against me while I swallow down the sweetest nectar of my life.

Then she shocks me. She fucking moans. No sound has ever

rattled me more. It's like a siren song.

I hold her tighter, squeezing her as close as I can at this angle, her back against my chest.

"More. More, War."

The nickname has a whimper slipping out of my lips. They don't leave her throat as I adjust her on my lap. Her full ass is pressed against my now fully alert cock, now that I've fed.

I'm about to remove my fangs. I haven't taken too much, not even close. I don't know why I doubted myself with Ember, I'd never take it too far.

But then her hand snakes around my neck, tugging me closer to her throat.

"Don't stop. Fuck. Touch me. I'm so close. Holy Hecate," she says breathlessly.

Touch? She'll let me fucking touch?

With both hands, I cup her breasts, squeezing and kneading her considerable tits that I'm bedeviled by. They're more than a handful, and all I can imagine is sinking my teeth into one while I fuck her. I can't help it when I grind against her ass.

Her warmth, her sounds, everything about this witch is fucking addictive.

I was obsessed before, but now? Now I'm absolutely, devastatingly impassioned by everything that is Ember Hallow. I'd fantasized about having her like this, her freely giving me her blood, but I never conceptualized what it would be like to actually have her.

She fucking owns me and I'm a wholly eager prisoner to her capture.

Ember grinds back on my lap and she whimpers, grabbing one of my hands and sliding it down her front, over her soft stomach and under her bunched up dress.

"More. Please. Please, War."

My witch is begging for me and I'm fucking wrecked over it. I want to take the gloves off, feel her wet heat against my fingers, but there's not enough time. I need to stop feeding. I'm barely drawing in any blood right now, but it seems to be an aphrodisiac for us both.

Instead, I slide her panties to the side, the tips of my fingers dragging down her slit, feeling the wetness even through the leather.

I've barely circled her clit as her fingernails dig into my neck, drawing my mouth even closer to her throat.

"Suck. Hard. Now," she demands.

I moan as I do what she says, toying with her pussy, strumming my fingers against her clit, not penetrating her under the current circumstances, but little does she know I'd fuck her, devour her, any time of the month.

It happens so fast, her head falling against my shoulder and her thighs quaking as she shudders out her release. Her body trembles against mine as I hold her close.

Never in my life have I felt as strong as I do now. I'm gentle as I pull my fangs away from her throat, licking a trail up the column of her neck to the back of her ear.

My one hand is splayed against her stomach as I bring the other from her pussy to my lips. She watches. Those big beautiful green eyes don't blink as I put my gloved fingers in my mouth, tasting her pussy for the first time.

Her full lips part, her heart still racing from the excitement, the feeding, and her orgasm. The scent of her arousal and blood is entrancing. I'm nearly about to come in my pants as her flavor hits my tongue.

Her blood and come paints my tongue and I can't help but to

savor it, my eyes shutting as I hum around my fingers.

I slip my fingers out of my mouth, bite the glove, tugging it off my hand as I prick my finger with a fang. I drag my blood over her throat, healing the wound before bringing the finger to her mouth.

"Suck," I tell her.

She shocks me by being obedient, parting her lips and never looking away from me. She sucks on my finger and all sense of control leaves me as I jolt against her ass, my release spilling in my pants.

Ember gasps as I pull my finger out of her mouth and we're both panting now.

"My blood will heal any of your injuries from earlier. But we should probably look you over for any pieces of glass," I tell her, and she blinks at me.

Her hand slides up to her throat, her fingers trailing over her now perfectly smooth skin where I bit her.

She swallows, her throat bobbing as her pulse increases.

"Will it…will it do anything else?" she asks, her eyes searching mine as she looks at me over her shoulder.

"It could have other effects," I say casually.

That has her hopping off my lap, and she clears her throat, flattening out her dress.

"No, no, no. We did not just do all of that for you to lie to me or talk in riddles. You said you were going to be honest, that you want to be a better man. What will your blood do? Why do I want to peel my clothes off and let you bite me again? What the fuck is wrong with me?"

She starts pacing, not even letting me answer.

"Nothing has ever been like that," she says, waving a hand at me, tears streaming from her face. "Nothing, Warin, not even close. You're violent, manipulative, and secretive." I go to open my mouth and she points at me to shut up. "Then there are these moments where you make me feel like I'm the only person who matters. You've proven you want to keep me safe, that you're attracted to me. Ugh, I'm so overwhelmed with every emotion, I want to crawl out of my fucking skin. So consider your next words wisely. They better be honest. So tell me, why? Why does it feel like this?" She's nearly shouting at me, pointing with accusation.

"Then I suppose we need to go back to 1933. Take a seat. I'll show you everything," I say.

She takes a deep breath, her chest shifting up and down as she breathes heavily. Her pupils are huge and her arousal and blood are still thick in the air, but I'm not dumb enough to bring that up now.

It takes her a few moments, and she licks her lips. She takes a few steps before sitting next to me on the bed, her wand in hand.

I go to reach for her face to wipe away her tears and she thankfully lets me. I want to taste them too, but I wisely decide not to.

"The truth, Warin. I need the truth," she says.

"Okay, the truth," I whisper and Ember takes a breath, holding up her wand, doing the basis of the spell I gave her access to.

This will either fix everything or ruin it as she slithers into my memories.

Chapter 25

Chicago World Fair

"This is pathetic," Oz says, as we roam around the World Fair.

People are elbow to elbow pushing through the different spectacles, some completely despicable while others are rather fascinating.

"I think I'll find myself a companion for the night. Maybe find one worth keeping for a few more weeks while we're here. What are you thinking? I know you enjoy the redheads. I'm sure we can find you one here," Oz goes on.

I sigh, waving a hand at him. "I'll catch up with you later tonight."

Oz glares at me, irritated with my mood, irritated that I no longer view him as the second coming of Christ. The steel wool has been removed from my eyes and I see him for who he truly is now. He's still powerful, made me rich, gave me eternal life, yet, I still feel listless.

I thought that when I had the money, the influence, that I'd have everything. I'd be content. Don't get me wrong, I love all of those things, but the cost was higher than I realized it would be. I had to cut ties with my Ma. She thinks I'm missing, or dead. The sun is an enigma now; the moon is my only constant.

There's also this rigid codependency Oz has to me, like I'm his reason and I can't stand it. He released me from the sire bond, saying it was archaic, but I'm still under his thumb. I think he likes knowing he controls me without the sire bond, because truly I have no other options.

Follow Oz, or he'll kill me himself—those are my two options.

Sometimes I wonder if things would be different if I were out on my own, if I could join a new nest and make my own way, maybe things wouldn't be so morose. But Oz won't allow it. He's directly told me that my allegiance belongs to him. If I detract from him, vampire council be damned, he'd chain me to a pillar and let me burn in the sun.

Oz digs in his back pocket, pulling out a few crisp bills and handing them to me, like I didn't earn this money outright.

"Be good," he says, pointing at me and turning his back.

We've made more money than we could ever imagine bringing moonshine and authentic bayou gin to the city of Chicago. They have their own nests of vampires, but Oz is older and reigns over the entire eastern half of the country.

There's nothing truly bad for me to get into. If I thought about stepping out of line, any vampire would go tattle right to Oz.

I just need a moment to catch my breath. I need something that is mine.

At least I have a few moments to myself. I'm not hungry, we gorged ourselves on those cocktail waitresses last night and then compelled them not to remember.

Life as a vampire is full of overindulgence. Anything I want, I can have it with a single word slipping out of my lips, yet something is missing and I don't know what it is.

The fair is boasting, a small child is shoving his face with Cracker Jacks and I almost wish I could taste the sweet treat. I don't particularly miss food or crave it, but I miss some of my humanity.

I can feel myself losing it, with no direction on how to get it back, or if that's even possible.

Life as a vampire is different, and I need to accept my new normal.

A pink tent stands in the distance, glittering lights covering the outside. The word 'Fortune' is embroidered in gold and something beckons me to the tent.

Surely it's some human making a quick buck off the insecurity of mortals. Who wouldn't want to know what their future holds? Even I, an immortal being, wants to know what awaits me in this exceptionally long life.

I approach the tent and cautiously look around, making sure no vampires are watching as the silk fans my fingertips as I pull it back. The moment I do, an earth-shattering headache wrecks my brain. My hands come up to my head and I want to scream but can't.

"What are you doing in my tent, vampire?" a voice asks, the headache subsiding for a blissful moment.

Definitely not a human. When I glance up at the slender woman with short dark hair, she glares at me, her wand in her hand.

Vampires don't fuck with witches, and I just strolled into this one's tent.

"Here I thought I was going to have my fortune read," I groan, giving the woman a smile.

She rolls her eyes.

"Vampires aren't welcome here," she says, giving me her back, unafraid as she sits back down at her crystal ball.

For some stupid reason, maybe to fucking feel something, I sit down across from her.

"Is the crystal ball all for show? Or does it actually do something?" I ask.

The witch lights her cigarette with magic, the cigarette holder floating in the air as she takes a huff, smoke flowing out of the side of her mouth.

"For show. Do you need to be told more aggressively to get the fuck out?" she says, another unbothered huff of her cigarette.

"Tell me my fortune and I'll leave."

"How does one tell the fortune of someone without a soul? Without a heartbeat? What is the fate of the dead?" she says, shuffling tarot cards with her hands, always keeping eye contact with me, her wand in immediate reach.

"Surely I still have a soul?" I ask, unsure.

Her inhale of her cigarette is dramatic, her dark eyes on me.

"Nothing I've seen of vampires proves otherwise. Always willing to hurt whoever you need to in order to get what you want. Why would I do anything for you?"

"Because I'm a paying customer?"

She arches an eyebrow and I place a substantial amount of cash on the counter, probably more than she makes in a week at the fair. She clicks her tongue and nods.

"What do you want to know, vampire?"

"Is there something more worth living for?" I ask, being completely blunt.

She shuffles her cards, shifting them between her two hands.

"The price has gone up," she says. "A vial of your blood, some of it needed for the spell."

"What will you do with it?" I question.

"Hmm. I don't see how that's any of your business, pay the fee or fuck off."

I bite my wrist, a goblet floats in the air, ready to collect my blood. When she's satisfied with the amount, she dips her wand into my blood before bringing it to her mouth.

The result is instantaneous as her head flings back, her eyes going white for a long moment, and she takes a deep inhale. She's back to normal quickly, a small cackle leaving her lips as she shakes her head.

"I'd heard the rumors that vampires could have mates, but I didn't think them true. I always assumed you all fucked and ravaged, never forming true bonds beyond perhaps your sire," she says.

Her hand picks up a glass of liquor and I wonder if it's something we imported for the fair. She holds it up and inspects the glass.

"You know you'll need to find a new business with prohibition being lifted."

"What were you saying about mates?" I ask, leaning forward. I've never loved anyone besides my ma. The concept sounds unbelievable.

"Some more gin and I'll tell you."

"Whatever you want," I reply.

She smirks and I wonder if she's fucking with me, if I'm just another fool sliding into her tent and she tells them what they want to hear.

"It's more common with wolves, a person who is destined to be theirs, a fate you can not outrun. You could have feelings for another, but nothing as strong as your mate. They are perfect for you in every way. The wolves are born with this knowledge, but it seems it's become less common with vampires, maybe it has to do with the growing population or perhaps tension within the supernatural community. You're rather hated, you know?"

"Well aware," I say sharply.

She smirks, lighting a new cigarette. "A blood mate is another supernatural destined for you. Their blood will call to you like no other and your blood will affect them exponentially. It will heal them faster, ruffle their desire for you. Just as their blood calls to you, the same to them."

"And you see one in my future?" I urge.

"Hmm. Unsure. I think more money would help."

I throw down all the money in my wallet on the table, and she nods happily.

"She is magical, fire, sugar, and flowers. Though it's uncertain that she will ever be yours, only that she is your blood mate, you'll have a very long road ahead of you to make that happen."

"When will I meet her? Soon? Where? What does she look like?"

She takes a deep inhale, her head flaring back again. Her heart rate is skyrocketing, and her breathing is heavy when she looks back up at me. Her face is resolved, saddened but resolved.

"I will tell you her name, but in return I need you to make an unbreakable vow to me," she says, her eyes watering as she takes a shaky inhale of her cigarette and downs the rest of her liquor.

"What vow?"

"Here I thought someone robbing me for my ring was a good enough reason to not wear it today. Lot's of unsavory types in the city at a fair so big. I should have known better." She laughs with a sarcastic sigh.

"I need you to preserve my grimoires, save them for your blood mate, but do not destroy them. And you must promise that you won't let your sire seek retribution against my coven."

My brows furrow as I look at the witch.

"Vow it," she says with a trembling voice, holding out her hand.

I take her hand in mine and nod. "I vow it."

"They're in the Greyhound bus, fifth seat back."

"Why do I need to preserve anything? What's her name?"

"Because I let a fucking vampire into my tent. Her name's Em—"

Before she can finish her sentence, Oz is behind her, his teeth in her throat before he snaps her neck. Her blood is dripping down his chin, covering his white shirt as he drops her body on the floor with a thud.

"Naughty, naughty, Warin," he says, taking the goblet of blood she collected and drinking down my blood, something I'd never willingly do with him. Vampires exchange blood, but it's usually done in a sexual nature.

"You gave this filthy little witch your blood, while you wouldn't even dare give it to me? Did she trick your young mind? Did she promise you something?"

I blink wildly, like I'm confused.

"I…I don't remember," I say and Oz clicks his tongues.

"Old witches like this are disgusting. It's important that we stick to our own, that we stick to our nest," he says calmly, placing a bloody palm on my face. "I knew I shouldn't have let you out of my sight tonight. Sometimes I forget how young you are. Come, let us retire for the night."

I look down at the witch's body; I didn't even know her name, yet a deep sense of regret fills me. She's dead because of my curiosity. Oz killed her simply because she was a witch and I gave her my blood.

"Warin. Now," Oz grates out, and I stand up, looking down at her listless body, knowing I'll need to sneak out later tonight.

Oz is like a warden as we sit in the basement of the humans he compelled. It's then that I have an idea, a way that I don't even have to leave the house to get what I want.

I have to wait until the sun rises. Oz is asleep. He rests more than a typical vampire, and I wonder if that's how he's continued to stay in power. The ones who don't sleep tend to spiral into madness.

It's dangerous as I walk up the cellar stairs, slowly creaking the door open. A beam of sunlight slips through and I'm careful to not open it any further.

"Clarissa, come here," I whisper.

She's an affluent woman, Oz wouldn't let us stay in a home anything less than expensive.

The human woman comes to the door, her face through the crack, her pupils wide.

"Yes?"

"I need you to retrieve something for me and for your family to keep it safe until I get it, no matter how long that may be."

"What do you need me to get?" she asks robotically.

I look down the steps, assuring that Oz is still asleep as I tell her where to find the grimoires, where to get a safety deposit box, and the information she needs to pass down for each generation.

Over ninety years pass before I collect the grimoires on the day Oz is found dead from Clarissa's great-granddaughter.

Chapter 26

I pull out of Warin's memories with a jolt. My eyes are even more watery than before when I look at him.

A blood mate? That's what I am to him?

My first reaction is joy. Being a mate to someone is a gift. I've seen it firsthand with Silas and Violet. It's like I finally found the missing puzzle piece under the couch and everything makes sense. There's a reason why I couldn't feel anything with another man. They weren't him; they weren't my destined person.

I'm also met with fear and anxiety over the whole situation. Maybe part of me thought that no matter what I was feeling, Warin was just a bump in the road of my stupid decisions. That eventually he would get bored and send me on my way and I'd just have to go on with my life. But if he's my mate, this is forever. Nothing will ever compare, and with that comes a lot of other problems to solve.

He lives forever and I don't.

My coven won't accept him, and if the vampire council is anything to go by, they won't accept me either.

"What do you need?" he says, a hand on my back and I lurch

off the bed. His touch is making my critical thinking skills go out the window, though maybe they've been long gone.

I stand, facing him with my arms crossed over my chest. He's beautiful again. His face completely healed because of my blood, because I'm his blood mate.

It all makes so much sense now, why I find him so handsome, why I couldn't help but fall for his charms even when he's scheming. He's fated to me, and I can't help but to find it so ridiculously romantic and also hate myself for it at the same time.

"When?" I question him and he tilts his head.

"When what?"

"When did you know what I was to you?" I ask.

This question has him shifting in his seat, he's uncomfortable, but nods, knowing he has to give me an answer.

"Your twenty-first birthday. You came to my bar looking fucking innocent and perfect. The only person I ever told about having a blood mate was Samantha. I'm not sure why I told her. Maybe I thought the witch was full of shit and that it wasn't going to actually happen. But Samantha, she believed it, so when she saw a pretty, naïve witch in line at a vampire bar, she brought you to my office. I was suspicious that Aster sent you, or that you wanted some of my blood. But in reality, I think you were seeking me out, something deep in you knew you were fated to me."

"And why don't I remember that?" I ask him. I already know the answer, but I need him to say it.

"I compelled you to forget. You told me your name, and I tasted your blood. I knew what you were to me, but I also knew that, to keep you safe, I had to keep you far away from me."

"Why?" I croak as I look down at my finger that's tingled so many times I've been around him.

Warin stands, his speed human-like as he approaches me as if

I might run away as he cups my face, his hands cool and comforting.

"Oz would have killed you, and I knew you'd be fine without me. It was more important that you were safe than for me to have the thing I wanted most in the world."

"But you indulged," I reply. "You watched me from afar. You kept tabs on me."

"I did. The bat in your shutters—"

"You can turn into a fucking bat?" I say a little too loudly and Warin smirks, shaking his head.

"No. My familiar, Betty, she kept tabs on you. When I could, I would watch you, make sure you weren't getting into trouble."

"Why didn't you come and find me once Oz was dead? You waited until the Slayer attacked."

His thumbs stroke my cheeks. "Don't ever doubt that I haven't wanted you every single moment in the last century. The moment I found out I had a blood mate waiting for me, I never touched another. The second I tasted your blood, I never drank directly from a human again. My devotion is only to you, Ember Hallow, and everything I've done has always been because I thought it was in your best interest. The only reason we're here right now is because I'm inherently selfish. I thought I could stay away, that I could do what was best for you, that I could protect you from me."

He leans forward, his lips nearly touching my forehead.

"I told myself that I'd ruin you, that you were far too kind to be tethered to a wicked creature like myself. Then Baptiste was murdered, and I saw an opening. Oz was dead. You were in danger and I took the opportunity in the only way I knew how, manipulating you into an arrangement where you needed to spend time with me, hoping you felt something too. I watched you for years, but being around you? Fuck, Ember. I'm greedy, and self-serving, but I couldn't let you go."

I swallow thickly, looking up at him, feeling nothing but true honesty falling out of his mouth.

"You feel it too, just a little bit?" he asks, seeming the most insecure I've ever seen him.

I grab his wrist, squeezing tightly.

Despite myself, despite what would be easier, I also feel this connection. I nod and place my head against his chest. His hand cradles the back of my head and I sigh.

How is it that a vampire's arms are the ones that make me feel safest, and why is it such a relief knowing that something isn't wrong with me? All these years I've been fascinated with the beings of the night, and now I finally find out why.

It was fate, not something wrong with me.

Warin is gentle as he pets my hair, a complete juxtaposition to the man I watched stake a vampire for talking poorly about me. He holds me close, a comfort I haven't had in a long time, and I just lean into his strength.

"I never meant to deceive you. All I ever wanted since I learned about your existence is you," he whispers in my ear.

I want to be mad about the time lost, the time we could have had together, but then I realize how long Warin waited for me.

"There was really no one since you found out?"

"No. Never," he promises.

I rest my ear on his chest, which is eerily silent. I let out a sigh as I play with the lapel of his jacket.

"This doesn't magically solve our problems, either. This is going to take work. There's so much to figure out. I-I want to make this work, but that's going to be a big ask. I won't leave my coven. I'll always be a witch," I say.

Warin doesn't stop his petting, which he's truly great at.

"I know. I don't want to change you."

It's open-ended, like he's worried that I want to change him.

"I don't want to change you either, but if we're going to do this, we'll need to make some adjustments. No more secrets, no more scheming without me."

He pulls back. "You'd like to scheme with me, little witch?"

"I mean, yeah, I think that some will be involved if we're going to make this work."

His hands are back on my face, and my hands slide up and down against the expanse of his solid chest.

"If I knew honesty would work this well, perhaps I should have gone with this approach sooner."

I narrow my eyes at him, because haven't I been saying that from the beginning?

"Tonight is the full moon. I need to be with my coven," I say sternly.

"No fucking way," he snaps back, taking our progress and little honesty session a few steps back.

"Achille has Conner locked up. The Slayer has been MIA. You and the council will spend the night hunting him and will stay away from coven land. I need to see my friends. I need some time to figure out what to do next. Also I need to stop at my cabin so I can stop my fucking period so I know I'm thinking straight," I huff out, straightening my dress.

There's a slight flashback of him sticking his fingers down my panties and how I'd really like to do a hell of a lot more right now. But there can't be any more of that until we figure some things out.

I might be slightly delusional, but I need some assurances. I need Violet and Iris in my corner. I need to know that I won't lose

them.

Warin's jaw is tense. "Betty will come with you. If anything is wrong, she'll alert me immediately."

"Okay," I say, not pushing back. "My entire coven will be there too, ya know."

"Yes, but you're my witch," he says, his thumbs stroking my jaw.

His.

Someone to call my own. Someone who wants me so deeply he'd wait a century for me, stalk me for years until the time was right. My mind is probably warped that I find this all endlessly romantic. But at this point, I'm pretty sure I'm over societal norms.

"What does being your witch mean to you?" I say in a sultry voice. This endless need is still thrumming in my veins. All I want to do is to succumb to this sensation and give into him.

He presses closer, a hand at the base of my skull and another cradling my chin.

"It means that I'll always protect you, that I'll cherish you, care for you. You'll want for nothing, Ember. My life is yours."

My heart stutters in my chest and no matter how stupid it is, I lift on my tiptoes and crash my lips against his.

He kisses me like a man starved, like everything in his life has led to this kiss. His hold on me is firm, yet gentle, as he deepens the kiss, his tongue sliding into my mouth as I moan.

There's a lingering taste of blood on his tongue, and I find that I don't hate it. If anything, I'm more turned on thinking about what we did earlier, the way his teeth sunk into my throat and how easily I fell apart at his touch.

I feel wholly woman in his arms and I know this feeling could never be recreated with anyone else. As scary and unknown as this all is, he's my fate.

This complicated vampire is what the universe has chosen for me, and I'm not mad about it.

I lightly tug on his bottom lip as our lips part. I'm nearly out of breath and he's in shock still, staring at me like I'm the reason the earth rotates.

"I still don't like it," he says, not letting go of me.

It's like now that he's been given access to touch, he never wants to let go, and I find it precious.

"You'll use any magic necessary to protect yourself. If you need me, call on Betty and I'll be there in a moment."

"Okay," I whisper.

"Begging and obedience in the same day. Sunshine, don't make me make a fucking mess of myself again," he says, his forehead resting against mine.

I glance down at his crotch, loving that I have the same power over him as he does over me, and bite my lip.

I'm not sure if I'll always feel sexually charged or if it's a matter of having his blood in my system, but something tells me it's the former.

"I need to go," I tell him, tugging away.

"Have Samantha take you home. Be safe."

He kisses me on the forehead. I'm careful with the door as I open it, making sure none of the sun slips through, as I walk over to the SUV.

When I hop into the backseat, Samantha arches her brow at me in the mirror.

"You know everything?" she asks.

"Just about. At least I hope. I need you to take me home though."

"For good?" she says, her concern for her sire written on her

face.

I shake my head. "No, just for tonight."

"Thank god, he'd be insufferable if you left," she says, but deep down, I think her snark is actually relief that I'm not leaving Warin.

In fact, it's quite the opposite. I have to find a way to make this work when his life is endless, and mine is not.

Chapter 27

Today was somehow one of the most horrifying yet gratifying days of my life. I feel complete, like Ember's magical blood is coursing through my system, giving me a strength that I never imagined.

I wasn't thrilled over the idea of her spending the full moon with her coven. But Betty will keep tabs on her, plus it's for the best that she isn't around while I do what needs to be done.

Since my retaliation could get me in trouble with the vampire council, I told Achille to bring our little problem to the bunker.

The sun hasn't set yet, and Conner is attempting to get away from Achille as he drags him into the bunker.

"Get your fucking hands off of me, you fucking lap dog."

His face is covered in one of our UV protectant balaclavas. I rip it off of his face before slapping him.

"That was a very unkind thing to say to Achille. He's been nothing but kind to you, apologize," I say, keeping my voice even.

"You're nothing. You're fucking ruining the nest, everything Oz built. Treating that witch like she's meaningful to you. She should be dead or drained of her blood. You're fucking pathetic—"

Before he can continue spitting vitriol, I grab the stake I

had Samantha retrieve, the one that nearly took my life and my witch's, the one Conner stole from my office. Then I promptly shove it in his stomach, knowing it won't kill him immediately.

I push it so far into his gut, the moment the tip pops through his back has me smiling.

He collapses to the floor, and I no longer need Achille to hold him, knowing he isn't going anywhere.

Conner whines in pain, bleeding from his stomach as I grab his chin.

"I thought Oz was special too, once upon a time. Then I learned what an insecure, irrational, psycho he is. You're young, it's not a surprise you worshiped him, but fuck he's only been rendered ash for a little over a week. You've already made such a critical assessment of my leadership abilities?"

"You…you…c-could never b-be him," he stutters out in pain, trying to pull the stake from his gut.

"Pesky little bitch, that stake is. You'd need someone who isn't a vampire to pull it out. Don't see any of those around, do you, Achille?"

"No, sir," Achille responds, leaning against the wall, bored.

"You could have left the nest, gone nomad. Instead, you betrayed me, you almost killed Ember. If I wasn't fast enough to get her out of harm's way she could have died. Burned the shit out of my fucking face, too. Thanks for that. I kind of pride myself on my face," I say with a roll of my eyes. "Now, you're going to die."

"Just do it al-already."

"Well, I'm kind of testing a theory. Want to make a bet, Achille? My bet's ten minutes."

"I'll give it seven," he says, holding up his phone, showing that he already started a stopwatch.

"My theory is the stake will still kill you if it's left in, even if it's not in the heart. Would make sense why most people don't live to tell the tale of a slayer. Lucky me, I had a pretty little witch take mine out. You know what's sad for you? If she were still here, she would probably take mercy on you and pull it out. That's what kind of person she is."

Conner's grim reality must be catching up with him as he looks up at me with pleading eyes. "Please. Take it out. I'll do whatever you want."

"Oh, that wasn't even on the table. It was just a hypothetical if Ember was here. But she's not. You're stuck with me and I fucking hate you. She might have shown mercy, but you won't get that from me. All you'll get from me is pain."

Red tears of blood spill from his eyes. I can tell he's either about to plea for his life more or make up some pathetic excuse and frankly, I don't have time for that shit.

I consider staking him again, but I don't need to. Not as black veins creep along his neck, and his demise becomes evident. His jaw drops as he falls to the floor, becoming nothing but a shriveled pile of goo.

Achilles holds up his phone. "Five minutes and thirty-seven seconds."

"Fucker. What victory prize would you like?"

"Not cleaning this mess up," he says, and I let out a huff.

"Fine," I groan, and Achille takes a seat in the corner.

I grab some of the cleanup as he crosses his arms. "Things have changed," he declares.

The mop soaks up his guts as I glance over at him. "They have."

"I thought it would be a bad thing, but I think change is maybe good."

I pause cleaning, and stare at him. "You do?"

"I've known you for a long time. This is the happiest I've ever seen you. It gives me hope," he says the last bit softly, and I wring out the mop.

I feel like a selfish dick, all these years moping and thinking

I'm the only vampire out there having a crisis about who I am and what my purpose is. Achille may be doing the same thing.

"I didn't realize you were having these feelings."

He glares at me with an arched brow. "Yes, because we all talk about our feelings so much. Sometimes I wonder what it would have been like to grow old, have a family, say goodbye to my grandfather. I've been wondering if there's more to this life, or if it has run its course. So, yes, now I have hope."

I stare at my friend I've had so long but have never confided in.

"You're not tethered to me. If you want to see what else is out there, I'd never stop you."

He adjusts in his seat. He still has on his gear, minus his face covering, as he runs a hand over his head.

"You mean that?"

"You will always be welcome in the nest, but yes. If you're feeling unfulfilled, life is too short, or too long, to not actually live it."

As I say the words, it sinks in deeper. The fact that I have tethered Samantha to myself, that she's right, she was my only reason for continuing this life.

Ember has given me a deeper purpose, and it's due time that I do the same for everyone else around me.

"I'll consider it, maybe take some vacation days," Achille says, scrolling through his phone.

"You do that," I reply as I mop up the guts.

The door to the bunker opens and Samantha comes strolling in with her night time clothes on.

"Smells like dead vampire in here," she says solemnly. "You boys ready to go, I'm sure the council is getting antsy."

"Achille, I'll meet you in the car."

"I think I'll take the long way home," he replies, zooming out of the room.

"What's up? Also, you missed a spot," she says, pointing to a speck of blood.

"I release you from your sire bond," I say simply, and she gasps. The tie between us broken.

I'm not sure what I expect, for her to run away, for her to curse me out.

What I don't expect is a bloody tear from her eye as she comes up to me and hugs me.

"I'm proud of you. Now…" she says with a sniffle, wiping the blood away with an eye roll. "Let's go keep the council busy so your witch can do whatever it is witches do on the full moon. Do they get naked together? Are you cool with that?"

"Samantha, I just released you from the sire bond."

"Yeah and?" she asks like I'm stupid.

"I thought you wanted to travel, to get as far away from me as possible."

She punches my arm a little too hard.

"War, you're a fucking idiot. No, I don't want to leave you. I just wanted you to get out of this funk and find your blood mate."

"I don't deserve this life."

"Nope, you likely don't. Now let's get the fuck out of here before they start asking questions."

"Warin. How was your daytime stroll?" Sebastian says as we all stand on the edge of our property.

"Lovely. Did you rest?" I ask, ready for this asshole to fuck right on off.

"Could have been better," he says, glancing over at Samantha.

"How much longer will the council insist on staying here? What if the Slayer realized they're no match for the nest and went hunting elsewhere?"

"Hmm. I haven't considered the possibility." He snaps his fingers. "It's a full moon. The chances of finding him tonight are higher than ever, so are the chances of running into a wolf or a witch. We're to stay away from their running grounds."

"Speaking of witches, where's your guest, Warin?" Joyce says in her grating voice.

"If you must know, she has a life outside of me. It is the full moon, after all," I reply confidently.

"You mean like a ritual with vampire blood on the full moon. It's not like you don't have a reputation of being manipulated by witches," Joyce says.

"And you have a reputation for being a pain in the ass. Can we get this over with?" I ask.

"Yes. Sebastian, can we get this over with?" Samantha says sweetly, all the curiosity dripping from his face as he looks at her.

I might not hold the sire bond over her now, but she will always be my progeny and I don't like how intrigued he is.

"So right, Samantha, darling, let's go hunting."

That's just what we do, my mind open to Betty in case Ember runs into trouble.

Chapter 28

Samantha dropped me off at my house and the first thing I do is make the quick potion to stop my period.

There's a fluttering around my ear and I bat it away.

"Miss Ember, is everything alright?" Tabitha says, her tone far nicer than usual.

"No and yes."

"The vampire isn't keeping you captive?"

I turn as I crush up the flower with the mortar and pestle.

"No, and I don't want anyone talking negatively about him. If you're not okay with him coming around, you all can leave."

I'm sharper tongued with her than usual, and I don't know if Warin is rubbing off on me or having some time away from the cottage has shown me just how demanding the fairies are.

"Miss Ember. Are you of sound mind?" Domingo asks, and I roll my eyes.

"Yes, I'm of sound mind," I say, though am I really?

The fairies are just a small taste of the pushback I'll get with being with Warin.

"Feel her head. Does she have a fever?" Tabitha says.

"Stop, I don't have a fever," I reply, resting my hands on the table. "Warin. The vampire. He's…he's my mate," I say. I figure it will be easier to test the reaction on the fairies before I tell Iris and Violet.

"Your what?" Tabitha shrieks, her wings flapping behind her. Today she's wearing a Barbie minidress.

"My mate, okay. Fate. We're meant to be together."

"Oh, no. Oh, no. He's compelled her. Someone call a priest," Domingo cries.

"Priests are for demons, you idiot, not vampire compulsion. We'll need to get one of the witches to help us," Tabitha says, both of them ignoring me as I rub the bridge of my nose.

"But then we'll have to leave the garden," Domingo complains. Tabitha also agrees that it's a serious problem to leave the garden.

"Stop it you two. I'm not compelled, I'm completely me. I know you are afraid of him, but he wouldn't hurt you. He wouldn't hurt me," I tell them.

"He said he was going to pop our heads off and drink us dry," Tabitha says.

Well, that adds an extra layer to me assuring them.

"I've made a vow with him for your safety. I promise you're fine. Warin wouldn't hurt me or anyone who means something to me."

"Oh no, Tabitha. I think she loves him," Domingo says, Tabitha's hands are on her face in horror and I clear my throat.

"It's too soon for that, right? I mean, these feelings are intense, but that would be crazy, right?" I say, trying to rationalize all of this with the fairies.

They both blink at me like I'm insane. I dump the mixture into water and chug it when there's a knock on my door. I take a deep breath and go to answer it.

Violet and Iris stand on my stoop. Violet looking beautiful, radiant, and happier than ever. Meanwhile, Iris looks like she's anxious and like she could use a good night's rest.

"I didn't realize you two were coming here first?"

"Where have you been?" Iris demands, walking past me into my house, looking around the cottage like there's some sort of mystery, before facing me. "You're alright?"

"Why wouldn't I be?" I ask her with a tilt of my head.

"She's in love with a vampire! She's been compelled. Exercise her from his evilness," Tabitha shouts in a high-pitched voice.

Violet and Iris both turn to me at the same time, Violet looking shocked and Iris resigned.

"Fuck," Iris hisses.

"What did that fairy just say?" Violet asks.

"Okay. Yeah. So we're just going to rip off this Band-aid then."

Violet's bright blue eyes blink at me wildly as she motions for me to continue.

"Did you know vampires could have mates?" I ask her and turn to Iris, who rubs the bridge of her nose.

"This is so fucked," Iris says, as she starts pacing back and forth, mumbling under her breath, like she's talking to someone.

"What's wrong with her?" I ask, pointing to Iris.

Violet looks over at our friend with concern and then back to me.

"We're starting with you first. All that talk about vampires in the past, I thought it was a fantasy, maybe something you'd try once and get out of your system. I didn't think you were serious."

"Me either, okay? I didn't expect it. I tried to resist him. Well, maybe not super well. But it makes sense now. We're mates, Violet. You should understand that," I say.

"Who is he?" Violet says in return, not questioning the bond I have with Warin.

"Warin Auclair."

Violet sighs. "Yeah, okay, I can see the appeal. He was at the meeting when I saw Silas again for the first time."

"He can't stop, he won't stop," Iris says, and Violet and I are now fully staring at her as she seemingly talks to herself.

"Iris, honey, is everything okay?" I ask.

She turns to face me, her amber eyes that are like a kaleidoscope of autumn leaves, blinks at me.

"I think the…thing…man, living in my house who claims to be my mate might be the one who tried to kill your vampire."

"The Slayer is at your house?" I say. "Wait. What? He's your mate?"

Iris rubs her temples, pulling out a chair and sitting down. Her elbows rest on her knees as she tries to get the words out.

"Yes. The psychopath in my house is my mate, and he's dead set on killing Warin Auclair for injuring him."

Violet and I both pull up seats at my worn dining table and sit in silence for a few moments.

"You're both sure?" Violet says.

"I'm positive," I say, more cheerfully.

"Yeah. Unfortunately. I'm sure," Iris says.

"Okay. Wow. I thought maybe you were feeling down about the date with Bobby not going well. As far as you, Iris, I thought something was bothering you but didn't know what," Violet says.

Iris grimaces, and I feel like there's more information she isn't telling us.

"Warin and the vampire council are searching for the Slayer now," I say, and Iris waves me off.

"They won't find him. My store is warded, and he's still healing. He won't leave. What I'm worried about is what happens when he's healed. He'll either get himself killed or kill your vampire."

I tilt my head at her, realizing she sounds more affected than she wants to let on about the Slayer dying.

"You know that he staked a vampire near me, and showed up at my house?" I tell Iris.

"I'm sure the psycho did," she says with a nod, back to rubbing her temples. "Listen. I don't like him much either, but I can't let him die, okay?"

I stand from my chair. "Well, I can't let anything happen to Warin. I actually like him."

"Even though he's a vampire?" Iris asks.

"Yes. He's not perfect, far from it, but he's protected me from the Slayer and from the vampire council. He's the one I've been waiting for. I don't know how to explain it," I say, exacerbated.

Iris holds up her hand. "I'm sorry, Ember, I don't mean to question you. I haven't slept much. Having a demon, well, something adjacent in your house along with other nuisances has me exhausted," Iris says.

"Wow. Okay. I thought my life was dramatic, but I think you two take the cake. So you both have supernatural mates of a… unique variety and they're both trying to kill each other. Cool, awesome. What do we do now?" Violet says.

"For now, we go to the moon ritual. We act like everything is normal. You know your grandma is going to lose her shit when she finds out, Em. You being with a vampire may be the thing that sends her into an early grave. I'm sure some of the coven might have an issue with it at first, but they'll have to get over it," Iris says, assured.

"What about you and your Slayer?" I ask.

"I don't know what to do with him yet." She sighs. "I just know

that every magical particle in my body doesn't want him hurt."

"I can understand that."

"So we get through the ritual, then what?"

"I think Warin could maybe be reasoned with, a peace treaty. The vampire council is another thing all together though," I say, biting my nail.

"He'll be more difficult." Iris sighs. "He's not just the Slayer, he's a human, too. The Slayer has more control though, and he's proven pretty fucking difficult to reason with. We'll probably need magic to deal with him. We'll need to hit the books and come up with a magical solution on that front. Maybe your vampire council, too?" Iris questions.

I lick my lips. "Warin. He gave me some old grimoires. A witch who specialized in offensive and defensive magic against vampires. It's come to me more naturally than I could have ever thought. Maybe there's something in there?"

"That's a good start. I'll visit my aunt tomorrow, see if she has any suggestions. What about Delphine? Has she seen any of this?" Violet asks Iris about her grandmother.

Iris huffs. "All she's told me is that she's sorry for my ancestral burden. She was right about that. I'm not sure she could see anything involving vampires or slayers, but I can ask."

"Okay, so in the meantime, you keep your Slayer. What's his name?" Violet asks, being polite, and Iris sighs.

"It's complicated," Iris says.

"Alright then. You keep your Slayer safe locked in your house, do whatever you need to do to keep him there. Keep him preoccupied so that he doesn't go after Warin. And Ember, figure out if you can reason with Warin, and what would make this council fuck off?"

I scrunch my nose and nod.

"That's it. That's the solution? You should be saving her from the bloodsucker," Tabitha cries.

"Tabitha, if you don't shut the fuck up," Iris grates out, pulling her wand out, and I grab her wrist.

"Tabitha, go back with the other fairies. Now."

She huffs, flapping her wings, before retreating to her fellow fairies.

"God, how do you deal with them all the time? Someone constantly talking your ear off when all you want is for them to go the fuck away?" Iris asks, and the question doesn't seem so hypothetical.

"Iris, is there something else?" I ask, grabbing her shoulder.

She holds my hand and shakes her head. "No, we've got bigger problems right now. Let's just get through tonight, alright?"

I search her eyes and nod. "Alright."

"Just another standard day for the Celestial Coven." Violet takes a deep breath. "Ready to get the show on the road?" she asks.

I nod, realizing that while there's so much I need to figure out, a lot of my problems have been solved today. Conner is out of the picture, the Slayer is out of commission, and I'm not fighting this pull toward Warin anymore.

There's still the issue of the vampire council, the Slayer wanting Warin dead, and the whole issue of him being a vampire and me a witch.

But at least Violet and Iris have my back, I never should have doubted them. They might not fully understand Warin, but they both know what having a mate feels like, and no matter how complicated everything is, we'll always have each other.

The future is still up in the air, things are still complicated as ever, yet somehow, I feel at peace.

Chapter 29

The ritual goes fine, the moon water has been collected, the strength of the coven is revitalized.

Blah, blah, blah.

All I can think about is fucking my vampire. I'm like a witch possessed as I enter my cottage. Just now realizing that I have no clue on how to get to Warin's house.

Knowing that the Slayer isn't a problem, Conner is likely dead, and the vampire council can't enter my home, I make a quick decision. I'm frantic with my magic, turning all my curtains pitch black, so that we don't have to worry about the sunrise, and set a bunch of candles alight.

It's like a fire lit under my skin. Maybe it's Warin's blood, maybe it's accepting this connection we have, or maybe I just want to get absolutely fucked by my hot vampire mate.

Whatever it is, I'm not fighting it. Just the opposite. I'm going to seduce the shit out of this man.

I shower quickly, shaving everything, two razors magically wiping around at once, making me smooth all over. When every inch of me is scrubbed to where I'm pretty sure I have on a new layer of skin, I dry my hair with magic, the pink waves slightly wild as I dig through my panty drawer.

The selection is sad, but there's one matching purple and pink set. It isn't overtly sexy, but at least they match. I tug them on, scooping my hands into the cups of the bra and making sure they sit high, and I look at myself in the mirror.

I've never been skinny or plus size, always somewhere in between. Enough to get compliments that include, 'you have such a pretty face', or small quips about my curves. Sometimes I've been more self-conscious, wishing that maybe my thighs didn't rub together, or that my stomach was more toned. But no matter what I was feeling, I appreciated the body I had. Right now I feel sexy, nervous about being fully naked around Warin for the first time, but just excited, too.

I grab my black robe, covering myself, knowing exactly what I have to do next.

I don't text Warin, instead I step out on my front porch and stare at the shutters.

"Um, Betty?" I ask.

Her dark little head pops out between the shudders, her beady eyes taking me in as she tilts her head.

"You're very adorable. Could you tell Warin to meet me here, please?"

She tilts her head to the left, a small squeak leaving her, which I assume is a yes.

"Thank you, Betty," I say, shutting the door.

"You're inviting him over?" Tabitha shrieks and I groan.

"Yes. Like it or not, he's coming over. I suggest you head back to the fairy garden."

"She's serious," Domingo says, his small eyebrows pinched in. He sighs, his wings flapping behind him. "Perhaps we could have a proper introduction to him another night, then?"

"Domingo, are you crazy?" Tabitha shrieks.

"No, Tabitha. We won't find a place better than this. Nothing is like Ember's garden and no witch will put up with us like Ember does. If we want to stay, we need to accept this."

I take a sigh of relief. Finally, a fairy on my side. I arch an eyebrow at Tabitha, waiting for her response.

She just huffs and flutters away.

"I'll work on it," Domingo promises, following her to the small door on the trim of the floor.

There's a light knock on my door, and I take a deep breath. I'm really doing this. I grab the doorknob and pull the door back.

Warin stands there, looking refined as ever as he holds on to the doorframe he rebuilt. He's wearing dark trousers, a black leather belt, and a dark shirt with three buttons undone at the collar.

His gaze starts at my bare feet, trailing up my legs to where my robe hits mid thigh. He doesn't stop his perusal there as he leans further in, his eyes finally meeting mine.

"You beckoned me, witch?" he says, his tone sultry.

"Were you busy?"

"Never too busy for you. May I come in?" he asks, though I doubt he needs a second invitation.

I pull the door back and he walks in, glancing around my house.

"You did some redecorating."

"I didn't want you to have to worry about the sunrise."

His fang slightly bites his lip as he shuts my door, approaching me in two easy steps, his hands gripping my hips, fingertips making indents against my flesh. The sigh that leaves me is heady, like my body calls to him, his touch calming some of the madness

I've felt all day.

"I thought I was rude, manipulative, and scheming?" he says with a grin, his nose dragging along my hair. "You have no fucking idea how much I appreciate this effort. How badly I want to peel this robe off you and worship your body all night long, but we can't stay here."

I slide my hands up his chest and have to repress a moan. I feel obsessed, consumed, and, most of all, undoubtedly horny.

"We're safe here," I say, hoping he will take it at surface value and let it go and do just as he promised.

"Let's go back to my house where I can do everything I want with you," he says, being all seductive, but I shake my head.

"No. I don't want to go there, not with the vampire council still there."

He moves his hands from my hips to my waist.

"You warded the room. It's soundproof."

I lick my lips and I'm trying to form the words that don't make me sound like an absolute lunatic. I already feel like one.

"Your blood is doing a real number on me, vampire. The least you could do is handle the situation," I say, my hands sliding down to his belt. "I know you've been patient. Waiting so long for me, haven't you?" I tug him by the belt, my breasts are pressed against his chest as I stare up at him. "You're stronger than me, because I'm not feeling very patient."

His one hand slides up my back, fisting my hair.

"Do you enjoy torturing me, witch? You're rather good at it."

"Aren't you tired of waiting? Tell me, War, did you watch from my window all the nights I touched myself, wishing it was you?" I ask him, knowing I'm being a menace, that maybe I've ripped out a page from his book on scheming.

He tugs on my hair harder, pulling my head back.

"What did you think about when you were making yourself come? When you'd have one hand under your blanket, and the other gripping your breast, sunshine?"

"I didn't know it then, but I'm pretty sure I was thinking about you," I whisper.

"Let me take you home," he says, nearly panting, the evidence of his erection pressing against my stomach. "I need you safe and in my bed."

"But what if I want you in mine?" I say, shoving him against his chest and hightailing it to my bedroom.

It is a strategic choice. I know how fast he can move, that I don't stand a chance. He lets me get to the end of the bed, before pressing me down face first on the sheets, his body on top of mine.

He grinds his cock against my ass before leaning down, his teeth dragging against my throat.

"You're so fucking wet for me. Your heart is racing, your blood calling for me. You're aching for it so bad you can't wait, can you, witch?"

"No, I can't."

He eases off me, rolling me on my back so quickly I nearly feel dizzy. Warin straddles me, none of his weight on me as his hands tug on the tie of my robe. I swear there's a slight tremor in his hands as he tugs the knot out, exposing my body.

There's no time to be self conscious. Not by the way he looks at me like he just opened the best gift he's ever received. The cool touch of his hands spanning my waist has me gasping, his thumbs rubbing my rib cage.

He leans forward, his face against my breasts as he kisses the exposed flesh.

"You win, witch. You fucking win," he says against my skin.

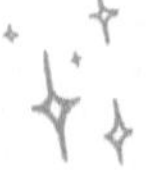

I run a hand through his soft, dark blond hair and he shivers. His fingers grip the hem of my panties and I don't stop him as he glides them down my thighs.

His eyes meet mine as his hands grip my thighs, spreading me wide. His eyebrow arches and I lick my lips.

"You're fucking beautiful," he says, kissing up my calf, his fingers indented against my thighs. "Are you going to let me taste you this way, Ember?"

I lick my lips, watching as he kisses further up my thigh, his fangs dragging along my skin. He smirks as he licks my skin, his tongue just barely reaching my lips.

"I can't tell what part turns you on more, the idea of me devouring your sweet little cunt, or sinking my fangs into your thigh?"

"Both. Definitely both," I reply.

"I already took too much from you today. You'll just have to come from my tongue alone," he says, no longer toying with me as his mouth is on me.

One of his hands holds my thigh wide, while the other slides up my chest, tugging on the cup of my bra and freeing my breast. He moans against my pussy as my back arches off the bed.

His tongue is inhuman with its speed and strength, outdoing any battery-operated device I've ever come across.

"Oh fuck," I moan out, gripping on to his hair, holding him against me. He likes it when I pull on his hair. He rewards me by eating me out with more rigor.

I don't know how to explain what it feels like to have him so solely focused on me, on making me feel good.

His hand moves from my thigh, his lips momentarily leaving my body as he slides his fingers around my wetness before slipping them inside of me. I gasp at the cool feel and pressure as his mouth joins his fingers.

"Right there, Warin, right there," I urge him.

He doesn't disappoint, keeping the same movement of his fingers and tongue. I'm not gentle with my grip on his hair as my back arches off the bed and my orgasm rips through me. It's a moment of pure bliss, like none of my problems exist. The only thing in the world right now is me and Warin.

This blissful little bubble of pleasure I never want to pop.

He licks me one more time and I shiver as he moves and kisses his way up my body. Pulling the other cup of my bra down, both of my breasts pushed up against the fabric.

"These fucking tits." He sucks a nipple into his mouth and sucks hard, only the slightest bit of fang dragging along the skin. "One day, I'll feed from here while I fuck you," he promises.

I'm still panting and getting myself together from my release, letting him have his fun sucking, licking, and kissing my chest. When I've finally caught my breath, I'm wiggling under his touch, gripping his shirt, and tugging him toward me.

His lips meet mine without hesitation, the taste of myself stark on his tongue.

Warin is gripping my chin as we kiss and all I can think is that he needs his clothes off now. I need him desperately. I've never wanted anything more. Maybe it's because we shared blood, maybe it's fate, maybe I'm an idiot for not giving a single fuck.

The hopeless romantic in me just knows that he's mine, that this can't be wrong. Even if no one ever truly understands this connection between us, I do. There's this physical tug between us and I need him to take away the ache.

"Your clothes," I get out between kisses.

He's off me in a blink of an eye. I can't help the needy whimper that falls out of my mouth. He's so quick that I don't even see him undress.

Warin Auclair is just easily naked in front of me, looking like an absolute dream. His body is toned in a way that I can tell he did hard labor when he was a human, but nowhere near a body builder. The veins on his skin stand out against his skin, and his cock stands at attention.

He strokes himself, eyes not leaving mine.

"Do you want what belongs to you, sunshine?" he asks, his thumb rubbing over the tip.

I bite my lip and curl my finger at him, beckoning him to the bed.

He's on me in an instant, his cool body against my warm one, his length pressed against my entrance as he kisses me with a reverent dominance.

Chapter 30

Part of me thinks I'm dreaming. That maybe the Slayer really staked me in the chest and I've died and am somehow now living the life of my dreams.

But when Ember bites my bottom lip, I know that somehow this is reality. That her plush, warm body is beneath mine.

That despite everything I am, everything I've done, she wants me. Maybe it's the sharing of blood that has her that way, and maybe I'm considering keeping her on a steady diet of my blood, so she never changes her mind. Or maybe she's my second chance.

"I don't fucking deserve you," I tell her, kissing down her throat.

I'm endlessly greedy, wanting to sink my teeth into her, but I can't. Not with how much I took earlier. I'll have to give her the grimoire with the blood replenishing potion as soon as possible.

"I don't care," she rasps out, tugging on my hair and digging her nails into my back.

I love that she's rough with me. The small bite of pain makes me feel alive.

With the utmost reverence, I swipe my thumb over her full bottom lip before kissing her mouth and sliding my hand between us, gripping the base of my cock.

Her pussy is warm, wet, and eager as I rub the head against her clit before sliding it down her entrance.

I push into her slowly, watching as her pupils dilate and her lips part on a moan. Her hand is clasped around the side of my neck as we lock gazes, and I can't help the whimper that falls out of me when I'm completely inside of her.

"Don't stop," she says, her heels digging into my ass.

"Oh, Ember. I'm just getting started," I tell her, grabbing her thigh and thrusting in and out of her.

It takes an effort to not move too fast, to not piston in and out of her with my vampire speed.

She's so wet that every time I pull out, the base of my cock is glistening and our flesh slaps together. She moans, writhes, bosses me around, and begs. Every second inside of her is the best moment of my life, but I know I won't last much longer.

"I need to feel your pussy gripping me. I need to feel you come. I've waited so long to know what it feels like to have you gushing on my cock, witch."

Her head falls back, the beautiful column of her throat exposed as she shouts and I can't fucking help myself, all sense of self-control lost as I lean forward and sink my teeth into her throat, tasting her sweet blood as she squeezes around me.

Ember's nails are digging so hard into my skin. If they could leave marks, they would as she moans and screams my name. I fall completely apart, my dick jerking inside of her tight pussy as I feel the greatest sensation of relief of my life.

I lick her throat, slight guilt hitting my gut, but as she scratch-

es my head and rubs my back, it falls away.

When I pull back to look at her face, she's heavy lidded, a smile on her face.

I can't help but to grin back. How many times have I seen her smile, wishing that I was the reason why?

"Okay?" I ask her, pushing her adorable pink hair from her face.

I may or may not glance down at her perfect tits before looking back at her face.

"Okay? That might be better than magic." She laughs, shaking her head and catching her breath.

Her throat still has two small puncture wounds, little beads of blood pebbling against her pale skin.

"You'll need to drink more of my blood. I took too much. I lost control of myself."

"I liked it," she says, her hands not leaving my body.

I'm addicted to her touch. I've never particularly liked anyone touching me before, even when I was human. But Ember, I never want our flesh to part.

My fangs dip into my wrist, and I bring it to her mouth.

"Drink," I tell her.

She looks maybe slightly skeptical, but doesn't question me as I bring my wrist to her mouth. My cock jerks inside of her when she does, and she moans as she swallows it down.

When I think she's had enough, I pull my wrist away; the skin knitting back together immediately.

"So, how long is that going to go on for?" she asks, looking down at where we're connected.

I give her a wide grin as I play with her hair. She smells so goddamn good I want to rub myself against her and carry her scent.

"Oh, sunshine. One of the many perks of being mated to a vampire? As long as I have a steady stream of blood, everything is more than operational."

She licks her lips and grabs the back of my neck.

"Thank Hecate," she says as she crashes her lips against mine.

I've lost track of time. I have not a clue what time it is or how many times I came or made Ember fall apart over the course of how many hours it's been. All I know is these have been the best hours of my life.

I haven't slept, and I only consider it now as Ember sleeps next to me. Her lips part as she breathes, a slight snore escaping her lips. She's fucking precious, insatiable, and completely mine.

She doesn't stir as I stand from the bed, hunting down my pants to find my phone. It's two in the afternoon and I laugh at the absurdity.

I don't even feel tired and I assume it has to do with drinking her blood. I've never felt stronger, more alive.

I've never felt this happy. Nothing even comes close.

There are a few messages from Samantha.

Samantha: I'm keeping the vampire council very busy.

Samantha: Eggplant emoji. Water emoji.

Samantha: If you know what I mean.

I want to gag, but put the phone away. I crawl back into bed with my witch, holding her tight, and despite this endless energy I feel, I close my eyes, feeling at peace for the first time in my life.

When I wake, Ember is not in the bed, and I groan into the pillow that smells like her. The scent of chicken and something else is thick in the air. I ignore the scent as I grab my underwear and crack Ember's door.

She hasn't removed the darkening curtains and I go into the kitchen where she's magically cooking, spoons stirring on their own, dishes washing themselves in the sink as she hums to a song I'm not familiar with.

I stare at her for a long time, watching her ass swish in her dress as she cooks and the way she tastes things by putting a finger in her mouth. It all feels so utterly domestic in a way I didn't think I'd ever experience.

"What are you making?" I ask.

She jolts, jumping a little and turning to face me, clutching her chest.

"Didn't we talk about you being louder with your stalking?"

"My apologies," I say, taking a seat at her dining table.

"Just some chicken and rice, nothing fancy. I woke up starving. It won't be sundown for a few more hours, though."

I shrug. "I like it here more than I thought I would."

"More than your fancy mansion?"

"Don't get carried away now," I say, and she comes to stand between my legs and I grip the back of her thighs.

"Am I always going to feel this insatiable around you?"

"I don't know. I've tried finding more information about blood mates, but witches weren't willing to talk to me, and I was too afraid to discuss it with other vampires. I'm not complaining though," I say as I slide her dress up her thighs.

"There is probably something we should talk about, though. I asked you to be honest, and that street goes both ways."

"What do you have to be honest about?" I ask, hoping that she needs to get it off her chest about how badly she needs to be back on my cock.

"Right. Well…theslayerismybestfriendsmateandyoucan'tkill-him." She says it so fast that if I had human hearing, I probably wouldn't have picked up every single horrifying word.

I push out of the seat to my full height and look down at her grimacing face.

"Excuse me?"

"We need to make a truce with the Slayer."

I rub my jaw, staring down at the witch like she's gone mad. "Did I fuck all the common sense out of you?" I ask and she shoves me hard in the chest.

"Don't even start with me, Warin Auclair. You remember what you said to me the other day, that you would do anything for me? Well, I need you to make a truce with the Slayer."

"He tried to kill me, Ember, he tried to get to you," I say, raising my voice more than I'd like.

"Okay, the killing you part is true, but he's hard-wired to do that. It's not his fault. Iris is working on a spell to fix it and I'm reasoning with you to let this go."

"Let it go? He staked me in your garden and if you wouldn't have pulled it out that I would've died? Who's to say that I don't make a truce with him and he goes back on his word immedi-ately? Not to mention the fact that the fucking vampire council won't leave my fucking house until he's dead. No, Ember. I can't do it, I can't make peace with a being whose sole purpose is to kill beings like me," I say, and she places her hands on her hips and pouts.

She fucking pouts at me. Her big green eyes look at me like she's disappointed.

"You're going to have to figure it out," she demands.

"Figure it out. Figure it out, or what?" I snap back.

She lets out a puff of breath. "I don't want to give you an ultimatum, Warin. I don't want to start this out on the wrong foot. It's clear that what's between us is undeniable. It's the same for them. I understand that this puts you in a hard position. I truly understand that. But I need you to also understand that my coven is still and will always be important to me. They're my family. Their situation is complicated, but at the end of the day they're still mates. So I'm asking you, as my mate, as the man that I've forgiven for hurting me, to please forgive him. You don't have to become friends or even like it, but I'm begging you, for me, to help me figure out a way to come to an agreement."

I stare down at the formidable witch, the one I promised to do anything for, the one who's looking past my worst traits. I've told myself repeatedly that I'd try to be a better man for her, that I would work on being honest.

"This isn't going to be easy. I still don't like it and I haven't a clue how to get the vampire council out of my house."

Ember's arms are suddenly wrapped around me tight as she squeezes, and I hold her back.

"That's all I'm asking. Thank you, War. We're in this together, alright?" she says, her chin resting on my chest as she looks up at me.

"This honesty business might just kill me," I tell her, smooth-

ing my hands up her side and cradling her face.

"Or, maybe, you'll be rewarded," she suggests, pushing me back down on the chair and standing between my legs. "Do you want to see what happens to good vampires?"

"What happens to good vampires?" I ask as she falls to her knees, her hands gliding back and forth on my thighs as she pulls out my hard and ready cock.

She licks the slit, and my hands tangle in her hair as she licks and sucks on my shaft.

"You like being good for me, don't you, Warin?" she asks, her pink hair pushed to one side, her cheeks flushed as she fists the base of my length. She pauses her movements as she waits for an answer.

"Only for you, witch."

She bites her bottom lip, stroking me some more.

"I like you like this. Honest, sweet, and doing what I tell you," she says, before I can answer, she leaves me speechless by taking my dick all the way down her throat.

I throw my head back and moan.

Maybe honesty has its perks after all.

Chapter 31

Exhaustion doesn't begin to cover it. Somehow I'm able to walk straight as the sun finally sets and I watch Warin put his clothes back on.

His body is a work of art. His tongue is the eighth wonder of the world. All I want to do is drag him back into bed and continue to act like the rest of the world doesn't exist.

"Are you sure we have to leave?" I complain, and maybe I tug on the string at the bodice of my dress.

He tugs on his belt, hooking it on the latch and all I can do is look at his deft fingers, which are probably the ninth wonder of the world.

All these fantasies I'd unknowingly had about him over the last decade didn't do him justice.

He leans over the bed, grabbing the strings and tying it into a bow.

"Such a tempting little present. I'd prefer to keep you naked and wet all night long, but we have things to do, don't we?"

I grumble, but nod. He's right. We have a lot that we need to figure out. He grabs my left hand and kisses the ring on my finger.

"Remember that how I act in front of the council is just that, an act," he reminds me.

"Right," I say, grabbing his belt and tugging him close. "I'm your little obedient pet, aren't I?"

He shivers, grabbing my wrists and pulling my hands away. "You're insatiable."

"You love it," I joke.

"I do," he replies, but his tone is more serious as he leans down and presses a kiss to my hair. "Now, let's get to work on getting these vampires out of my goddamn house, yeah?"

"Ugh. Fine."

He smiles as he holds a hand out for me, and we're out the front door. Achille has the SUV parked out front waiting for us.

But suddenly all the fairies that live in my garden congregated out front.

"Are they going to attack?" Warin jests and I elbow him in the stomach. He doesn't even flinch.

"What's this about?" I question them, and Tabitha takes center stage.

I wouldn't call her their queen, perhaps their unspoken leader, because she always has so much to say.

She takes a deep breath, her hands on her hips. "We'd like to… well, we'd like to say…um, yeah."

"What she's trying to say is that we're sorry and that we would like to formally meet your mate," Domingo interrupts.

"What he said," Tabitha adds in. "As long as he doesn't make any more jokes about popping off our heads and drinking all of our blood."

"It was a joke. Drinking your blood would be too tedious," Warin says.

"Warin," I snap and take a deep breath. "I appreciate your

apology. I take it that means you and the other fairies plan on staying here?"

"If you'll still have us," Domingo says.

"No more being rude to Ember," Warin says sternly. "And there's a chance that she won't be here as often, so that would make you all the wardens of the cottage."

This has Tabitha beaming, fluttering closer to his face.

"Wardens you say?" she asks.

"Of course, we need trusted beings taking care of the cottage when Ember isn't here. Are you up for the task?"

"Certainly. We're more than capable. We can monitor the place and make sure the flowers are up to Ember's standards."

"That would be a huge help," I tell Tabitha, and her chest puffs out.

"We won't let you down."

"I know you won't. I'm not sure when I'll be back, but I'll figure out a way for us to communicate long distance. Until then, you'll keep an eye out?"

"I'll, I mean, we'll be the best wardens for your gardens."

"Thank you, Tabitha," I tell her, grabbing Warin's arm as we head to the SUV.

"How did you do that?" I ask him. "The fairies have been nothing but meddlesome and demanding since the day they moved in."

"I don't think it hurts that they're terrified of me. Some beings just need a purpose, a direction," he says as we slide into the backseat.

"Is that how you felt?"

"For the longest time I wondered why I had this long life, but with you? Forever doesn't seem long enough," he says.

I force a smile, and lean in and kiss the corner of his mouth.

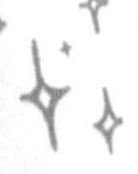

Neither of us bring up his words, because he has forever and I don't. He hasn't outright asked me if I'd be open to becoming a vampire. Maybe he already knows the answer.

Would he be alright with me aging and him always looking young and beautiful? Would I?

His hand kneads my thigh as we drive to his mansion, knowing the role I need to play, and what information we need to find out.

What exactly will it take to get the vampire council off our radar and prevent them from killing Iris's mate?

The mansion is quiet and I can't decide if it's because vampires can be exceptionally quiet, or if it's because they're out hunting for a Slayer that they will not find.

Either way, I don't say shit as we walk through the halls and head to Warin's room.

The moment the door is open, Gus is scurrying over to me.

"Ember Jeanette Hallow, where in the fuck have you been?" he says, his small hands grabbing my clothes and searching my skin. *"I've been here worried sick."* I arch an eyebrow as I look at his collection of plates, cups, and the small little nest he's made himself in the corner.

"Clearly you've made yourself sick over it. I'm fine, Gus, I promise."

"I'm assuming you figured out the vampire is your mate, or whatever?" he asks as he scurries back to his nest on all fours. *"If shit is going to get freaky in here, I'm going to need my own room, spelled to ward off all the vampires, of course. They're fucking weird,*

Ember."

I blink at him a few times. "You knew?"

"I mean, I didn't know. I assumed. But you know what they say about assumptions. Plus, it's not like you would've listened, anyway. You're hardheaded."

"I'm not hardheaded. You're hardheaded," I snap back.

"I know you are, but what am I?"

"I'm going to strangle you. You knew, and you didn't at least give me a heads up."

Gus rolls his eyes, his fist going into a bowl of what look to be hand made pretzels, before he pops one in his mouth and begins crunching away. He doesn't say anything and I narrow my eyes at him.

"This one sided conversation with your familiar is riveting, but I have to see what the council is up to. We'll figure out more when I get back. You know where the grimoires are?" Warin asks.

"I do," I say, and Warin leans down and places a soft kiss against my lips.

"Yeah. My own sound proofed, vampire-free room stat. I might throw up."

"Shut up, Gus," I hiss at him.

"Keep her safe for me," Warin says with a wink to Gus, who is now puffing out his chest.

"Oh, real smooth. You had the fairies and Gus convinced you were going to drain them dry, and now they're all seeking your approval like lost puppies."

"He knows talent when he sees it. Now, what do we need the grimoires for?" Gus asks.

"I'll be back as soon as I can," Warin assures again, giving me a smirk, before zooming out of the room.

I sigh, plopping down on Warin's bed. I'm still exhausted, but there's so much that needs to be done.

"We need to figure out what it will take to get the vampires out of town, how to make sure the Slayer and Warin don't kill each other. Oh, and there's the whole thing where Warin will live forever and I won't," I pout about that last part, because it's something that I've been keeping to myself.

Gus leaves his nest, a trail of crumbs following him on the floor as he hefts himself up on the bed and cradles himself against my arm.

Little shit definitely missed cuddling.

"I don't know how to solve your first two problems. But I might have an idea for the one that seems to weigh on you heaviest."

I glance down at Gus, and tilt my head.

"Me turning into a vampire is not an option."

Gus snorts, like he's disgusted by the thought. *"Of course, it's not an option. Disgusting. The only reason I'm okay with your vampire is because of the quality of life he can provide me, plus you, like, care for him or whatever."*

"What's your idea then?"

"I don't want to get your hopes up, but I'll reach out to some of my contacts."

"Are there a network of raccoon familiars who share information?" I joke, and Gus nips my arm. "Ouch, Gus."

"Do you want my help or not, witch?" he asks.

"I want it," I say, squeezing him harder. My body betrays me, too exhausted from my long night/day of activities with Warin, and I can't help it when I drift off to sleep with Gus in my arms.

Chapter 32

Ember is passed out, my stomach churns when I think about why she's so tired.

Disgusting.

What's even more disgusting is what I'm about to do to ensure her happiness. But, in the long run, even I can agree the more time I get with my witch, the better.

The magic I'm thinking of is as old as time and complicated. I scurry out of the vampire's room, knowing Ember is safe with the wards she's placed. I might not have been pro-vampire from the start, but I can't deny the change he's had on her.

She trusts her magic more with the vampire. Not to mention I don't think I've ever seen her as happy as I did when she strolled into the room this evening with a wide grin on her face.

Ember's always been happy around others, but I see who she really is, when no one is around. She needed this, and if she needs help, it's my job as her familiar to do whatever I can with my power.

So as much as it fucking pains me, I teleport off of the vampire's property to the home of the familiar I think may help me.

The large purple mansion is overkill, though I can't deny Violet and her wolf have substantially made it less tacky. I round the house where the gazebo is.

Sure enough, Walter is sunbathing, Marie next to him, though she doesn't allow him to touch her paw.

"Ugh, what do you want?" Walter asks, though he doesn't even move, his furry round belly facing the sky.

"Lovely to see you, as always, Marie. Surprised you're still sticking around this sourpuss," I say.

Marie bunches her shoulders, rolling onto her stomach, where she licks her paw. *"I have nothing better to do."*

"Right, that tracks."

"I supposed you're here to discuss this vampire and slayer debacle these witches have found themselves in?" Walter asks. *"I swear if it's not one thing, it's another with these three idiots."*

Marie slightly hisses at him and I can't help but to give her a smile. The cranky bastard rolls over onto his stomach with an eye roll and appraises me.

"I've told Violet everything I know about slayers and vampires. Which isn't much. They're the types of beasts you stay away from," Walter says.

"Actually, not here for that."

"Then what? To ransack our kitchen?" Walter says, looking me up and down.

It takes everything in me to not bite him.

"Maybe Scarlett will have the information I need," I say, and that has Marie perking up.

"No. We can help you, that busybody acts like she knows everything when this is her first cycle. It's annoying," she says.

I hold back a grin as I climb the gazebo steps.

"Familiar magic. Do you think it would work on other super-natural beings?" I ask.

"You can't be thinking about what I think you're thinking about doing," Walter says.

"I think it's romantic. Wanting someone so much that you'd search the world for just the right magic to spend eternity together," Marie says.

"Right. Romantic," Walter says, glancing over at Marie. *"I suppose the same magic could work, connecting two souls together in the same way, tethering them to one life force and preventing aging like it works on us with our witches."*

"And where might a raccoon get his greedy paws on this type of magic?"

"You're not going to like it," Walter says, and I swear the cantankerous little shit is grinning.

"Just tell him, Walter. I'm bored of this," Marie purrs.

"For the type of magic you seek, you'll have to go to Sarephine Fontenot," he says, a light chuckle in his voice.

I grit my teeth, and Walter plops back on his back.

"Let's hope she doesn't try to add you to her little collection," Walter snickers.

"Right. Thanks for all your wisdom," I say with a roll of my eyes and teleport back to the vampire's mansion.

There's no way in hell I'm going to that witch's swamp by myself. I got the information. I'll give it to Ember and she can do with it what she wants.

I crawl up the bed, back into my witch's arms, and try not to have bad dreams about the swamp witch and all the rumors surrounding her.

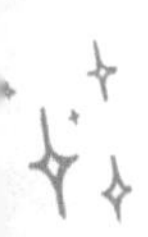

Chapter 33

Another fruitless night of hunting for the Slayer, and I can tell that the council is beyond agitated. It's more than the fact that we haven't found the Slayer. It's clear that they're becoming suspicious of me. Or perhaps I'm a jaded, paranoid, immortal being who thinks everyone is out to get me. But we're going with the idea that I'm completely rational and these fuckers need to go.

Sebastian and Samantha hunted together again. They're all smiles as we walk back into the home. The rest of the council, however, looks like they're out for blood.

"We need to bring the vampire who brought these allegations to us back into the fold. I know Warin has confirmed the account of the Slayer, but isn't it curious that the whistleblower is nowhere to be found?" Justin asks.

That would be because he is now serving as fertilizer, but they definitely don't need to know that.

"Who was the whistleblower again?" I ask.

Joyce rolls her eyes. "As if you don't know. Someone in your nest mysteriously leaves, and the council appears. Don't be such a dumb blond, it's not attractive."

"God, Joyce, you're giving me whiplash. Do you want to fuck

me or see me burned in the sun? Neither is on the table, by the way."

"This cun—" Joyce hiss, her fangs bared to me.

"I grow bored with this," Magnus drawls. "Slayers aren't built to lie in wait. With the amount of new vampires in town, there's no way they could tame their beast enough to not attack."

Unless they found their mate, that would trump everything. Fuck, I hate that I had to agree to Ember's terms. I really was looking forward to gutting him and watching the life leave his eyes. Yes, I'm trying to be a better man for Ember, but a man still needs his hobbies.

"Perhaps the deputy of the area would agree to call on us if there are any future sightings. Warin wounded him enough that he did perish," Beatrix says.

"Or maybe our gracious host is lying to us," Joyce says.

Her ugly, comfortable shoes clack against the floor as she circles me.

"Maybe he's hiding the Slayer. Just like he locks his witch in her little tower and we're unable to access her," Joyce says, and I hate how close to the facts she is.

"Why would he hide a Slayer, Joyce?" Sebastian asks, bored with all of this.

I can't help but notice his hand is on Samantha's shoulder.

"Same reason he hides his witch. Why we executed so many witches in Chicago all those years ago? Warin isn't one of us, not really. You've been working with the witches again, haven't you?" Joyce says, and I keep my face passive.

"It's not illegal to fraternize with witches," I say.

"He's right. It's odd, but it's not forbidden by the council," Sebastian says.

"It is still suspicious, no? A member of his nest comes crying to the council, telling us he needs our protection and that there's a slayer his previous leader didn't notify us of. He lives to tell the tale of being staked by a slayer and has his little live-in whore warded away in his bedroom."

My jaw ticks and Sebastian looks like he wants to shut her down, but she's talking too much sense.

"We will interview Ember again," Sebastian says pragmatically.

Beatrix, Justin, and Magnus groan in irritation. I have to swallow down my fury of them being near her. Not after I've had her, not after this connection of ours has been solidified.

"Are you afraid of what we might find out?" Joyce taunts.

"Just worried that you might have a temper tantrum over how much she enjoys my company, is all."

"Right. Go get her," Joyce demands.

I jerk my head in a nod and head toward my bedroom, leaving Samantha and the council in my wake.

When I open the door, she's in my bed, her pink hair splayed all over my pillows, her raccoon snuggled against her.

Fuck.

If I had a heart, it would be pulsating and racing over seeing her like this, alongside the nerves of deceiving the council. Ember is a brilliant witch, but lying directly in the faces of multiple old as fuck vampires will be a challenge.

I push her hair off her face and cup her face. When she stirs she presses her face against my palm and smiles.

"You're back," she says, blinking away sleep, and grabbing my wrist. "Good. I need you."

"As much as I wish that's why I was in here, we have a problem."

Her brows furrow, and I stroke her face.

"The council is getting restless. They're demanding to interview you again."

Her eyes widen in shock and fear. This wasn't part of the plan.

I was supposed to figure out how to get the council off our backs while she and her friends work on making sure the Slayer doesn't kill me.

She swallows thickly, untangling herself from her familiar, who barely stirs.

"What if they don't believe me? What if they can tell I'm lying?" she says, looking at me for guidance.

I glance down at her ring and shake the idea away immediately. There's no way I'm leaving her vulnerable with them.

"Do you know any spells to calm your nerves?" I ask, rubbing my hands up and down her arms.

"We're waiting!" Joyce screams from the sitting room.

Ember nods her head sharply, holding her wand and doing a small incantation.

"Should I get changed?" she asks. She's wearing one of my shirts. I shake my head, at war with myself over them seeing her like that, but realize it's a good thing.

"No. I'll protect you, above anything else. You're safe with me, okay? Just do your best to answer their questions like you're being compelled, alright sunshine?"

She nods, some of her nerves fading away from whatever spell she cast on herself.

I grab her by the waist and walk her barefoot, messy-haired self, to the sitting room. It's reminiscent of the night they showed up, and I do exactly what I did that night, plopping her on my lap.

"Do what you must, Joyce. I'm ready to go home. You know I have my favorite little blood bags waiting for me," Magnus says.

Magnus stands with his back to the wall, Justin and Beatrix sit boredly on a couch together. Samantha and Sebastian are exceptionally close together as Joyce paces, staring down Ember.

"Ember, have you seen the Slayer?" she asks.

"No," Ember says a little too robotically, and I rub her thigh, giving her reassurance.

"So you can not say whether Warin was injured by one?"

"I just know that I removed the stake from his stomach," Ember says.

"I see. And has Warin given you his blood?" Joyce asks.

"Why in the fuck is this relevant?" I ask.

"I'd like to know as well," Magnus chimes in.

"Only to heal wounds," Ember says.

"Never directly on your tongue? Never to use it for a spell, perhaps?" Joyce asks.

"No."

Joyce snatches Ember's wrist, and I can't help the hiss that rips out of my throat.

"Simmer down, War. Just checking your little pink toy's pulse."

Joyce does just that, her fingertips dangerously close to where Ember's protection ring sits on her finger.

"Does Warin drink from you?"

"Yes."

"Do you enjoy it?" Joyce asks.

"What the fuck does this have to do with the Slayer?" I interrupt.

"Yes, Joyce, what does this have to do with the Slayer?" Sebastian says, getting to his feet. "We came here to hunt. There's been no sign of him. Warin has been a gracious host, despite your blunt rudeness. This is enough. I will stay, make sure that the Slayer does not return. The rest of the council will go home."

Joyce glares at Ember, still holding her hand, and I can sense that Ember is holding her breath. She eventually drops her hand and turns to Sebastian.

"We never split up," Joyce says, straightening out her cardigan.

"Did I ask you how you felt about it?" Sebastian retorts, and Joyce tightens her lips. "Come nightfall, you will go back to HQ while I ensure that everything is safe here."

The three other council members look relieved, while Joyce turns and glares down her nose at us.

"Very well," she says, turning away and heading to her room.

"Does that compromise suit you, Warin?" Sebastian asks.

"Yes, thank you," I reply.

Even though I want all these motherfuckers out of my house, especially the most powerful one who keeps touching and giving my progeny saucy looks.

"Very well. Everyone have a good day and I'll see you off tonight with instructions," Sebastian says. The council leaves.

Samantha, Ember, and I stay seated, all sharing looks, knowing no words can be shared between us. I haven't told Samantha about the Slayer, but she looks at me suspiciously, before giving us a tilt of her head and retiring for the day.

"Come, let us go to bed, you need more rest," I tell Ember, holding her hand and bringing her to our room.

As soon as we're in the room, Ember starts breathing heavily. I cup the back of her head and bring her to my chest.

"You did great. You were so brave. We'll just have to deal with Sebastian, but it has solved a big portion of our problem."

She nods against my chest, holding me tight.

"Come on, let's get some sleep, okay?"

"Okay. You really don't think she noticed I was hiding something?"

I bring the blankets over both of us, we're lying on our sides facing each other and I have a hand on her hip.

"Even if she does, Sebastian doesn't, and that's all that matters. She'll be leaving and you won't have to deal with her ever again. Things will be less tense with only Sebastian here. Although, we'll still need to be vigilant."

"Does Samantha know about Iris?" she asks.

"No, I haven't told her anything."

"I'm sorry you have to lie to her."

"Whatever it takes to keep you safe," I tell her, and she shifts her body so her head is on my chest, and I'm holding her tight. Her soft hair is pressed under my nose as I inhale her delicate scent.

Her thumb moves back and forth on my chest and she sighs like she has something else to say, but drifts off to sleep.

I don't slumber immediately, my head filled with problems and solutions. It would be kind of nice if Sebastian killed the Slayer. Then it wouldn't be me who did it, but he would be out of the picture.

Groaning, I shake that thought from my head. She asked me to spare him, and that's what I'll do. It will make her happy, and that's my life's mission.

My life. My endless fucking life, while Ember's is much shorter.

I'd never condemn her to this. She's far too radiant. I'd love her no matter how she looks. I'll have to accept the years I have with her as a blessing.

But I make a vow to myself that the moment she leaves this earth, I'll leave it with her.

I kiss the top of her head, trying to not think of such morbid things. I've spent so much of this immortal life hoping for more in the future and I finally have it. Thinking about the moment this happiness is ripped away from me will only cause me pain.

I will live in the moment with her, though I don't deserve it.

My sleep schedule is entirely fucked up. Being with a vampire is definitely going to be interesting as far as that goes. But I find myself hopeful that I'll get to figure out a new normal.

We can fix up the cottage some, and make it more vampire safe beyond my little curtain fix, and while Warin sleeps I can work on the garden. There can be other days where we disappear in this big, giant house. The idea has me smiling to myself. I like the idea of creating a life with Warin, no matter what it looks like.

I'm trying to not dwell on the immortal elephant in the room, though as I flip through the journals, I look for any mention of slayers or becoming immortal outside of being a vampire. Which sounds wrong, so I give up, shutting it, and putting it back in the safe.

Warin, Samantha, Sebastian, and Achille are out looking for the Slayer during the day, and since the other council members left, I'm finally free of this room.

I choose to explore the rest of his house while Gus watches his show. My familiar has been a little odd recently, but I chalk it up to living his new life of luxury.

Needing the sun on my skin, I go out to the gardens, placing a blanket on the ground and lying on my back. The sun feels like a balmy blanket surrounding me and I soak it up.

We should definitely build a pool out here. I'll have to bring it up with Warin. Gosh, I went from thinking he was the world's biggest asshole to making demands on how we make this place more comfortable insanely quickly. I laugh at the craziness of my life, but smile anyway.

Part of me always wanted a big romantic gesture, some epic story that I could tell people, and well, I got it.

I roll over to my stomach, pulling out my phone and text the group chat I have with Violet and Iris.

Me: How is everything on your front, Iris?

Iris: I haven't found anything to subdue or overpower a slayer. He's finally healing. There's only so much I can do to keep him occupied.

Me: But you'll let me know the moment he leaves your house?

Iris: Of course I will Ember. What about on your end? Just the main vampire guy is there?

Me: Oh, yeah. To be totally honest, I don't think it has anything to do with the Slayer and everything to do with his massive crush on Samantha.

Violet: Who's Samantha?

Me: Warin's daughter.

Violet: Pause. Rewind. You're a step mommy?

Me: Gross no. His progeny. I think we're kind of the same age. She may be older? I don't know, vampire years are weird.

Violet: Speaking of vampire years...

Me: Nope. Hey Iris, do you know anything about blood replenishing potions?

Iris: I know that they don't work on slayers. I can have Scarlett drop the potion at your house. You're being safe right?

I laugh at the text. Does she mean safe sex with my vampire mate? Wait…he does finish. He said that everything is basically in working order as long as he has a steady stream of blood. I close out of that chat and open one with Warin.

Me: I can't get pregnant right?

He answers super fast, considering he's supposed to be hunting a slayer and has the president vampire down his neck.

Warin: Unless it's the second coming of Christ, no.

Me: You said as long as you had a steady stream of blood everything was in working order.

Warin: In the sense I can get hard and direct my blood flow, witch. So no, I can't get you pregnant, but we can pretend if you want.

Me: You're insatiable. Speaking of which, Iris is getting me some blood replenishing potion. When things settle, I'll figure out how to make it on my own.

Picturing his burned face sends a jolt to my stomach. I never want him to hurt like that again. He promised me that he would be completely safe, covered head to toe like Samantha was. But even so, I worry about him. Sebastian decided since the night hadn't dug up any results that they would see if maybe the Slayer is only coming out during the day. Which Warin and I both know he isn't.

I laugh and decide to torture him some more by sending a picture of my tits nearly bursting out of my dress. I bite my lip and watch as three little dots appear and disappear as he decides what to type back. I'm like a lunatic with a grin staring at my phone, waiting for him to respond, that I don't hear any steps behind me.

I gasp as a sharp object digs into my neck. It isn't fangs; I know that much as I slowly turn around, my gaze going hazy.

A person covered from head to toe in black clothing stands before me. Two human men on each side of them.

"I hope you enjoyed your last day in the sun, witch," she says, before everything goes black.

Chapter 35

Looking for the slayer during the daytime is fucking pointless, but I had to play along.

So here I am, sitting at my desk at the bar, covered in my UV gear, wanting to pull my dick out and jerk off to the picture my witch just sent me.

We haven't even scratched the surface of all the things I want to do with her. Whatever fantasy she comes up with, I'm happy to play along.

I'm about to send my picture back when a nagging voice infiltrates my thoughts, killing my boner immediately.

"She's been taken!" Betty screeches in my head.

I can tell that she's exerted, that she's flying hard, she struggles with daytime flight, but whatever is happening, she's doing her best.

"What are you saying?"

"She…she was out in the garden and suddenly three figures took her. One vampire, two humans. I'm tracking their van now." Betty pants like she's out of breath. *"They're driving so fast, War. They're headed west."*

"Do your best to keep up. I'm on my way."

I pull out my phone and message Achille and Samantha together, giving a rundown of what's happening and that I need them immediately.

Instead of waiting for a vehicle, or worrying about what might happen to me, I pull the protective hood over my face and I run like I've never run before.

I head to the only roads that lead west, but even my energy has bounds. After about twenty miles, I'm starting to fade and have to take a break. All I want to do is rip this mask off and scream into the fucking sun.

She can't be gone. What was I thinking, letting her roam the house while no one is there? I thought what? That the Slayer would hold up their end of the bargain? That with Conner dead, there wasn't a threat? She'll never be truly safe. It's the reason I stayed away for so long.

My sunshine, my beautiful Ember, what have I condemned her to?

I'm about to collapse on this highway, take my clothes off and give myself what I deserve when a SUV pulls up, three familiar faces inside.

"You're so fucking dramatic. Get in. Sebastian has a tracker on Joyce. We know where they're going," Samantha says, annoyed, like I'm being ridiculous. "You'd know if she was dead, Warin, god. Get in!" she screams at me and I agree.

"I knew she was pissed, I didn't think she'd go fucking rogue," Sebastian seethes. "I'm sorry, War—"

I don't let him finish as I grab his jacket getting into his face.

"I will kill your entire fucking council if she's harmed. I'll fig-ure out how to summon slayers and I'll make as many as I can to kill every single last one of our kind. Then I'll walk into the sun, hoping that maybe even for a moment I'll be reunited with her." Sebastian tilts his head.

"She's your blood mate?" he questions, not even seeming threatened by me.

Achille drives like he's in a supervillain movie, our bodies shifting as he rushes to save Ember.

I glance over at Samantha. "You told him?" I say, my heart breaking over her betrayal.

"No, idiot. You've been so far up your own ass, you haven't been paying attention. Sebastian's mine, that's why he knows," she says, seemingly shy.

"What?"

Samantha shrugs. "I thought he was hot, and I don't know that maybe fucking the head honcho might be a good thing for us, and well, one thing led to another and we tasted each other's blood and it was like this cosmic revolutionary thing. Why do you think he left Ember alone and sent the council away?"

I blink at my progeny, and she lets out an irritated groan.

"You told him to?" I ask, glancing at Sebastian.

"Yeah, she asked me to, so I did. Fuck, you think I enjoy being in charge of these self-centered pricks? I've been longing for something else, and that thing is Samantha. You mean something to her, so when I say I'm on your side, I mean it. I want you to get your mate back and I'll deal with the council," Sebastian says.

"Joyce is mine," I growl out.

"Fine. She's been haunting earth long enough, anyway."

"What of the others?" I ask.

"They're bored to madness. If they become a threat then we'll handle it," Sebastian says easily.

Samantha grins. "You're like a million times hotter when you're not wearing business casual clothes and talking about murdering people."

Sebastian smiles back, a stupid fucking dimple showing up on his face, and I grimace.

"Knock it off. Where are we headed?" I complain.

"It looks like they're headed to New Orleans," Sebastian says, holding up his phone and I swallow as we drive back to where it all began.

The sun is falling as we approach the ancient warehouse. It's been converted to a distillery of some sort. The type of place where they make beer that tastes like raspberries and all the pretentious dicks that run it have mustaches.

They market the place for being a prohibition hot spot, not having a single clue how much bloodshed has happened here.

I stare at the building confronted with my harrowed past and the bright future that was just within reach.

Sebastian is right. I'd feel it if she's gone, but I can't sense her pain. I have no idea what Joyce is doing to her and I'm shaking with anger and fear. I knew Joyce was a bitch, but I didn't think she'd take it this far, her motive makes no sense.

"Here," Samantha says, handing me a few silver stakes. They're easier to throw than wooden ones, easier to aim too. "She's going to be fine, War."

I nod sharply and look at the three vampires around me. Samantha and Achille who have been by my side through it all. Then there's Sebastian, the wild card.

"If you betray us," I say, pointing a stake at him.

"Yup, slayers, ripping out hearts, stepping into the sun, got it," he says with an eye roll.

The sun is finally behind the building as we get out of the vehicle, trying to not make much noise. The only upside of the new age distillery is that it's loud. Our cover might not be completely

blown.

I take the front as the rest follow. There are muffled voices in the distance. We have stakes drawn as we walk down the steps, trying to not make much noise.

"How kind of you to finally join us," Joyce's voice calls out, and it feels like I'm dying as I approach the middle of the warehouse.

It looks nothing like when I was turned, but I know that it's the exact spot where Oz made me a vampire. It's curious she chose this spot to bring Ember. Why does she want me to be haunted by this place forever?

Ember is tied to the chair, her head lulled to the side, her pink hair covering her face.

"What the fuck, Joyce?" Sebastian says behind me.

"Oh great, I was hoping you'd be here," Joyce says, coming to stand in front of Ember.

"Seriously? Why? Because you're jealous?" I ask.

Joyce laughs, throwing her head back, her throat fully exposed, and all I want to do is rip it out.

"Please. You think this is all over her? Over you?" she says, looking me up and down like I'm irrelevant. "This is about loyalty. You were always the favorite, always so pretty, the thing he couldn't have. But me? I've been loyal for over a century. I've passed the tests, I'll be rewarded," she says, like some sort of maniac.

"What are you even talking about? Have you succumbed to madness?" I ask, my gaze going back to a passed out Ember. Her heart is still beating. I just need to keep Joyce busy enough so that I can formulate a plan. She has a few human guards, all of them with modified cross bows with stakes attached.

Joyce laughs again. "God, you didn't even wait for his blood to dry on the pavement before trying to destroy his empire, did you?"

I tilt my head. "This is about Oz? Oz was your sire?" I'm

confused as hell, I thought Joyce turned around the same time as I was, at least that's what she's said. Oz said none of his other progenies worked out, that's why he usually had his henchmen change humans to vampires.

Joyce's smile is feral as the clacking of expensive leather shoes slap against the ground. His bigger than life frame coming into the warehouse. If I could breathe, I wouldn't be able to any longer.

Back from the fucking dead, Oz stands before me. This can't be real, his clothes, his watch were with what was left of him.

"Yes, Joyce is my progeny. Did you miss me, Warin?" Oz says.

He comes to stand behind Ember, pushing her pink hair from her face. I want to storm across the room and rip off his hand for daring to even touch her.

"I can see the appeal. How long were you hiding her from me, anyway?"

"You're alive?" I say, because there are no other words.

Oz rolls his eyes, his hand on top of Ember's head. I think about how easily he could snap her neck, lean forward and drain her dry. It's the same nightmare I had from the day she walked into my bar and let me taste her blood, it's why I stayed away.

"You know, faking your own death is far easier as a vampire than it is as a human. I mean, sure, putting my plan into place took endless plotting, but when you have loyal vampires on your side, it makes all the difference. It's a shame Conner isn't here to see it, but every grand scheme needs a sacrifice."

"Just let her go and you can have whatever you want," I say.

"What I want? You've never given a shit about anyone other than yourself. I created you. I gave you everything and you couldn't even give me a single ounce of loyalty, could you? You were mine, you belonged to me, you still do," Oz says, his tone manic.

He's been on the edge of madness for so long, I wonder when the last time he rested was. It doesn't bode well for us getting out of this situation.

"Just let her go and I'll go back to being whoever you want me to be."

Oz clicks his tongue. "I knew the moment you no longer loved me. When you no longer realized how much I gave to you. It was that night in Chicago, you were never the same after that. That witch filled your head with evil, but I tried to look past it. We were creating an empire. We had everything. I thought maybe if we had more, then you would be settled."

I go to take a step closer and Oz tugs on Ember's hair.

"Not a step closer. I couldn't have planned this all better if I tried. It was a convoluted process, I'll admit. It started with figuring out how I could fake my own death and get the attention of the vampire council. Wouldn't you know scaring the right humans and giving them the means to protect themselves can get a lot done in a short time? It took some time for them to summon the Slayer and even more time to lure it into our parish, but once he did, it was the first thing I needed."

I glance over at Samantha and she's typing away on her phone. What the fuck? I ignore her as I look back over at Oz. He's let go of Ember, walking away from her and puts a hand on Joyce's back. She seems overjoyed from his touch.

"Joyce, ever the loyal progeny, she's been my secret little weapon, telling me every little thing the council is up to. Neither of us were happy how things were being run. It should be me who is in charge of the council, I'm older than Sebastian and far less lenient. What I didn't account for was you throwing a celebration over my death and shacking up with some fucking witch when my planted remains hadn't even been scraped off the pavement. I'd planned for us to take over the council together. Me and my progenies in one place, Samantha, as an extension, was going to be included in that."

Oz puts his hands on his hips, looking around the warehouse.

"I thought the location was fitting, don't you think?"

"Oz, please. Whatever you want," I beg, not that I think it's going to work. I just need time, a moment to think of how the hell I'm going to get us out of this situation.

Oz shakes his head back and forth, pursing his lips, like he's debating it.

"Kill Samantha, and I'll think about it. You'd, of course, have to share this one," Oz says, rounding Ember again, tilting her head back and exposing her throat. "Nothing hits like witches blood, my mouth is watering thinking about it." He grins. "Kill Samantha, and maybe we can work past this. I mean, Sebastian is going to have to go." He scrunches his nose. "Achille, you can stay."

Oz trails his fingers down Ember's throat.

"So, Warin, what's it going to be? Your progeny or your witch?"

I stand there, involuntary tears of blood running down my face. This place was my last human memory, and it seems like it's going to be the last place I see anything.

Oz laughs. "Ever so soft. Where did I go wrong with you? Maybe she'll listen better. I can't quite decide if I want to drain her dry or make her mine."

He leans forward, his teeth about to sink into Ember's neck, but they can't touch her skin.

"What the fuck?" Oz hisses, trying to bite her again.

My witch's eyes meet mine and I look down at her glittering ring and she gives me a small nod.

"Now," I shout, knowing that if I die, at least I went out swinging.

Chapter 36

Keeping my pulse even and my head lulled for this entire villainous monologue nearly had me falling asleep.

Witch on a stick.

How many more big bads do I have to deal with in a lifetime?

I kept my hand bunched in a fist, thankful that my protection ring wasn't discovered. I've never been more grateful for a piece of jewelry in my life or a charm that hides it from the world.

When Oz tries to sink his teeth into my throat, I know that it's now or never. I slowly lift up my head and see Warin's face, blood staining his cheeks as he looks me over. His eyes glancing down to my ring and then back to where Oz holds my hair.

"Now," he shouts, as total pandemonium takes place.

Vampires and stakes are zooming past my head at unbelievable speeds, it's unnerving and I know I need to get out of the crosshairs. The human guards are shooting off their crossbows, but that doesn't seem to last long as Samantha rips their throats out one by one.

I make a mental reminder to not get on her bad side as I work my way out of my own confines. For the first time in my life, the ability to use fire finally comes in handy, as I burn away the ropes that were holding my ankles and wrists. I singe my skin slightly and hiss through the pain.

I'm not sure what to do when I'm free from the ropes, but sitting here like an idiot for sure isn't the answer. Sebastian and Warin are fighting Oz, while Achille takes on Joyce, Samantha joining that fight once all the humans are out of the picture.

Though I'm very anti-killing, I understand how necessary their deaths are. I do my best to not look over at the soldiers as I scurry behind some brewing tanks, holding on to cool metal as I watch in horror as they all fight each other.

The fight against Joyce is going better. With Achille's size and Samantha's quickness, I have no doubts that either of them is in danger.

With Oz, though? I'm not sure what to think. It's almost like he's toying with Sebastian and Warin.

"I'm older than all of you in this room combined. In the end, I'll get what I want. It's just a shame so much blood needs to be spilled," Oz says, his dark eyes glancing over at me with a smirk. "Maybe when you're dead, I'll turn her, anyway."

Warin lets out a frustrated scream, he and Sebastian rushing him at the same time. Oz is faster than any vampire I've ever seen, and stronger, too. Shoving them both off him, tossing their bodies into some of the brewing materials.

They're momentarily distracted as Achille holds Joyce's arms behind her back, he's grunting with the strength it takes. Samantha cups the vampire's chin, grinning in her face as she presses the tip of the stake against her chest.

"Bye bye, Joyce," Samantha coos as she shoves the stake into her heart.

It's just like that night at Howl and the Moon. She quickly

shrivels up, blood and guts everywhere. My wand is now in the goop that was formally known as Joyce. Samantha picks it up and looks over at me, throwing it in my direction.

I grimace as I pick it up and hold it close in my fist.

"Four against one, that seems hardly fair," Oz complains, as he lets out a piercing whistle.

It's then that nearly eight more vampires enter the brewery. Oz backs away from the fray, letting his minions attack the vampires that are here to save me.

There's no way they can win, not against this many. If I don't figure out a way to help, they're dead along with myself. I can see the fear in Warin's eyes as he glances over at me mid-fight. He hasn't given up, but he knows that this is over.

No. It's time to do something great. It's time to prove that I'm a formidable witch.

I think back to my skills, the way I saw Warin's memories, the way I fought Conner off. The emotion inside of me is raw and dangerous. My life is just getting started and there's no way I'm going to let this asshole take it away from me.

There's no way with so many vampires that I can direct the pain to specific ones. I haven't practiced enough for that. But I try with all my might to work with intention, letting my magic know who's here to do harm and who's a friend.

Every ounce of me slips into their minds quietly, not lingering to search their memories or find information. I can feel their thoughts, but my magic doesn't touch them. There's a chance I'm in Achille's or Sebastian's minds, but I don't let that stop me as I take a deep breath.

I put every ounce of energy into causing pain, sending alarm bells in their mind, causing chaos. My eyes are cinched shut, but I can hear the wake of my magic. Bodies are hitting the floor and vampires are writhing in pain. I don't stop, and continue my assault on their minds.

Some of the moaning stops, and I can feel the exhaustion deep in my bones as I shudder, no longer able to hold the spell.

I slouch against the cool metal as dark eyes peer down at me.

"Hmm. Maybe you are more valuable left intact. I haven't seen a witch take down that many vampires in a long time. In fact, I ripped out her throat. That was fun," he says, tilting his head at me. "Tell me, witch, was he worth it?"

I glance around the room, not seeing or hearing anyone else, and tears fill my eyes. He can't be gone. We can't lose everything, not when we just found it. I know it was messy and it wouldn't be easy, but I liked that he was difficult. It was fun bantering back and forth to each other. All my life I wanted a great love, and I finally found him. Life doesn't seem very much like living anymore.

"He was worth it," I croak.

Oz gets down on his haunches and tsks his tongue. "It's a shame you and your coven will have to die because you got involved with the wrong vampire. But I can assure you, I'll have the utmost fun draining them all dry. Who should I start with? Violet, Iris, or maybe your bigoted grandmother. Maybe I'll let her live."

Tears are falling down my eyes and my wand is so tight in my hand it feels like I might break it.

Of course, this maniac knows all about my coven. At least Iris has the Slayer, and Violet has the wolves. Maybe they stand a better chance.

Oz's hand touches my face, his thumb and forefinger squeezing my chin. "He always had a soft spot for sweet, pretty, little things. Now, if you give me the protection item you have, I'll make it painless," Oz says.

I look around again; I don't see Warin's body, I don't hear anyone moving, until I do. It's a quick glimpse, something not vampire, something else. I lick my lips.

"Vow it," I tell Oz.

He laughs. "I don't need to make a vow with a dead woman. They're gone, all of them. It's just you and me here, but the difference is, I have more vampires and what do you have? Nothing."

"I have a family, people who care about me, more than I can say for you," I reply.

Oz laughs, squeezing my face harder. "You think I give a shit about that?"

"I don't know, you tell me? You're how old and throwing a tantrum over your progeny not loving you?"

"You know nothing. You're an insignificant little bi—"

He doesn't finish his sentence as the wooden stake slams through his heart, his blood splattering my face in the process. He holds the wood in his chest, like he can't believe it, his veins going black as he falls to his knees and collapses to the ground.

I hope to see Warin behind him, and hope floods my veins, until I see the man that was standing outside of Iris' store the other day. He stands tall, black tattoos covering his skin as he tilts his head at me in an in-human gesture.

"She's unhurt," his deep, spooky voice says.

Suddenly, Iris is on her knees next to me giving me a hug. The Slayer watches with an almost jealous gaze as Iris squeezes me tight.

"How?" I rasp out.

"Samantha. She sent me an odd text message that included emoji's saying that you may be out of your depth and that Oz is the whole reason Adam was turned into the Slayer. We teleported here."

"I wish to have a hug of my own now," the Slayer says, and Iris rolls her eyes.

She stands and holds her hands out for me, pulling me up to my feet.

"Give Adam control, and I'll give you a hug," Iris counters.

"No. Me. I would like the hug, not the man," the Slayer retorts.

I'm wiping tears from my eyes, trying to see if Warin is still there. The room is a mess of blood and bodies, and I can't help the sad little hiccup that falls out of me.

"I'll give you a hug and then you give Adam control. He's the only one we came here to kill. None of the others," Iris says, her hands on her hips.

"A kiss. A kiss and I will not kill the other blood suckers and I will let Adam have control for an hour."

Iris takes a deep breath, looking up at the ceiling for guidance.

"Others?" I interrupt, something hopeful in my voice. It must be what gets Iris to agree.

"Fine, a kiss and you do everything you promise."

The Slayer leans down, their height difference is staggering as his dark eyes search hers. She seems less than impressed as she leans forward and places the chastest kiss against his lips.

I expect the Slayer to pout about it, complain that it wasn't much of a kiss. Instead, he grins from ear to ear, which is horrifying.

"The best half second of my tremendously long life," the Slayer says.

"Give Adam control," Iris demands.

The Slayer looks pissed. "If anything seems suspicious with the undead, I will take over immediately," he tells Iris. She just flicks her hand at him.

Suddenly his demeanor changes, along with his eyes. A regular man now stands before me, though he looks just as irritated as Iris.

He looks down at where Oz's body was and he sighs.

"He's the one who gave my family the summoning spell?" he asks, talking to Iris.

"Yes, I'm sorry, Adam," Iris says, grabbing his arm, far more friendly with the man than she was the Slayer.

Adam nods, the toe of his shoe pointing in his guts.

"This piece of shit ruined my life," Adam says.

"Mine too," a deep voice croaks behind him. I look over Adam's shoulder and I see Warin, a stake hanging out of his side. "Sunshine, you mind ripping another one of these out of me?" he asks.

Tears stream down my face as I run toward him. I'm not as delicate as I should be as I throw my arms around his neck and squeeze. He winces, and I pull back and look at him. He's a blurry mess with how much I'm crying.

"I thought you were gone?"

"Just another stake to the side. Nothing I can't handle," he says, cupping my face.

He's covered in blood. It's horrific looking, but I nod and grab the stake, tugging with all my might as it falls to the floor. A sigh of relief fills me as his skin knits together immediately.

"What about the others?"

"As soon as the Slayer got here, we got out of the way so that he wouldn't turn on any of us. Oz didn't expect or sense him, thought we were dead in the fray."

"How did Samantha know to text Iris?" I ask. Even if Warin told her, I can't even be mad, her knowing about the Slayer probably just saved our whole lives.

"It seems as though she may have cloned your phone that first night I brought you back to the house. I can't even be mad about it. Also, she's Sebastian's blood mate, or whatever. All of them are fine," he assures, looking at me like he can't believe I'm still alive.

The feeling is mutual.

"You scared the fuck out of me," I say, grabbing his shirt.

"You did so good, you saved us with your magic. Without that, we wouldn't have had a fighting chance. The Slayer wouldn't have gotten here in time. You're magnificent," he says.

He's holding me tight, like I might disappear when there's a growling noise behind us. When I turn around, Adam is long gone. The Slayer is back in charge of the body.

"Nope. Hell no. I kissed you and you promised you would listen," Iris chastises him.

The Slayer glances down at Iris, not liking her reasoning at all, as he glares at Warin.

"I don't like it either, man. We both tried to kill each other, so let's call it even," Warin says, and I'm proud of him for agreeing to my terms. The Slayer killing his problematic maker might be part of it too.

"Another kiss and I let them walk away," the Slayer says and I have to bite my lip as Iris looks so irritated with him.

"Fine. Can you two please get out of here quickly? Oh, wait. Here, Ember," she says, tossing me a potion bottle. "Now, can you two get out of here?"

"Gladly," Warin says, tossing me over his shoulder and moving so fast I may just throw up from the movement.

I hold on to his back and despite everything, I can't help but to smile. We made it.

We're both still here, despite everything. If that isn't fate, I don't know what is.

Chapter 37

I'm quick through the night, holding Ember until I get us to my townhome on Burgundy street.

I glide Ember down my body as I shut the door behind us and Ember glances around my oldest home.

"Another house?" she questions.

"To be fair, I bought this eighty years ago," I reply, cupping her face.

She's still here. She's still *her*.

I would have never forgiven myself if I lost her or if Oz would have changed her against her will.

She grabs my wrist and squeezes. "Are you okay?"

"I should be the one asking you that," I say, and she shakes her head. "I'm so sorry my selfishness brought you here. I wish I was a better man and that I could let you be free of me, but I can't. Every day, I'll try to be better for you, but I can't do that."

"I don't want you to," she whispers.

I clear my throat and look away from her for a moment. Nothing I've done in my life has led me to deserve her, yet she wants me anyway.

When I turn back to face her, I push her hair out of her face, cupping both sides of her chin. My thumbs rub against her smooth, soft skin. She already had some blood on her face, and I only added more by touching her.

I glance down at myself, realizing that I'm covered in blood, and sigh.

"Let's go get cleaned up?" I ask, not knowing how to say the words that are spiraling in my head.

That I love her, that I can't imagine a world where she wasn't in it. That my life is meaningless without her. But how, at the same time, I feel like I'm going to be the root of everything horrible in her life. It's an endless cycle of self-loathing and endless selfishness.

I lead her down the hallway, starting the shower and undressing myself. It's a massive glass rectangle with no door and I step in, needing to get the evidence of the night off me.

Red-tinged water swirls down the drain as I look at my feet and I finally let myself feel the fear of what could have happened.

I've felt pain. I mourned my ma when Oz changed me and again when she passed, but nothing could ever prepare me for what it would feel like to lose Ember.

I just need a minute to calm down, to accept the reality of everything that happened. That she's okay, that Samantha's okay, that Oz is actually gone this time.

The spray hits my shoulder blades and hair as I lean against the tile, red staining the perfectly clean white tile.

Is that what I do to Ember? Stain her? Hurt her?

I meant what I said. I'm too selfish, too obsessed to let her go, but is that what I should be doing?

Hands wrap around my chest, her bright pink nails in view as she rubs my chest.

"Hey. We're here, we're okay," she says.

She's the one assuring me.

What in the fuck is happening here? I should be the one comforting her, assuring her that we're safe now. Which I suppose we are. Oz is actually gone, Joyce is out of the picture, and her friend seems to have a true handle on the Slayer. Not to mention my progeny is fucking the leader of the vampire council.

Yet, there's still this lingering fear in my gut over how fragile Ember is, how she could be taken away from me at any moment.

I turn in her arms, giving her more access to the shower, since I don't feel cold. Her wet hair plasters against her magnificent body as water driblets drip down her skin, Oz's blood washes away.

Her hands are still on my chest as she looks at me inquisitively.

"I'm okay, Warin," she assures me and I lick my lips.

"I could change you. You could be immortal," I blurt out, just needing to say it, selfishly asking for even more than I deserve.

She sighs, her hands falling off my chest, so I grab her wrists and put them back there.

"I've never been so afraid as I was tonight. If you were a vampire, you'd live forever with me. You'd be safer," I try to argue.

"I need some time to think about it," she says softly. If I were human, there's no way I'd be able to hear her whisper.

There's no way I can push her on this. If she became a vampire, the only reason she would be doing it is to make me happy.

Selfish. Selfish. Selfish.

"Okay," I whisper, taking a step forward and wrapping her in my arms.

Her heartbeat is frantic and now that she's washed off any evidence of tonight, she smells like her again. If I changed her, I'd be taking those things away. She'd have to give up her coven, the sun, who she is, and I feel sick thinking about it.

Ember's nails slightly dig into my shoulders as we hold one another.

"We're safe," she repeats and I nod, kissing her wet hair.

"Yeah, we're safe," I reply, wondering just how true that is. I'm not even sure if I have adrenaline as a vampire, but it feels like all the fear and worry from the night is hitting me. All I want to do is hold Ember and put today behind us.

"Warin, look at me," she says, and I pull away from her body just enough to look down at her. "There's no one out there trying to get us. We have time to figure out how to make this work. But I'm here. I'm right here in front of you and I'm not going any-where."

I cradle the back of her head and bring my lips to hers. The warmth of her mouth is addictive. The way her curves press against my body is perfection.

Ember kisses me deeply, like maybe she's trying to convince herself that we're safe too.

Being wrapped in her embrace is keeping me tethered to reality. The rest of the night washing away.

Ember's fingers toy with the hair at the nape of my neck and I shiver as I grab her ass, lifting her into my arms. She doesn't hesitate, her legs wrapping around my waist as I press her against the shower wall.

She sighs into my mouth as my cock hardens between us. The scent of her arousal mixes in the shower and I yearn for the feeling of being inside of her, the way the rest of the world disappears when I'm blissfully lost inside of her cunt.

"Do you need my cock inside of you, witch?" I ask as I grip her ass and rub myself against her stomach.

"Yes, I need you," she says, her hands tangling in my hair.

Has anyone ever needed me before? Certainly not like she does.

I easily hold her up with one hand, using the other to push myself into her warm, waiting pussy.

She gasps, her fingernails digging into my scalp.

Her breasts press against my chest as I push into her as deep as I can. It's like the deeper inside of her I am, the more real she is.

"I'm so fucking obsessed with every part of you. This ass," I say, squeezing the full flesh, "is perfect. These tits? Do you know how often I think about feeding from you there?"

"Do it," she rasps out.

"After your potion," I hiss out, shifting back and into her. Ember's head falls back against the shower, exposing her beautiful throat. "You need it, don't you? My fangs and cock so deep inside of you?"

"Hecate, yes. I need it," she says, her nails digging in hard on my shoulders, making me shudder.

"I'm going to fill this pussy up so many times tonight, so much that you won't remember a time that I wasn't inside of you."

"I-I. Right there, War," she says.

A shiver passes through me as she uses my nickname as I thrust my hips at the angle she wants. I grip her ass hard, knowing there will be bruises in my wake, but when I give her my blood, they will heal.

"Are you going to come all over my cock, sunshine? Mark it as yours?" I ask.

Her lips part, her eyes going hazy as she does just that. Ember clenches around me, milking my cock, and there's nothing left for me to do but follow suit. Trembling, I finish, cum filling her magical, sweet cunt.

She's panting, her wet hair stuck to her face and shoulders as I lean forward and take her lips against mine.

"You're mine forever, witch, no matter how long that is," I say against her mouth.

She doesn't respond with words, just nods as she kisses me again. I turn the shower off and carry her over to the bedroom, a trail of water in our wake. Ember's lips don't leave mine.

I'm about to toss her onto the bed, spill that potion down her throat, and fulfill my promise of finally drinking from her perfect tits, when she whispers something, her wand careening toward her hand.

She flicks it with a little spell and suddenly we're both completely dry.

I smile as I kiss her again.

"That's extremely handy. Why don't you fetch your potion while you're at it, witch?"

"You're insatiable," she says with absolutely no heat, because she is too.

It's like no matter how many times I have her, it won't be enough. No matter how many inches of our skin touch, I can't get closer. There's no world where Ember Hallow doesn't consume my thoughts.

"How do you feel about Ember Auclair?" I ask her, taking her off guard as the potion comes whipping through the room and landing in her hand, as I toss her on the bed, climbing up her marvelous body.

"I could be convinced," she says, biting her bottom lip.

"Is that so?"

She adjusts us so that she's now on top, and I can't focus, not as her tits hang right in front of my face.

Ember uncorks the potion, tossing the cork across the room

as she swallows it down, her throat bobbing while she does. She doesn't hiss at the taste, and actually licks her lips after, which pleases me.

"Now. What was I promised?" she asks.

I grab her ass, shifting her on my length, rubbing her wet pussy that's dripping with my cum over myself.

"Hmm. I think ladies first, right?" I ask, squeezing her left cheek for good measure before bringing my hand to my chest.

I could bite my wrist, prick my finger, but the idea of her lips against my flesh sucking my blood has me harder than I've ever been in my life. I know when she's had my blood, she'll be voracious. I want her to orgasm with my blood in her system and hers in mine. I need to be part of her in every fucking way I can.

With my free hand, I open the nightstand, grabbing the lancet ring, and slicing a small cut on the base of my throat.

Ember looks at me with wide, green eyes.

I toss the ring onto the nightstand and trail my hand up to her spine until I have a fistful of her hair, bringing her mouth to my throat.

She's hesitant as her tongue swipes against my skin, but quickly she becomes ravenous, her full lips pressed against my skin as she drinks.

I can't help it as my cock leaks and I thrust myself against her pussy lips.

This witch is mine in every way I can have her.

Chapter 38

As I swallow down Warin's blood, I feel my wounds from my escape healing, and it fuels every inch of my body with a sense of desire.

Nothing I've ever done in my life compares to this feeling. I'm not sure if I should feel ashamed about how much I like drinking my vampire's blood. It's not like it sustains me in the same way, but it fills me with something else.

Unfiltered want.

All I can think about is Warin, how he's mine, how we're fated to be with one another.

He's rubbing the head of his cock against my clit and I feel like I'm already so close. The sounds of where our bodies are rubbing together is salacious and wet, and his hold on me is possessive and endearing at the same time.

Part of me wants to give him what he wants, to tie our souls together for an immortal life together. Maybe I could do it, for Warin, I could be a vampire.

I shake the thought from my head and go back to how good I feel now, how consumed I feel by the taste and warmth of his blood.

When I pull back, I watch in amazement as his skin stitches back together, only a small smidge of blood on his flesh, and I can't help but to lean forward and lick it off.

Warin groans, his grip on me brutal.

"Are you trying to make me come before I'm even inside of you again?" he asks.

"That's the perk of having a vampire mate, isn't it? You can fuck me as much as I need you to?"

He groans, like I'm torturing him. His hands move up my sides until both of my breasts are in his hands.

Warin's touch makes every single one of my nerve endings greedy for his skin on mine. His thumbs circle my nipples, and I can feel myself getting wetter with every growing second.

"Are you going to let me fuck these too, pretty witch?" he asks, pushing them together and leaning forward, taking a nipple in his mouth.

There's the slightest bit of fang and I can't help it as my thighs shake with anticipation.

"Whatever you want," I tell him truthfully.

When I'm with Warin, when we're sharing blood that is fated to be together, it's like nothing is off the table. It's not something I'd ever considered before, but the idea of Warin having me in a way that I know he wants turns me on.

His tongue swirls around the hard bud, teasing me. Or maybe he's delaying the pleasure for himself. He sucks hard on my nipple, and all I can do is grind down on his cock, creating friction.

The pleasure is almost too intense and I'm uncoordinated and dizzy with greed as I seek out my release. Warin doesn't let up. Knowing that I'm close, he just keeps sucking and nipping, but not sinking his teeth in me.

One of my hands is tugging on his hair as the other holds the headboard as I take what I need, my abdomen tightening as my peak hits me, a loud moan ripping from my throat as I soak us even more.

I'm shivering, not sure if I can take anymore, as Warin pulls away from my breast, his thumbs back to rubbing the sensitive tips.

"You're getting my cock nice and wet to give me what I want, aren't you?" he says, which shamelessly has me clenching around nothing. "I think we can do better, though."

His dick slides into me easily, and I'm thankful for his immortal stamina as he thrusts, fucking me from below.

I'm out of my mind as he fucks me, so oversensitive and consumed with our connection.

When he leans forward, no longer toying with me, and sinks his teeth right into my left breast, I think I see stars.

My vision goes black, my hearing goes out, as he drinks from me and fucks me. I'm almost positive I'm crying, because nothing could ever feel this good, nothing could be this cosmic and perfect.

He holds me tight, like our bodies couldn't be any closer, almost like we're one thing, and I fall apart.

My weight completely on him as I shiver, moan, and writhe. He takes one last long pull of my blood, and when his teeth pull out of me, I think I just might fall apart.

I can't stop the shaking as Warin quickly flips us, my breasts bouncing with the motion, my hair sticking to my face as he looks down at me like I'm an actual goddess.

It's what I always wanted, someone who was thoroughly obsessed with me. Did I think they would be a century-old vampire with slightly ambiguous morals? No, but I wouldn't have anyone else. Warin Auclair is mine, and I'm his.

He looks down at where his bite is, and I watch as it heals, his fresh blood still pumping through my veins.

I lick my lips, my eyes are heavy lidded and I'm oversensitive as Warin slides his hand over my pussy, making me hiss as he collects the wetness between us and rubs it over my chest.

It's dirty, salacious, and so fucking hot.

He rubs his length between my lips again, making himself even wetter as he straddles my sides, pressing my breasts together.

"You spoil me, witch," he says.

I don't even have a retort; I feel boneless, fucked out of my mind. Somehow, I still get even more turned on watching him. I doubt any of this is normal. Our need for each other is driven by this deep, soul binding connection few others could understand.

"You're so beautiful, so lovely. I love every inch of you," he says, and I blink at him. He said my body, not me. Yet, I feel everything else he's not saying.

I love him.

I really fucking do.

Maybe it's not the most romantic moment to realize this, but I wonder if Warin is thinking about it too as he holds my large breasts together, sliding his cock between them.

His thumbs rub my nipples as he thrusts back and forth, the head of his dick lost in my voluptuous chest.

"Are you going to mark me with your cum, War?" I ask him, knowing how me calling him his nickname drives him crazy.

"Fuck," he hisses out, his hips going faster than any human man could fathom.

I help him, taking over, pushing myself together as he grabs the headboard. His gaze fluctuating from where he's fucking me to my face.

The headboard makes a loud cracking noise as he pants over me, pulling out between my flesh and fisting his cock. Ropes of cum splatter against my breasts and Warin's eyes devour my body as he makes yet another claim on me.

When he's spent, he looks down at his work for a moment, a masculine sense of pride and a grin on his face, before he shifts his body, his tongue lapping up some of his mess before his mouth meets mine.

I swallow down his taste as we kiss. When he pulls back, he looks almost as spent as me. That's a lie, I'm pretty sure he could go like five more rounds.

"You might have fucked the memories of tonight out of me, but I still need sleep," I say.

Warin smiles, with that slight fang smile I used to think was him being a smug asshole, that I now find endlessly charming.

"Be right back," he says.

He's back quickly with a warm washcloth. He starts by cleaning off my chest. He's thorough, overly so. Before sliding it down my body, delicately cleaning the rest of me.

Warin adjusts the blankets, shifting us so we're both covered.

He cradles himself behind me. "Too cold?" he asks.

I shake my head.

"No, just right," I tell him.

The words *I love you, goodnight* sit on the edge of my tongue, but I let my eyes close. I let go of all the bad memories of the night and cling to all of the amazing ones instead.

Warin and I have spent days in New Orleans, fucking, drinking, and for me, eating amazing food that Warin has delivered to the house.

It's been magical.

The idea of slipping back to reality is a tough one, I have to face everything that happens now.

Sure, Iris and Violet have accepted me. The fairies and Gus have made peace with my decision. Hell, a big portion of our coven is progressive, but unfortunately, that doesn't include some of my family. Not to mention the fact that I have a big decision to make.

Do I let Warin change me? Do I leave everything I know behind? Would I be happy as a vampire, even if that meant forever with Warin?

Warin grabs my thigh in the backseat. Achille came to pick us up and bring us home.

"Do you need some time at your cottage?" he asks.

My heart swells at his perceptiveness.

"If you don't mind?" I ask him. As much as I would like to stay in our little bubble forever, I can't think rationally when I'm around him.

"Betty will be right in the shutters, if you need me you can tell her or call and I'll be right there," he says.

It's sunset, and as we round the one lane road to my cottage, my stomach sinks into my chest.

Waiting on my porch are my grandmother and mother. No doubt, Warin can hear my heart rate picking up.

Part of me wants to ask him to stay in the car. Maybe to spare him from their wrath, or myself, I'm not sure.

But Warin doesn't give me a chance as he rounds the car with his super speed and opens the door.

I feel like I'm going to puke as I see their appalled faces. I'm a disappointment, I always have been. They didn't consider my magic anything special. In fact I'm pretty sure they thought that of me as a whole. Never skinny enough, never quiet enough. I was too much and too little at the same time for them and the feeling hurt.

When I glance over at Warin, his beautiful eyes assessing the situation, I realize that I've been more than enough in every way to him.

He's made me a stronger witch, praised me for my magic. He always takes the opportunity to tell me how beautiful and selfless I am.

To him, I'm not too much. I'm more than he could ever ask for.

I grab his hand. Approaching the steps to my cottage, my grandmother's nostrils flare as she looks at the two of us, her lips pursed.

"Pack your things, Ember. We're leaving the coven," my grandmother says and I shake my head.

"No, I'm not leaving," I reply sternly.

"This coven has gone to hell in a handbasket. First the filthy dogs and now my own granddaughter is defiling herself with a dead man?" she asks, waving her wand around like a threat.

Warin says nothing, almost acting bored with the situation.

"If you want to leave the coven, that's your choice, but good luck finding a new one. Celestial Coven was one of the few covens still stuck in the old ways, you aren't going to find a coven who thinks like you. I'm not leaving, and I'm with Warin whether you like it or not."

"Fleur, talk some sense into your daughter," my grandmother says.

My mother sighs, looking down at the ground, and I wonder if maybe this is the moment she finally grows a spine.

"I don't want to leave the coven, either. Lavender is doing amazing things. I don't like that Ember is with a vampire, but it's still her choice," my mother says, shocking the shit out of me.

She's always been a wet blanket, doing what grandmother always said instead of sticking up for herself.

My grandmother's face is pinched as she takes in the surrounding scene. I'm fortunate that she might be a bigoted old bitch, but at least she's not insane, like Violet's grandmother.

"Consider yourselves singed from my family tree. The coven might be more progressive, but they'll never accept this. Losing my magic, my wealth of knowledge in magic, will be a detriment to the coven. Losing you would mean nothing," my grandmother says.

Unfortunately, that's when Warin opens his mouth.

"Then leave, you old bitch," he says.

I grimace as my mother's eyes go wide and my grandmother looks at Warin like he's evil incarnate.

"What did you say to me, vampire?" she hisses, holding her wand up.

Warin sighs, rolling his eyes. He moves at the speed of light, my grandmother too old to keep up as he grabs her wand. He's standing back beside me as he dangles it in the air.

"Fuck off or I'll crack it in half," he says.

"You disgusting—" Warin goes to snap it on his knee and my grandmother makes a placating gesture. "Wait. Fine, I'll leave."

Warin hands me the wand, bypassing my grandmother and mother as he enters the house.

"You let him into your house?" my mother gasps and I sigh.

"Yes. As amazing as this little family get-together has been, I'm over it."

My words shock both of them. I've been so ready to please in the past, putting up with their harsh words and quiet digs. But being with Warin has shown me that there's power in standing up for yourself.

"Grandmother, I hope you find the coven you were looking for. And mom, I guess I'll see you at the full moon ceremony," I say, not sure where I want to leave things with her.

She's not a mean person, just weak.

My grandma still looks pissed as hell with her arms crossed, and she doesn't look at me as she takes a step down the stairs.

She trips on the last step, falling in the dirt, and I have to hold back a smile, because it feels like karma.

But it isn't karma.

It's Tabitha and Domingo holding a small length of string. I hear them chuckling before they fly away.

My mother goes to help her up, and I toss her wand on the ground.

"You're no longer a Hallow," my grandmother seethes, as she gets up dusting herself off.

"No. I'm not. I'm an Auclair," I say, shutting the door behind me.

Chapter 39

When I close the door, Warin is on me in a second, pushing my back against the door as he kisses me senseless.

"You mean it?" he asks.

"Why would I want a family name that doesn't want me?" I ask him.

"I want you, more than anything I want you," he says, his forehead pressed against mine.

He would do anything for me, and I suppose this needs to be me doing anything for him. I'll just have to live without magic, without Gus, maybe without my friends.

I'm panting heavy as a knock sounds on my door. I groan, not wanting to deal with my family anymore.

Warin's brows are furrowed which makes me more confused as I break out of his grasp and open the door.

It's Samantha with Gus eating popcorn in her arms.

"Oh, my fuck. Take him. He wouldn't stop nipping all of us, I'm guessing, because he wanted to see you. Either way, take the gigantic menace," Samantha says.

Her arms are outstretched with Gus, and he nips her fingers one last time as I take him.

"Oh also, I may have threatened to drain your grandmother dry," Samantha says with a grin. "Well, I have much more interesting things to do. See you at home, I guess," she says with a shrug before running away.

I didn't even get a word in, but I look down at Gus with an arched eyebrow.

"Nice to see you, too. Thanks for checking in with your familiar after being kidnapped and nearly turned into a vampire. Plus, menace is a compliment. But seeing as I don't speak undead, I had to get their attention somehow. I think I have a solution to your little problem."

I glance over at Warin, who has no idea what Gus is saying.

"What do you mean?"

"You're not gonna like it, but it's way fucking better than being turned into a vampire."

My eyebrows raise in surprise.

"You found something in the grimoires?" I ask him.

"Worse. We need to pay Sarephine Fontenot a little visit."

"Sarephine?" I question.

"The psycho witch that specializes in familiar magic. She sent me to you, Walter to Violet, Scarlett to Iris. She's in charge of bringing our souls into these forms and connecting us with the right witch. She's straight up crazy, but good at what she does."

"What's he saying?" he asks.

"Tell him he owes me a life of luxury for what I'm about to do," Gus says, and I put my hands on my hips, not answering Warin.

"Why would the familiar witch have anything to do with Warin being a vampire and me a witch? And why now are you telling me where you came from?" I ask Gus.

"Sarephine is…unhinged. But the magic is strong and would work for the situation. As long as you are alive, I'm tethered to you, never aging, never changing. What if she could do the same for you

and my rich, slightly annoying step daddy? Plus, I can't have you turning into a vampire or else I'll get reassigned to a new witch."

I sigh at him and then I really think about it. What if instead of me being a vampire we could link our lives together?

"What am I missing?" Warin says.

"Gus thinks that this nomadic, psycho swamp witch might help us. Maybe instead of me becoming a vampire, she could tie us together like witches are to familiars."

"My job here is done," Gus says, scurrying to the couch. *"No way am I going to that place again,"* he sighs.

"Oh, you're absolutely coming with us," I say back and he lets out a pained groan.

"Why would this witch help us?" Warin says.

"She's broke as a joke. Make her an offer she can't refuse," Gus says.

"Gus says she needs money," I relay to Warin, and he nods his head, like that's a simple solution.

"Then let's go. Right now," Warin says, ready to make this connection between us official.

We haven't even said the words yet, and here we are ready to beg a swamp witch to tether us together forever. Totally normal.

I grab Gus, he claws into the couch but eventually I get him free and we get back into the SUV.

Against his will, Gus tells us how to get to Sarephine Fontenot's swamp.

It takes us hours, and I'm not even sure what we're on is considered a road. It's the dead of the night, and I wonder if she'll even see us.

As we pull up, there are bright eyes everywhere. Raccoons,

cats, foxes, and alligators?

Gus groans next to me, like being back here is horrific. When we pull up to the house, lights immediately turn on, and a witch with braided gray-white hair, wearing a blue muumuu, and holding a mangy cat, comes to the front porch. The wood is cracked and worn, and she holds her wand tightly in her spindly fist.

She doesn't immediately acknowledge us, instead she zeroes in on Gus.

"My Augustus, have you come back to me?" she asks.

Gus curses under his breath and the old woman laughs.

"You always were a little shit. What does your witch and her vampire want?" she asks, again to Gus, not us, the talking people right in front of her.

"They want their lives tethered together like a familiar is to their witch," Gus says.

The old crone laughs, the cat in her arms trying to get free, but unable.

"Why in the world would I offer that?" she asks.

"The vampire is rich," Gus tells her, and her demeanor changes. *"I know it's not cheap feeding all your wayward familiars waiting for witches to be born. Not to mention I don't think you've changed your nightgown in over a decade,"* Gus says.

I squeeze his middle, and he yelps.

"What he was rudely—"

"Shut up, witch," Sarephine says, looking back down at my raccoon.

"Tell her I only talk to familiars," she says to Gus, even though I'm standing right here.

Warin looks skeptical next to me, like maybe he wants to strangle the swamp witch, but this is the only lead we have.

It's this or I make the decision to never see the sun again, never use magic, untether myself from Gus and my coven.

"Five million and some of the vampire's blood," she says.

"Done," Warin says quickly.

"Ten million and some of the vampire's blood," she updates her offer.

"Done," Warin replies again.

"Fine. We do this now. Gladis, go get mommy's banking information," she says, putting the cat down, who trots back into the house.

The cat comes back with a piece of paper in its mouth, and Sarephine hands the paper to Gus, who then hands it to Warin.

Warin pulls out his phone, clicking away at an unreal speed.

"The transfer is complete."

"Your blood vampire," she says.

"Blood after the spell," he retorts.

She pinches her lips, but tilts forward.

"Tell them to come to the porch," she says to Gus, even though she was talking to Warin about money. This woman is totally cracked out and I wonder if we're getting scammed.

Gus holds on to me for dear life, like this woman might snatch him up and add him to her little collection of creatures.

"There's no guarantee this will work. I've only tied magical creatures to witches before," she says, of course after she has her money.

Awesome. I'm going to be a fucking vampire.

"For the spell to work best, I need to understand their intentions. It's how I pair familiars with witches, understanding their signatures. Since he doesn't have a heartbeat," she says, tapping her finger against her chin. "Blood, I will sense the connection in the blood," she says, grabbing a bowl that really looks like it needs to be heavily washed from the porch. "Augustus, tell them to put their blood in the bowl," she says.

"*You heard her,*" Gus says.

Warin bites his wrist, putting his blood in the bowl first, his wrist heals immediately, and he grabs my wrist, lightly pricking it with a fang and I add mine.

Sarephine gasps when they combine, and she holds it up to her nose.

"I've never seen such a connection," she says.

"*Maybe this was a bad idea,*" Gus says quietly.

"A verbal confirmation will make the spell stronger," Sarephine says manically, as she stares at the blood. "Tell them to state their intentions out loud," she directs Gus.

"*Again, you heard what she said.*"

Warin takes a step closer. The old porch creaking with each step. He grabs my waist, since I have Gus in my arms. It's probably the most vulnerable I've seen him as he looks down and back up at me.

"My love started for you the moment you walked into my bar. I know you don't remember that night, but I made a vow to protect you every day since then. I hold true to that vow, but it's more than that now. I not only love you because fate destined us together, but because of who you are." He steps even closer, Gus squished between us.

"I never thought I would see the sun again, but you are the brightest thing I could have ever asked for in my life. You are beautiful, brilliant, funny, and don't put up with my shit. I love you for you, Ember, and I don't care what forever looks like, as long as it's with you. I promise to protect you, care for you, and put you first," he says as he cups my chin.

My eyes are watery as I lick my lips.

"I'm not sure how we got here, but I'll admit that I was starting

to have feelings for you well before we shared blood. I just didn't want to admit them to myself. No one has made me feel more confident than you do. I know that your past is complicated, and the future might be too. But there's no one else I want to walk this life with other than you. I love you for your faults and for your charms. You're persistent, generous, and thoughtful. Ever since I was a little girl, I dreamed I'd have a fairytale romance and while it might not be conventional, it's more than I could ever dream of. I love you, War," I say.

He leans forward, Gus protesting between our arms as Warin kisses me.

I feel it then; the magic surrounding us as Sarephine chants. It's not in English and I wonder how she was imbued with this magic, but it doesn't matter.

Our lips don't part as the magic washes over us, connecting us forever. It's like a tether wrapping around my heart and latching on to Warin's. Our life lines become one, my soul forever tied to Warin's immortal life span.

Every nerve ending in my body cools a few degrees, and when we finally part from our kiss, I can see it in Warin's eyes.

He rubs his chest like he feels it too.

"Give this to the vampire and tell them to get the fuck off my property," Sarephine says, handing a vial to Gus.

My familiar's hands are shaking and I wonder if the magic has somehow trickled to him as he hands the vial to Warin.

Warin doesn't look at the other witch, and barely looks down at what he's doing as he fills the glass with his blood, his eyes never breaking away from mine.

"Tell them as long as the vampire lives she lives, she's frozen in time, blah blah blah. Oh, and Augustus? Whenever he gets staked and they both die, you belong to me," the witch says, cackling.

Gus's eyes go wide, and he clings on to me for dear life.

Warin shoves his blood into Sarephine's hand, and grips my waist, as he leads us off the precarious porch and back toward the vehicle.

None of us speak until we get in the car.

"*I told you she was fucking insane,*" Gus says, and Warin immediately turns into the backseat to stare at Gus.

"You heard him?" I question and Warin looks back at me with a sigh.

"I suppose we're all connected now," he says, placing his hand in mine.

"*Don't forget about me,*" a female voice says and my eyes go wide.

"Just me, you, a raccoon, and a bat," Warin says deadpan and I laugh.

Gus however doesn't find it too funny as he grumbles in the backseat with his road snacks.

"My life is quite literally in your hands," I say, and he brings my hand to his mouth, kissing my knuckles. I haven't let everything tonight sink in yet. I guess I won't age anymore?

"Finally, a real reason worth living," he says, placing my hand back in my lap.

Maybe it's not the fairytale where we ride a horse-drawn carriage into the sunset. I think I was always meant to ride off into the darkness in a bullet proof SUV, anyway.

Chapter 40

Epilogue

My witch is a bridesmaid at her best friend's wedding or anniversary. The details are a little hazy, all I know is my witch looks delicious.

Her friend, Violet, who is getting married is a little less complicated than Iris, who unfortunately brought her Slayer to the wedding.

What an absolute fucking vibe killer.

Right now, it seems like the man is in charge. He sits at the back, looking pissed off, per usual. At least with Ember's life attached to mine, I don't have to worry about that specific problem. I'm pretty sure Iris keeps him on a relatively tight leash. At least I hope so.

The love of my life, my blood mate, the reason I exist's eyes are watering as she listens to the bride and groom speak. I'm overcome with joy as I look at her, to realize that somehow we have it all. My glasses and umbrella shield me from the sun as I watch the nuptials, but Ember stands in the sun where she belongs, her hair glistening, her skin full of life.

My witch belongs to the sun and her coven almost as much as she belongs to me.

She wipes a tear as the couple kisses and I wonder if she wants an official wedding.

Ember has my last name, her life is tied to mine, my ring on her finger. I don't need the government to get intertwined with our affairs. However, if she asked for a wedding, I wouldn't be able to deny her.

She has me wrapped around her pink manicured finger and there's no place I'd rather be.

Everyone cheers as the ceremony concludes and we're ushered to the reception space, which is literally just the other part of the backyard. Ember finds me quickly, grabbing the train of her dress and rushing up to me. She grips my waist and kisses my chin, joining me under the umbrella.

We get some looks from members of her coven, but for the most part they keep to themselves. I may not completely understand Ember's friendships, but I can appreciate how much they protect and stand up for Ember.

I can already see Iris glaring at one older witch as she openly stares. The woman purses her lips and walks away. Ember doesn't even notice.

"It was beautiful, wasn't it?" she says dreamily, her head resting against my chest as music plays and people

"You were beautiful," I say, pushing some hair off her shoulder.

She looks up at me, not able to see my eyes because of the glasses, and grins as she wraps her arms around my neck, toying with the hair on my nape. I hold on to her waist with one hand and the umbrella handle with another.

I glance down at her full breasts, that are abundant in this bridesmaid dress, and Ember laughs.

"My eyes are up here, War," she says.

"I'm a simple man, with simple needs."

"Simple?" she snorts. "Nothing about you or any of this has ever been simple."

I squeeze her tighter to me, her chest pressed against mine as she smiles up at me.

"You know, there might be something to this whole wedding thing?" I say.

"Oh is that so?"

"Maybe we could sneak away, have a little romantic moment of our own?"

"I think we could manage that," she says.

"What exactly would you like me to do to you, witch?"

"Push my dress up my waist, your fangs deep in my shoulder while you fu—"

Mid whisper there's a squeak as Gus grabs my witch's dress and tugs.

"*They won't give me any fucking cake*," he complains.

"Little cock block," I complain as Ember laughs, bending down, at least giving me a gratuitous view down her dress as she picks Gus up.

At least I never have to worry about her wanting children. The large raccoon is like a forever child demanding her attention, time, and disturbing us constantly during our time together.

"Cake and then we can sneak away," she says with a wink.

Gus cracks a mischievous smile and gives me the middle finger over Ember's shoulder.

I give him one right back and he cackles.

I follow them over to the cake and wait patiently as the party rages on. Eventually night falls and I can toss the glasses and umbrella. Everyone is enthralled with the night, laughing, drinking, and celebrating the couple as I grab Ember by the wrist and drag her into the forest, just far enough away from the party to give us some privacy.

Ember's fingers grip on to the tree bark as I slide my fingers up her dress, toying with her clit.

"You need me so fucking bad, don't you, sunshine?"

"Always," she whispers as I flip her dress, grab my cock, and sink myself into her warm pussy in one fast motion.

Ember moans as I sink my teeth into her throat, filling her completely.

She's my everything, nothing compares to all the ways I have her, mind, body and soul.

"Make me come," she rasps out.

My fangs retract from her shoulder, where I lick the small puncture marks.

"I think that can be arranged, Ember Auclair," I say, as she clenches around me. I follow suit, filling her up with my release.

She pants against the tree and I push my release back into her, before fixing her panties and dress before turning her to face me.

"Really?" she says and I bite my lip.

"Now you'll have a piece of me all night," I say, and she rolls her eyes playfully.

"You're insatiable."

"For you, always," I say, leaning down and kissing her lips.

"Vow it," she whispers, and I kiss her again.

"I vow it," I whisper against her lips, though there's no vow necessary.

This witch is my obsession for the rest of my hopefully very long existence.

Acknowledgments

This book was so much fun to write, this definitely won't be my last vampire romance.

A big thank you to my team who made this book beautiful, Sandra, Amarna, Val, Kay, and Marie. I'm so lucky to have you all willing to work with me and make this book shine.

To my Alpha readers, Jade and Marielle, thank you for being amazing cheerleaders and pushing me to keep going. I'm so excited that Marielle will also be the one translating this series to Portuguese.

My amazing Beta team for pushing me to make the story even better, Lindsay, Hailey, Jess, and Lainey. I was in my head a lot over this book and I'm so grateful I had people to bounce ideas off of.

Stephanie, thank you for proofing and sticking with me.

I'd also like to thank all the media that transformed my young mind into loving vampires.

My Louisiana rep team Amber and Dani for reading in advance so I do your state right.

Also by Sarah Blue

Other works by Sarah Blue
Omegaverse Romance

Heat Haven Heat Cutes
Mile High Heat

Heat Haven Omegaverse
Heat Haven
Omega's Obsession - (Jonah's Parents)
Protector's Promise - (Elliot's Parents)
Too Tempting
Heat Haven Holidays

Dead Palms MC
Nobody's Darlin' - (Axel's namesake)

High Roller Omegas
Queen of Hearts

Pucked Up Omegaverse
One Pucked Up Pack
Don't Puck With My Heart
Puck Around & Find Out

Lavender Moon
Lavender Moon
Lavender Moon Meets Las Vegas

The Carlson Brothers - Contemporary Romance
Swallow Your Pride
Forget Your Morals
Double Your Standards

Paranormal Romance

Celestial Witches
The Marriage Hex
The Fang Arrangement
The Slayer Seduction

Charming Series
Charming Your Dad
Charming the Devil
Charming as Hell

Love in the Veil
Petty Cupid
Lucky Cupid
Daddy Cupid
Jolly Cupid

About the Author

Sarah Blue is a USA Today Bestselling author of paranormal, omegaverse, and contemporary romance. When she isn't writing you can find her nose buried in a book or picking up a new craft she probably won't finish. She lives in Maryland with her husband, children, and two cats.

www.authorsarahblue.com
@sarahblueauthor on Instagram and TikTok
Sarah Blue's Reader Group on Facebook